...ER FO...

Qty...

Cut By: _____

Scanned By: _____

Scanned B... ...'s

Praise for *Last Call at Smokey Row*

Professional Reviews

Last Call at Smokey Row, *a captivating novel by Pat Camalliere, beautifully portrays a slice of life from a recently bygone era, blending the mundane with the bizarre. Engaging and masterfully composed,* Last Call at Smokey Row *by Pat Camalliere is an easy-to-read yet sophisticated story tinged with nostalgia and familiarity. The novel explores multiple themes, including loneliness, self-discovery, friendship, and the fragility of life. Character development is outstanding, featuring a range of personalities from good-natured barflies to unexpected villains … The pace is smooth and consistent, which, combined with one of the most impressive writing styles I've ever encountered, creates a relatable and immersive read. Overall, it is a truly excellent work that will appeal to fans of various genres, and I wholeheartedly recommend it.*

> – *Reviewed by Gaius Konstantine for Readers' Favorite*

Pat Camalliere's writing shines in her ability to create vivid, relatable characters. Camalliere's ability to balance humor, tragedy, and suspense is masterfully done. Her meticulous research is evident, and her passion for Lemont's history is undeniable. Last Call at Smokey Row *is a reflection on human connection and the impact of our choices. With richly drawn characters and historical intrigue, this novel is a must read for fans of character-driven stories and local history. Camalliere's storytelling leaves a lasting impression, making this book a memorable addition to her repertoire.*

> – *Reviewed by Carol Thompson for Readers' Favorite*

Last Call at Smokey Row *by Pat Camalliere is a historical novel about a woman named Jane Archer. Jane moved to a small town, Lemont, Illinois, feeling lonely and out of place, with hopes of starting a new life. One day, a co-worker invites her to Sami's Saloon, although she feels a bit uncomfortable in such an environment. Jane shares her story of how Sami's Saloon changed her life ... Her journey from feeling lost to finding purpose touched me; it showed how people can grow even after going through hard times. The writing is detailed with strong character development. The supporting characters all played a major role in making the book stand out. I recommend* Last Call at Smokey Row *to readers who enjoy books about self-discovery, friendships, and finding a sense of belonging in unexpected places.*

– Reviewed by Mary Clarke for Readers' Favorite

Last Call at Smoky Row *tells of Jane, who finds herself alone and unloved in her early thirties, despite having followed the formula for a good life, getting a solid education and marrying appropriately. Ironically, the very place she hangs out and the characters she meets there form a foundation for new beginnings that sends Jane into a direction different from either the successful path she thought she was on or the downfall she thinks she's experiencing now.*

 As Jane reviews the patrons of the bar, how they begin "dropping like flies," and the changing relationships and reputations that bind such disparate personalities together, readers enjoy a story steeped in character decisions and life experiences. It brings these oddballs to life, setting their courses in sync with events that propel them in new directions.

Pat Camalliere's story is as much about growth and adaptation as it is about a woman's ability to reinvent her future from a present which looks decidedly different than any definition of a successful life that she's absorbed in the past. Readers seeking a story that moves its main characters from a seeming end of life to new beginnings will find Last Call at Smoky Row *a thought-provoking tale of how change happens, relationships and connections form, and institutions as venerable and lowly as bars can become incubators for change.*

– Diane Donovan, Editor, Donovan's Literary Services; Editor, Bookwatch; Author: San Francisco Relocated

Recommendations from Other Writers

If you're a fan of character-driven stories, you'll love Last Call at Smokey Row. *Author Pat Camalliere sets her tale in Lemont, Illinois, a place she knows well and clearly loves. Centered on Jane Archer, a bright and observant thirty-something in search of herself, the story takes place mainly at Sami's Saloon, a local bar and pool hall that's well past its glory days but still has something to offer. Jane's quest is the framework for a colorful tapestry of human experience; the regulars she gets to know at Sami's may not all be lovable, but every single one—the pool hounds, the drifters, the fellow searchers for someplace to belong—is unforgettable.*

There's a quiet magic to Camalliere's writing, a vividness of place and people that draws you in and doesn't let go. Humor, friendship, unexpected loss, and a simmering conflict that ultimately leads to a startling act of vengeance, or perhaps rough justice, are expertly intertwined by a storyteller who's a master of her craft. Don't miss this one.

– D. M. Pirrone (Diane Piron-Gelman), author of NO LESS IN BLOOD *and the* Hanley & Rivka Mysteries

What a lovely and thoughtful look at the characters who find themselves drifting together at a small-town bar. Aware of it or not, whether likely to succeed or not, each one searches for what's missing in their lives. A careful, well-written exploration of how we escape our pasts and try to move forward with new people and new pursuits. Not all goes according to plan, of course, and a delicious thread of intrigue grows to a very clever ending. Satisfying at so many levels.

– Sandra Cavallo Miller, author of OUT OF PATIENTS

The main character and narrator, Jane Archer, is someone many people can relate to. But at the age of 33, she finds herself a divorced ex-teacher, living alone for the first time in her life, working a dead-end job in a grocery store, and wondering if she has the stamina and

motivation to figure out what to do next. Invited by a coworker who participates in a pool league, Jane visits a local tavern called Sami's. There she meets a collection of people seemingly as adrift as she is. In time, Jane builds relationships at Sami's. With the help of one of her newfound friends, she slowly begins to find a new career path and perhaps even the hope of romance.

With such a diverse mix of personalities, problems in the group are sure to bubble up. One conflict gets resolved in a way that I guarantee you won't see coming. Through it all, Jane responds to the events around her by continuing to ask questions and to grow. Despite the large cast of characters, it is her story above all, and Camalliere brings it to a satisfying end.

– Ruth Hull Chatlien, author of KATY, BAR THE DOOR

Pat Camalliere's latest book, Last Call at Smokey Row, departs from her acclaimed Cora Tozzi historical mystery series while remaining a love note to the author's beloved geographical territory—Lemont, Illinois. The protagonist, Jane Archer, has retreated to Lemont to recover from a failed marriage and career. Relatively sheltered and limited in life experience, Jane accompanies a co-worker to a neighborhood bar, a landscape that is foreign and uncomfortable at first. Jane can't quite figure out what draws her to keep returning to the bar, but she gradually warms to a number of the regulars. As her relationships deepen and intrigue filters in, Jane opens up to new experiences, her attitudes broaden, and she is ultimately able to find her own way forward, fully embracing a new life. Camalliere offers readers a thoughtful meditation on change, how we find and build community, and the courage to begin again.

– Barbara Monier, author of PERFECTLY HUGO

Last Call at Smokey Row

LAST CALL
at
Smokey Row

PAT CAMALLIERE

CAMPAT
PUBLICATIONS

Books by Pat Camalliere:

Last Call at Smokey Row

Staying Alive Is a Lot of Work: Me and My Cancer

The Cora Tozzi Historical Mystery Series:

The Miracle at Assisi Hill

The Mystery at Mount Forest Island

The Mystery at Black Partridge Woods

The Mystery at Sag Bridge

Paperback first edition

ISBN: 979-8-9871624-3-9

Library of Congress Control Number: 2025910365

CAMPAT Publications, Lemont, Illinois 60439

Cover design by Jeff Waggoner. Photography by Pat Camalliere. Designed and typeset by Jeff Waggoner. Edited by Donald G. Evans. Line editing by Diane Piron-Gelman.

Dedicated to friends in low places.

There is a tavern in the town...

Prologue
2022

"Look at this, Jane," Rusty said. He passed his tablet to me where I was sitting at the other end of our sofa. I set down my phone and looked at his screen. It showed an article from today's Patch. The headline read, "Sami's Saloon, a Lemont mainstay, closes permanently after 130 years."

I skimmed the article. "The headline isn't quite right," I said. "The building has been a bar since the 1890s, but it was only named Sami's in about 1980. They're blaming Covid. Another business done in by the virus."

"It's terrible. Nick's, Tom's, Pollyanna, Main Inn—they all seem to be surviving, even with competition from all the restaurant bars in town. I'm sure Covid's been tough on all of them. I hope we don't lose more. Hate to see empty buildings all over town, especially ones in the historic district, like Sami's."

"That's true," I said. "Not that we go to Sami's anymore, but we do have a sentimental attachment."

"I wonder what might go into the building now. We don't need another beauty salon in town, do we?" Rusty looked off into space. I guessed he was remembering people and events from Sami's, as I was doing the same thing.

"Some boutique shop, I suppose," I said.

I looked fondly at my husband of—I did a quick calculation—over forty years! How had the time gone by so fast? His receding hairline left the entire top of his head bald, instead of the thick curly dark hair I remembered from the night we met at Sami's. My hair was thinner now too—white instead of light brown. He'd kept his trim figure, though, while I'd gained some thirty pounds. I sighed. It was time I got serious about losing weight.

We were empty nesters now. Our only daughter, Peggy, lived in Minnesota where she practiced as a radiologist alongside her husband, who was head of the department of surgery at a university hospital. There wouldn't be anyone to carry on the Dineff name, but Peggy had given us three grandsons in five years, then after another five years went by gave birth to our only granddaughter, now nearly three years old. Too bad they weren't closer, but we found time to visit at least once a month.

I handed the tablet back to Rusty, who returned to browsing the news. I pulled a handkerchief from my pocket and cleared my nose, then drifted into memory mode and pictured Sami's: the massive, well-worn old carved bar that ran the length of one wall, the pool table at the back, the old tin ceilings, manufactured right here in Lemont. I heard the jukebox, always too loud, playing a favorite from the eighties—"Take This Job and Shove It"—and smelled the alcohol, sweat, and smoke of a typical neighborhood bar in the days before indoor smoking was banned.

How could I explain Sami's? The place had rescued me at a low point and ended up changing my life.

Sami's was where I had come out of my protective shell and learned how another element, totally foreign to me at the time, lived. It was where the innocent, priggish woman I had been learned humility, tolerance, and inclusivity. Sami's was where I learned to walk in someone else's shoes—even better, I thought with a chuckle, on my own two stocking feet—before I turned my life in another direction.

I'd been grateful to the friends I'd met back in those days. The people I'd known at Sami's had seen me through a tough time, even as I shared the misfortunes of their own lives. I'd come to care for them. My memories of the evenings we spent there were poignant, fond, and yes, sad too. And toward the end, awful.

Now that I'd published a few novels, maybe it was time to drag out the old memories and write about Sami's. Maybe I'd even ask Sue from my writers' group to read my manuscript when it was done and invite her to write a poem to include as a preface, an homage to Sami's

Saloon.

I reached for the note pad and pen I kept on the table next to my customary place on the couch and jotted a note so I wouldn't forget my good intentions.

Chapter 1

I PAUSED ON THE SIDEWALK outside the nineteenth-century wooden building, wrestling with doubt. What made me think coming to this neighborhood bar would cure my boredom and loneliness, let alone help me accept my failures and find a way to my dreams of a better future? But, in a moment of weakness, I'd let Lindsay lure me into meeting her here.

"Sami's Saloon," the bright blue neon sign flashed in the window next to the double-door entrance. Wasn't the name spelled wrong? Shouldn't it be Sammy's? Or Sammie's? I pushed open the heavy door. Immediately a blast of cool air rushed out, welcome in the mid-evening heat of August 1981. Not as welcome: the stale odor of too many male bodies, the acrid smell of beer, the chaos of many boisterous voices shouting over the jukebox, "Take this job and shove it!" *And* a cloud of cigarette smoke.

Lindsay said this bar used smoke-eaters. Strike one. I was right—this wasn't my kind of place.

Resigned, I blew out my cheeks, then took in a breath of fresh outdoor air and stepped over the threshold into the smoky bar. This was the Lemont I'd heard about, where in the late eighteen hundreds and early nineteen hundreds this part of town lining the canals and railroad tracks was populated by an infamous red-light district known as Smokey Row, a hundred saloons, brothels, gambling dens, and other places of ill repute that catered to the barge, quarry, and railroad workers of the day. The same buildings, two-story clapboard structures with stores on the ground floor and living space or offices above, still filled the downtown area of Lemont. I supposed it was time I saw this element of town for myself, since I'd been here for six months now.

Standing near the doorway, I glanced around the noisy room, crowded with after-work drinkers. It was seven in the evening. Happy hour must be over, but the room was still full. These must be the regulars, the dedicated drinkers.

Dedicated drinkers—aka drunks. Something else to look forward to. I sighed and stepped away from the door, looking for Lindsay. I didn't see her. In fact, I was the only woman in the place…oops! No, a tall, large-boned woman of about forty sat on a stool at the far end of the bar, holding a pen and looking at some papers in front of her.

I was surprised she could read in here. The only light came from beer signs that advertised popular brands but produced dim illumination, except for a long, rectangular stained-glass light over a pool table at the end of the room. Even from where I stood, I could read the lettering on the light: Blatz. The walls were covered with glossy chipped paneling that looked more like a photograph of wood than the real thing. A well-worn, heavy, carved wooden bar ran the length of the long, narrow room on the left, the right wall lined with a few small tables and chairs, the noisy jukebox, and an equally noisy poker machine. Over the din, a sharp crack followed by a rumbling sound and a cheer came from the rear of the room. Patrons crowded along the bar, standing or sitting on stools, and a cluster of men gathered around the pool table at the back of the room where the bar ended, across from the restrooms.

The only person who looked my way was the bartender. The man was moderately tall, with a long, emaciated look. The top of his head was completely bald, the sides and back sparsely populated with straight dark thinning hair, a little too long, and thick, heavy eyebrows sat atop penetrating, almost-black eyes and a large, hooked nose. The spelling of the bar's name made sense now, as he appeared to be of

Middle Eastern heritage. He was dressed neatly in dark pants, a white button-down shirt open at the collar, and rolled-up sleeves.

Where are all the women? Maybe I should leave....

"Welcome, pretty lady, to Sami's exceptional drinking establishment," he called. "You have not been here before, I think. What is your pleasure?" His voice sounded precise and friendly, but his smile looked forced.

How would I explain to Lindsay if I left? But if I stay, of course I have to order something. Shit. I have no idea. A beer? I hate beer! Wine? Do they serve wine here?

What else did I have to do anyway. My only friend in town, Dottie Lou, was busy with her family in the evenings.

"Um...I'm Jane Archer. I'm meeting someone here," I said.

"Ah, I see. And who is this gentleman friend? He has not yet arrived?"

"No...um...it's a woman. She shoots pool here." I switched my purse strap from one shoulder to the other.

"You must be meaning Little Lindsay. She is your friend? She is usually here by now."

Little Lindsay. I haven't heard her called that, but it fits. Proves I'm in the right place at least.

I heard another sharp crack followed by a rattle and realized I was hearing balls on a pool table. I looked at my watch. Just past seven. Hadn't Lindsay said they started playing at seven? But there were only men around the pool table. *I am so out of place here!*

I ignored the bartender and walked to the end of the bar where there were a number of empty stools and sat on one of them to wait.

The bartender had called me pretty lady. I wondered if he did that to everyone. I certainly didn't think of myself as a pretty lady. I didn't think I was unattractive, but Plain Jane seemed to suit me better. Although I was at least neat, clean, and pleasant enough, I was too short and a little dumpy, with poor taste in clothing and an inability to handle my mousy brown hair or makeup well. My tortoiseshell cat's-eye glasses probably weren't fashionable anymore, since I'd not changed them in years. Education and accomplishment had always meant more to me than appearance. I should probably be working on that too, now that my life situation had changed so drastically.

While I waited, I studied the room. Some men appeared boisterous, some argumentative, some contemplative or even a little brooding. Other stared silently at one of two televisions that were mounted behind the bar, one near the front and the other near mid-bar. Both screens viewed sports events, but different games. No sound emitted from the televisions, which made sense since they would never be heard over the din. From across the street the horn of a passing train momentarily drowned out the laughing and yelling customers, cheers from the pool table, the jukebox, and bells from the poker machine. I wondered if these men had come here to escape things about their lives they were dissatisfied with and developed behaviors to hide that fact. I didn't think of myself that way, but now it occurred to me that perhaps I wasn't that different from them after all.

Why did I let Lindsay talk me into coming here?

The door opened again and Lindsay struggled through, carrying a large purse and a slender black leather-like case about two feet long and six inches wide. I assumed the case held her pool stick, although I could see a rack of sticks on the wall next to the table. She was out of breath and red-faced as she rushed up to me.

"Sorry. Car didn't want to start. Fortunately, a guy in the parking lot had a cable." A look of concern came over her face. "I hope it'll start when I leave here…"

"I'll be sure you get home," I volunteered. *Damn! What did I just do? Now I'll have to stay until she's finished…whenever that is.*

"Thanks." She started toward the back of the room. I followed.

"Lindsay! Let's get rolling!" called a man with a pool stick in his hand.

"That's Dixon," said Lindsay. "Look, sit on this stool next to the table. Hold my purse, will you, while you watch us play?" She pointed to a barstool near the head of the pool table and handed her purse to me. "Order something from Sami. A rum and Coke for me. He'll start a tab. It's my break."

Whatever that meant.

Pool was clearly important to Lindsay. Lindsay Wexford and I worked at Ordman's Fresh Market in State Street Plaza, a local grocery store, me as assistant service manager and Lindsay in the produce department. There was good reason the bartender, who I gathered was Sami, the owner of the bar, called her Little Lindsay. She was barely four and a half feet tall and weighed about ninety pounds, her short arms and legs of almost dwarf-like stature. Her square jaw, wide-set eyes, thick eyebrows, and prominent nose appeared almost masculine, but she had a full head of luscious honey-brown hair that cascaded thickly over her shoulders. She walked to the pool table with quick, energetic motions, unlike the hesitant, almost fragile meekness she displayed at Ordman's. But I noticed she kept her head down and didn't look directly at the other players.

During work hours, Lindsay rarely engaged in conversation with other workers and took breaks alone in a corner. "She's an odd one," the manager said, rolling her eyes. "She's a decent worker, but don't expect her to chat or even notice you."

But I did notice her, I felt sorry for her, and I'd always been accused of having insatiable curiosity. I made it a point to keep her company during breaks when the opportunity came up.

"What do you do when you're not at work? For fun?" I asked her one day.

"Pool," she said.

"Really? Where do you swim?" I hadn't been in Lemont long enough to look for pools nearby.

"No," she said. "Not swimming. I shoot pool."

That seemed odd to me. Wasn't pool a men's game? Not something I expected a tiny, meek, fragile-appearing woman to engage in.

She gave me a crooked little smile. "I'm pretty good. Would you like to come and watch me sometime?"

"Um…sure," I said without enthusiasm. I knew nothing about pool and didn't want to. That was something that happened in rough neighborhood bars, where people like bikers and losers hung out. But my curiosity was piqued, and I didn't want to turn her down. Which explained why I was here at Sami's Saloon.

The alternative was watching television and falling asleep, as usual. After my divorce and quitting my job, I had found an apartment and temporary job in Lemont, near my best friend Dottie Lou, hoping to get my life back on track. My marriage had been a mistake, as well as the teaching career I thought I'd wanted. Here I was, in my early thirties, with a master's degree and some post-master's education in biology, still wondering what I wanted to do when I grew up.

Almost immediately I realized I didn't like living alone. Out here in Lemont, where the wind turned around and came back, I felt isolated, no longer having anything in common with my former friends and teaching associates, and my parents lived half an hour away. I couldn't spend all my free time with Dottie Lou—she had her husband and kids to take care of. I no longer had a man to share my life. Isolation wasn't a bad thing if it got me moving in a new, better direction. But I needed a jolt. I needed to meet new people. I doubted this was the right place to do that, but I had to start somewhere.

I struggled to climb onto a stool, jostling two big, heavy purses. Should I put them on the bar, under my feet, sling them on the back of the stool, or balance them on my lap? No option seemed reasonable. Once settled, I pulled a handkerchief out of my purse and tried to look busy polishing my glasses.

The bartender—Sami—returned. "You are not comfortable. You are wondering if you should stay. Let me get you something to help you make up your mind."

"Why do you say that?" I said, slipping my glasses back on and putting my handkerchief into a pocket to avoid struggling with my purse again. "You know nothing about me."

"Ah, but I do," he said, his words clear despite his clipped accent. "I am the exceptional reader of people. You don't have that look of being ridden hard and put away wet, an expression I have heard that, I think, applies to many of my customers. So, you see, you are not comfortable. What can I get you?"

"You're right—I don't come to bars. I don't know what to order. Something only mildly alcoholic, I think…."

"Leave it to Sami," he said and walked away. He returned quickly, setting in front of me a tumbler filled with a cloudy, whitish fluid, ice, and a wedge of lime on the rim.

I sipped through a slender red straw. The taste was sweet, tangy, fruity, not like alcohol at all.

"What is this?"

"Vodka and grapefruit juice. You like?"

I did like, surprisingly. The drink was refreshing on a hot August night and didn't taste like alcohol or cloyingly sweet. Sami turned away, moving down the bar to draw another beer from the tap for a customer who was waving at him.

I swiveled my stool to watch the pool game, balancing the purses on my lap. From here I could see the front door and watch who came in or went out. "And I am a material girl," blared through the room. Next to the jukebox a heavyset man with uncombed hair and patched jeans fed coins into a poker machine, his vulgar shouts or ecstatic comments competing with the periodic electronic sounds.

A broad-shouldered, stocky man, the man Lindsay had called Dixon, approached the pool table. He appeared to be in his late thirties and had a reddish face and scars from adolescent acne. The top of his head was bald, the sides and back covered with a thick mat of wiry hair. He wore jeans, a plaid shirt, and cowboy boots. I thought he resembled a bowlegged redneck Einstein.

Dixon fed a quarter into a slot at the head of the table. Balls rumbled into a pocket under the tabletop. He placed a plastic triangular device on the tabletop, filled it with colored and striped balls, pushed them tightly together and rolled them back and forth a few times, then removed the device. The balls remained tightly together. His opponent set one hand on the table, drew his stick back and forth a couple of times, concentrating, then with a quick stroke drove a white ball into the others. Balls scattered on the tabletop, and one rolled into a pocket. He studied the remaining balls, then said, "Stripes."

The man continued to move around the table, lining up the white ball to make it hit another ball and drive a striped ball into a pocket. Lindsay stood at the side of the table, holding a stick, watching.

When the man missed, he walked away and Dixon took his turn. He apparently didn't do very well, because soon the game was over and Dixon eased himself onto the empty stool next to me, turning the stool around to watch the game. Sami immediately placed a glass of what appeared to be Coke on the bar in front of him.

The man at the poker machine banged his fist next to the control panel and yelled, "Fuck!" I winced.

Dixon turned to me. "That's Dirty Wally. Don't mind him. He's harmless. Must be havin' a bad night, though." Dixon's voice sounded friendly, soft and low, with a heavy Southern drawl. When he smiled, I noticed badly misaligned teeth. As for Dirty Wally, his stained shirtsleeves more than just his foul language indicated his nickname suited him.

I turned in Dixon's direction. "Dixon Parker," he said. "You're a friend of Lindsay's?"

"Yes. Jane Archer." He leaned his stick against the stool and held out his hand. We shook, after I struggled to free a hand from the purses on my lap.

"I won't see the table now 'til my quarter comes up agin. Little Lindsay's gonna run it." He took a sip from his glass and set it back down. He sighed and then smiled at me. "How'd you know Lindsay?"

"We work together." We watched for a minute. "How does she know which ball to hit?" I asked.

"You don't know the game?"

"Not at all. First time watching. Lindsay says she's pretty good."

"She's not exaggeratin'. Look...." He pointed. "See that line of quarters on the side of the table? Each one is for the next person to start a game, or break. My quarter comes up, I rack the balls, and then my opponent, who won the last game, breaks. The white ball is the cue ball—that's the only ball you can hit with your cue stick. The break scatters all the balls on the table. Some of the balls are solid color, some white with stripes. You sink a ball on the break, you get another shot and the ball that went in determines the balls you have to sink—the solids or the stripes. If you miss, the other player gets to shoot."

"And if you have stripes, the other player has to sink solids?"

"You got it."

"When the other player misses, you get to shoot again."

"Right." He grinned. "Unless it's Lindsay on the table. She don't never miss, so you don't get the table back."

"Is she the best?"

"Prid' near. There's a couple give her a run for her money. In fact, here's one comin' through the door now."

I looked up. At the door was a dark-haired man of average height and build wearing silver metal-framed eyeglasses and four-o'clock shadow. He appeared to be in his thirties. Unlike most of the men in the bar, he was dressed in a suit. He walked up to Dixon, slipped off his suit coat and draped it on the back of Dixon's stool. "Gonna be able to make it Saturday?" he asked.

"Sure thing," Dixon said. "Rusty, this here is Jane. She come to watch Little Lindsay play. They work together...at Ordman's, that right?"

I nodded. He stuck out his hand. "Rusty Dineff." We shook.

"Me and Rusty's golf buddies," Dixon went on. "We play every Saturday, weather permittin'. And Rusty's one of the ones beats Little Lindsay now and then...unless we gets lucky, that is."

Rusty excused himself, reached into a pocket and pulled out a quarter that he added to a line of quarters on the rim of the pool table. He stood watching the players as he took off his tie, folded it up and put it in his suit coat pocket, and rolled up his shirtsleeves. Then he walked over to a rack on the wall next to the pool table, selected a pool stick, picked up a little blue square, and rubbed the end of the stick on it.

Over the din, "Take this job and shove it," blared from the jukebox again and some patrons joined in the refrain. It seemed to be a favorite. Bells and burps continued to sound from the poker machine, and Dirty Wally continued to cheer or swear.

"Do you like this song?" Dixon asked.

"I actually haven't heard it before. I'm not much into country music."

"What kind of music *do* you like? There's lots of things on the jukebox—I'll play something you like."

I smiled. "Actually, I like classical music. Don't think you'll find any of that on there."

"I guess not," said Dixon. He paused, furrowed his brow, then: "What is it?"

"Classical music? Like the *1812 Overture* and music they play on movie soundtracks, stuff like that. Orchestras, not bands. I used to sing with a church choir."

"Oh. Well, you're right. Won't be any of *that* on there."

We watched Lindsay for a bit. Then I asked, "Tell me about Sami. He's from the Middle East somewhere?"

"He comes from Pakistan. Owns the bar, 'bout the past year or so. He's all right. Sometimes gets a little rough towards closin' time if too many customers buy him drinks. He'd never turn a drink down…it's business. But he keeps his wits about him even though. Most of the time he's all right," he said again. "Seems to be a good businessman."

"Where he's from, don't they disapprove of drinking? Why did he buy a bar, instead of a convenience store or a gas station, something like that? Isn't that unusual?" I bit my tongue, hoping Dixon didn't think I was stereotyping Pakistanis.

"Maybe—I wouldn't know. It's just business, and this is a busy place. He can make a lot of money here, if he doesn't drink up too much of the profit. I heard buying the place might have been his wife's idea."

Dixon elbowed me and pointed to the end of the bar, to the woman I had noticed when I came in, reading in the dark. Whatever she was looking at seemed to have all her attention, as she hadn't lifted her head from what I'd seen. "That's Whitney Murphy, Sami's wife. She's prob'ly looking over the receipts. People say she wears the pants here, keeps watch over everything Sami does."

"Really?" I was confused. "Sami's last name is Murphy? That's not Pakistani."

Dixon chuckled. "It's Sami Chaudhry. Whitney kept her maiden name. Born and raised here in Lemont, never lived anywhere else. One of them 'Long Time Lemonters' you prob'ly heard about. Not about to give up her name."

I studied her. "I haven't seen them talk to each other since I've been here."

"Not unusual. Gossip says they don't have the normal husband-wife thing. But she has a good job over at Argonne, workin' with figures some kind of way, accountant or somethin' like that. Makes a lot of money. Some say that's where Sami got the money to buy this place."

We sipped our drinks. Sami came back and placed another vodka and grapefruit juice in front of me. "I don't want another drink," I said. "I don't handle alcohol very well."

Sami gave me an angry look, then softened it with a smile. "Rusty bought it. The man wants to buy you a drink, you don't say no. It's bad for business. Don't drink it if you don't want to, but someone buys a drink I serve it." He walked away.

I got the message. But I had enjoyed the first drink and found myself sipping the second one.

No one had ever bought a drink for me, but then I hadn't ever sat in a bar before either. Should I be suspicious of Rusty? I asked Dixon, "What does it mean when a guy buys me a drink? What am I supposed to do?"

"Depends on the guy. But in this case, just wave to him and say thanks. Rusty don't mean nothin'. He's just a nice guy wanting to welcome someone new. He's not lookin' to pick up women."

I looked at the pool players and caught Rusty's eye. I smiled at him, held up the drink, and mouthed the word, "Thanks." He grinned, nodded, and turned back to the game. I noticed he walked with a confident stride, like a soldier. He had warm brown eyes behind wire-rimmed glasses and a pleasant, deep voice.

He seems friendly, I thought. Average in the looks department, more interested in pool than me. Dixon must know him pretty well, since they played golf and shot pool together, and he apparently didn't think Rusty was the sort of guy to hit on women. Who'd be interested in me anyway? I'd never been one to be noticed in a crowd, especially in a neighborhood bar. I relaxed.

I was enjoying talking with Dixon. The place was nothing like anything I'd experienced before in my sheltered, middle-class life. But the people were friendly, and it seemed safe, loud but not rowdy. It was near my apartment. It would be a change from vegging out in front of the television every night. Maybe I'd stop in from time to time, not stay too long, learn a bit more about this game of pool and the people who hung out here.

I glanced over at Lindsay. She was setting out the balls into their triangle and Rusty was standing by, clearly her competition for the next game. This should be interesting.

I'd stay to watch Lindsay play a game, then make my excuses and leave. I didn't have to return. Although I was intrigued by the people I'd met, and I had no social life or other place to go. Dixon and Rusty seemed like nice guys....

Chapter 2

I'D KNOWN DOTTIE LOU MEYERS since freshman year of high school, when we became best friends. She often told others I was her oldest and dearest friend. I was a whole five weeks older than her, but throughout our friendship we always laughed at the implied misinterpretation. Now, not only did we have the longest friendship, but she was the only longtime friend I had frequent contact with after my recent divorce. Even though I had moved to Lemont to be near her and my parents in Oak Lawn, she was busy with three children, a fourth on the way, and a husband who expected his perfect wife to take care of his house and family and to wait on him hand and foot. Tom was a nice enough guy, and Dottie Lou never complained, but I hated it whenever she told me about some personal pleasure she had to give up to satisfy some whim of his or stroke his ego. I never saw *her* desires being important to him.

It was to Dottie Lou I turned when I was lonely, when I needed a boost, a friendly ear, or an opinion. It was Dottie Lou who helped me through the bad times that led up to leaving my job and my husband, Dottie Lou who supported and encouraged me through the divorce and relocation.

And so, at the first opportunity I called Dottie Lou to tell her about my evening at Sami's.

"So, what do you think," she asked, after I'd described my evening. "Are you going to go back?"

I thought about the question. "Honestly, I don't know. I mean, I have nothing to stop me from going. I need to meet people if I want to start a new life. I can't depend on you for everything. The closest thing to a friend I've found at work is Lindsay, and she's the one who brought me to Sami's. It's not our kind of place, though. I sort of feel like I'm just putting myself into another place I don't fit. What's the point in that?"

"Yeah, well, true. You're not a pool shooter. Those guys you told me about, Dixon and Rusty, could you have any interest in them, do you think?"

"After Dick—"

"Who turned into a dick, didn't he?" Dottie Lou interrupted, and we laughed.

"I'm afraid to get close to another man after things didn't work with Dick. I just want friends to be with right now, and I can't put all that on you."

"You could. You know that."

"But I wouldn't do that to you. No, I have to find other ways to socialize. I guess this place could be a start. At least get me comfortable with being out and having fun, not just working all the time and our all-too-frequent bitch sessions. Maybe I should give it a try until something better presents itself."

"Do you want me to see if Tom will watch the kids one night and I'll go there with you?"

I thought that over. Sami's wasn't Dottie Lou's kind of place any more than it was mine. I was ashamed to admit, even to her, that Sami's had some sort of unexplainable attraction to me. Sort of like slumming. I'd always wondered why people hung out in bars. But it was one thing to talk to Dottie Lou about these ideas, quite another to actually bring her to the place where she'd see it for herself. I guess I'd already made up my mind that I would go back, and I didn't want her to watch me on unfamiliar ground. When I visualized such an evening, I saw her balancing her protruding pregnancy on a bar stool, shaking her head and saying, "Bad move, Jane. I just can't understand why you'd want to come here."

So, what I said was, "That's okay. I'll go watch Lindsay again the next tournament night, like I promised her. Then I probably won't go anymore."

Chapter 3

OVER THE NEXT FEW WEEKS I discovered that most of the major pool leagues started in the fall, but players often came to Sami's on other nights for the social life and to keep their skills up. Lindsay played on an in-house league on Wednesday nights. Despite my original reluctance to return to Sami's, I found myself looking forward to a regular night out. I transferred my wallet and keys to a small purse I kept over my shoulder or set on the bar top so I wouldn't need to struggle to make room for a large purse. I usually arrived a bit after the league started at seven.

Sami's reminded me of Irish and English pubs I'd seen in movies and read about in books. I'd never been to one of those pubs, but, like Sami's, they were neighborhood sorts of places. Often the patrons walked from their nearby homes to get together with friends and neighbors after work, or late in the evenings to socialize over one or more drafts of beer—usually more.

From reading about Lemont since I'd moved here, I knew that Lemont's earliest residents were Irish laborers who frequented places like Sami's. The buildings in the old area of town still remained, with some of their original furnishings such as thickly carved dark wooden bars and tin ceilings. The building Sami's was in dated back to at least the 1890s when there were a lot of single men working on the Sanitary and Ship Canal living in town and looking for places to cut loose in the little free time they had. Owners had changed through the years, but this building had always been a bar.

I didn't have much, if anything, in common with the people at Sami's, but despite my misgivings I was getting to know not just the pool players but the bar's "regulars." Underachievers for the most part, in my opinion, but I wasn't exactly a super-achiever myself at the moment. Although different than people I'd known throughout my strict religious upbringing, they seemed to be a mixed bag of nice people, some who were content with their modest lives, others who hadn't found success in life. Some were smart, some undereducated or slow. Some held regular jobs, others were underemployed, unemployed, or long-time public aid recipients. Some came to shoot pool, others to hang out with friends. All spent a good deal of their free time socializing and drinking at Sami's.

Besides Lindsay and Whitney, only a few other women came into the bar. Some were wives of male bar patrons, some loners looking for a good time who rarely returned, a few trying to *make* time with someone. There must have been a certain vibe those unattached women gave off, because I noticed right away that the men in the bar treated most women with respect but cussed freely in front of others. Fortunately, the men here were always polite to me. Otherwise, I wouldn't have returned.

One of the bar regulars was Angelico Raphael, known fondly as Angel. Angel was treated by most of the other patrons as a sort of bar mascot, because he was there every day and all day when he was in town. Dixon said Angel had been born in El Paso, Texas, to illegal Mexican immigrant parents who passed him back and forth between relatives on both sides of the border as a child. He was poorly educated, could only read a few words, had no skills, and was unable to retain even menial jobs because his drinking made him a frequent no-show.

Tall, slender, and dark-complected, with a full head of black, curly hair, Angel was rather nice-looking. I guessed him to be about forty. Bar talk was that he had a wife in El Paso. a nice lady who understood and cared about him, only more like a pet than a husband. With both their interests at heart, she sent him to Lemont for months on end, where they had friends he could stay with. He got a little day work to keep him in beer money, so she didn't have to support him and deal with his nightly drinking. From time to time he would return to El Paso, they would spend a month or two together, and then he'd wear out his welcome and she'd put him back on a bus to Lemont.

At first, I assumed Spanish was Angel's native language but was surprised to learn that his Spanish wasn't much better than his English. Raised on the border, he spoke broken English to most people and broken Spanish to Spanish-speakers, making conversation with him difficult. I thought of him as a sort of Mexican gringo. But he was so good-natured that I found it entertaining to talk with him nonetheless.

Drinking all day was Angel's life. He spent more than half of his waking hours—and some of his sleeping hours—at the bar. Now and then he cheerfully did odd jobs for friends or businesses nearby. Then, before Sami's opened for the day, he wiped down the counters, cleaned the sinks, swept up, and set the stools back on the floor, getting the bar ready for business. For that he was allowed a limited number of free beers and snacks. He took his customary stool toward the rear when the bar opened at one in the afternoon. His speech, never easy to understand under the best of circumstances, got more and more unintelligible with each beer he consumed as the evening wore on. It didn't take much. For someone who drank as consistently as Angel, it seemed he'd failed to build up a tolerance for alcohol.

But everyone liked Angel. When sober early in the day, he was always willing to lend a helping hand, so people called on him. He never charged, but most of the time friends slipped him a few dollars, and I looked for ways to help him out. He was a quiet drunk, never mean or angry, greeting men and women alike with a happy smile, showing interest in their lives, engaging them in his odd conversation that was part English and part Spanish—until he passed out, usually sometime after ten in the evening. Then he would doze with his head on the bar until closing, sometimes wetting his pants in his sleep, prompting disgusted outcries from those sitting near him. Eventually he'd wake up and teeter out the door. Other regulars kept an eye on him, bought him food now and then, and saw that he got home safely when necessary.

I wondered why Sami put up with Angel's behavior. I could only guess it was because he had a pretty good deal with the work Angel did for a few cheap beers. Perhaps they had worked out a compromise that kept Angel at the back end of the bar, where he would be less offensive to other patrons.

Most of this I knew from talk at the bar, since I usually left early, before Angel was seriously impaired, and I rarely had to experience that side of him. I liked Angel too. Since he was always around, he knew everything that went on and kept me informed about what was new. He fixed things or did heavy lifting for me, providing I got to him early in the day. A few times a week I'd run over to bring him food from Ordman's that would otherwise go to waste. I'd never had to witness him passing out or wetting the floor. The idea made me uncomfortable.

Another regular was a bit harder to know. John David Christopher was a small man, only a little taller than my five feet, three inches. He was painfully shy and talked very little. He came in every night about six and left about ten. He drank slowly, sparingly, sometimes non-alcoholic beverages. Even though the weather was still hot, he always wore a knit stocking hat pulled down over his ears. He was extremely protective of that hat, batting away any hands that tried to touch it. Knowing that, some rowdy bar patrons would tease him by trying to snatch his hat, but he was always able to keep it on. He had a slight build and was fair and clean-shaven. No one knew his hair color because his head was always covered.

Dixon and I had hit it off from the first night and now we usually sat on stools next to each other near the pool table where we could watch the games. I asked Dixon about John David. Something I'd sensed about the man reeked of mystery I couldn't resist. "It's hot in here. Why is he wearing that hat, do you think?"

"He always wears it. No one's never seen him without it."

"But that's odd—why? Does he have a bald spot or some disfigurement he's hiding?"

"Guess you could say that. Talk is he don't have any ears."

I glanced at John David. "Whoa! He's deaf? He doesn't act deaf. Was he born like that?"

"Naw, he's not deaf. His ears was cut off, supposedly."

"What? How did that happen?" An image of Vincent van Gogh popped into my mind.

"No one knows for sure. Story is somethin' happened in Nam. He should never of been sent there. Heard tell he was always a simple guy, quiet, and I guess the pressure was too much for him. He did something, no one knows what, that angered his soldier buddies, something about another buddy that ended up dead. Later they found John David cringing somewhere but safe. Guys from his own group, word is they never liked him much to begin with. They blamed him for their buddy that died, and they cut off John David's ears. He's never been quite right in the head since he come back. PTSD, they're callin' it now. At least, that's how the story goes."

I glanced at John David, who sat gazing at his beer with his elbows on the bar and his head resting on his hands. I felt pity for him, but in truth he made me uneasy.

"He's harmless," Dixon said. Dixon thought well of just about everybody, I was discovering. I, on the other hand, tended to be more judgmental.

We watched the pool shooters for a while, and Lindsay got up for her game. Dolly Parton's "Nine to Five" blared from the jukebox.

Sami was standing near the sink in the middle of the length of the bar. I saw him make a forceful downward motion followed by the sound of breaking glass.

"What is Sami doing?" I asked Dixon. "Breaking his own glasses? Why would he do that?"

"Nah," said Dixon. "He's just getting rid of beer bottles. There's a chute next to the sink that runs down to a bin in the basement to collect glass for the trash."

"But why does he throw the bottle instead of just letting it slide down?"

"He wants to be sure the bottle breaks into as small pieces as possible. More room in the garbage bin that way. Saves him from breaking them later."

I supposed that made sense.

"Say, how'd you and Lindsay get to be friends?" Dixon asked, thinking, I suppose, that I knew more about her than the pool shooters did.

"Actually, I don't know her that well. She's really close-mouthed at work. She lives alone, I think. I've tried to be nice to her at Ordman's, but I was still surprised when she asked me to come here. I didn't think she would have if it wasn't important to her, and I didn't want to let her down—she seems like someone who needs a friend."

I took a sip from my drink, the grapefruit and vodka I'd decided I liked, and looked around the bar. My gaze stopped on John David again, who was sitting three stools away, watching Lindsay run the table. Watching her very intently, I realized. I turned away, glad he wasn't watching me.

I suddenly remembered something Sami mentioned a week ago about John David having a thing for Lindsay. I had thought he was just making conversation at the time. Maybe he was right and she felt nervous about it. "It entered my mind she might feel like she needed protection from someone here. I hope I'm wrong about that."

Dixon didn't miss a thing. "Well, I hope you're not thinking she needs protection from John David. She must know he's harmless by now."

I studied John David. He sat quietly, taking an occasional sip from his beer. As usual he wore a stocking cap, a red one tonight. He slumped over the bar, occasionally glancing up to watch Lindsay. His eyes darted around, skittish, avoiding contact; then he stared back down at the bar.

"Maybe he likes her because she's little, like him," I said.

"Who was those guys in that *Wizard of Oz* movie?" Dixon asked.

I laughed. "You mean the munchkins."

"That's them."

Dixon tried to catch Sami's eye to refill his Coke, but Sami didn't see him. "So, you come here to watch Lindsay play?" he asked again.

"The first time, yes. But I have to admit I met some nice people and I wanted to get to know them better." I looked at him and smiled. "Like you. I have a lot of curiosity about people, too much sometimes. I ask a lot of questions, in case you hadn't noticed."

Rusty lost the game he was playing with Lindsay and came to stand behind Dixon and me. Sami came over and placed a beer in front of Rusty. Dixon left to join the pool shooters.

"You want to play with us?" Rusty asked.

"Pool? Or golf? Or did you have something else in mind? Regardless, I don't play either game, I'm afraid."

He laughed. "I meant pool. I can teach you, if you're interested."

I looked at him. He seemed a nice enough guy. I'd never seen him drink too much or get loud. He swore some, but everyone here did that. He seemed to be competitive and took his pool games seriously, but he was never mean or rude. Wearing his usual suit pants and button-down shirt with rolled up sleeves, he seemed a step above most of the men in the bar who dressed in dirty construction clothes or T-shirts and jeans. But there I was, being judgmental again.

"Dixon has already tried to teach me, and he says I'm hopeless. Apparently, I have a lousy bridge, whatever that is, and no stroke. I don't hold the pool stick right—I can't seem to get comfortable with it in my hand or get it to move smoothly. It jerks when I try to hit the cue ball, and the object ball, if I ever manage to hit the right ball instead of the table, never goes the direction I want. I can't even play the first shot right, let alone think about where the next one should go if I do get lucky and sink a ball. Position, I think was the term he used. I have enough trouble just following the game and learning the lingo."

I kept my words light, but the one time Dixon tried to teach me to shoot pool it was immediately clear I was out of my depth. To demonstrate, he had to lean over me from behind and guide my arm.

I couldn't loosen up and ended up feeling stupid and humiliated in front of skilled players. There were two things that made me angrier than anything else: doubting my truthfulness or intelligence, and being humiliated. I didn't like surprises, and I didn't like to play games. Therefore, I'd refused to try to shoot pool again.

Rusty laughed. "You do make yourself sound hopeless, but skill comes with practice. You just got to get out there and play."

"I'll think about it. For now, I just enjoy watching the games. There's a lot more to it than just having the talent to connect with the ball, isn't there? I've been trying to understand the strategy."

"Just keep watching. You'll learn a lot here. There are some pretty good players. You haven't been just watching the game though, have you?" He raised his eyebrows and then winked.

I laughed. "No, I guess you caught me. I've been watching people. That's one of the reasons I like to sit at the end of the room, facing the door, so I can see everyone who comes and goes, and watch what's happening. When you're not really a drinker, when you don't know the people and don't play pool...well, for me the entertainment is people watching. For instance, Sami says that guy..." I pointed at John David, "...has a thing for Lindsay. And Dixon says Lindsay shouldn't worry about it because he's harmless. What do you think?"

"Apparently so. At least that seems to be the talk around here."

"So, should Lindsay be concerned?"

"Why? John David is quiet, mild, doesn't give anyone any trouble, just stays to himself. He's a little weird, but he's like a kid, really. Someone picks on him, he just walks away. Never seen him get mad. Just needs a place to be and this is it. He's not likely to hurt anyone, especially Lindsay, if people are right about the way he feels about her."

I looked at John David again. He was staring at the bar top. He still made me uncomfortable. "Okay...I guess."

"Looks like Lindsay's running the table again," Rusty said. "I might have to leave before my turn comes up. Gotta get to work early tomorrow."

"Where do you work?" I finally had the opportunity to ask the only guy who came in here in a suit.

"I'm with an engineering consulting firm, Sargent & Lundy. I've been on assignment at Argonne. It was supposed to be a temporary placement, six months. But I've been there three years now and the contract just got renewed for another year."

His expression didn't show a hint of self-importance, but I was impressed. The suit he wore should have been a tip-off, but this man clearly was not the typical blue-collar worker that frequented Sami's. I didn't know Sargent & Lundy, but Argonne, located in Lemont on the other side of the Des Plaines River, was a world-class national laboratory and would use only top consultants.

"That sounds important," I said.

He chuckled. "Not even close. It's a huge place, some four thousand employees, fourteen hundred of them scientists and engineers, most with doctorates. With my measly bachelor's degree in engineering mechanics and all the geniuses around me all day, I feel more like low man on the totem pole."

"Doesn't Sami's wife work there too?"

"Whitney? Yeah, that's what I've been told—in accounting. Our paths don't cross. As I said, it's a huge place. The lab occupies fifteen hundred acres, countless buildings."

We sipped our drinks and checked out how Dixon was doing. He was standing at the side of the table with a frown on his face. "Nine to Five" was playing yet again—for at least the fifth time, but I'd lost count. Must be someone's favorite.

I reached for my purse and fished in it, trying to locate my handkerchief.

"Something wrong?" Rusty asked.

I shook my head and closed my purse. "I wanted to clean my glasses, but I seem to have forgotten my hankie."

He reached into a side pants pocket and pulled out an ironed and folded white men's handkerchief. "Here, use mine," he said, offering it to me.

I took it and slipped off my glasses. "I'm surprised. Most men don't carry handkerchiefs anymore."

"Grandma would be rolling in her grave if I didn't. She gave me a pack of new ones every Christmas and expected to see me use them."

I laughed. "Most women use tissues now too. But I don't like them. They're not soft enough. Give me a good old hankie any day. I'm almost obsessive about it."

I finished cleaning my glasses and handed the hankie back to him.

"Have you always lived in the area?" I asked.

"I don't. I live on the North Side, in Rogers Park. That's why I can't stay too late, since it's a long drive. I could shoot pool in my neighborhood, I suppose. But by the time my day ends at Argonne, with rush hour traffic, it's too late to make it that far by the time the leagues start. So, I play here and then go home. I've been thinking about moving, though."

Darn, I thought. And then I wondered why that had popped into my head. The last thing I wanted at the moment was to get involved in any sort of relationship. What did I care where he lived?

"What does your family think about that?" I asked.

"No family to consider. Divorced for almost six years. Never had kids. One sister, and we don't talk. How about you?"

"Divorced, but only a year. I don't have any children either. I have degrees in biology—Bachelor of Arts with a minor in education and then a master's. I thought I wanted to teach, but it turned out I don't care much for teaching, at least not at the high school level. I know the material, but kids don't want to learn and I'm an awful disciplinarian. I spent most of the class just trying to get their attention. So I quit my job after the divorce."

"What are you doing now, besides sitting at Sami's?"

"I'm an assistant manager at Ordman's, the grocery store in town."

"Oh yeah, that's how you know Lindsay."

"Right." I sighed. "I worked at a Jewel in Oak Lawn when I was in high school. After the divorce, I needed money to live on. Grocery stores pay decent and the work doesn't take much brain power. I needed time to figure things out—wasn't ready to put in the effort to start a new career right away—so I just took the first job I found and moved out here. My best friend lives here too."

"That must be nice for you."

"I thought it would be, but as it turns out we don't see much of each other. She's busy with her family and can't get out much. I work days, and evenings and weekends her husband wants her home." I sighed. "It's reassuring to know she's close if I need her, though. We spend more time on the phone than in person. Maybe if her husband will watch the kids one night I can bring her here for a little while." I doubted that would happen. Tom wasn't the kind of guy to watch the kids while his wife socialized in a bar.

I began to notice a little buzz and thought I'd better slow down on the drinks. It hadn't taken me long to find out I had to stop drinking *before* I got high, since the effects of alcohol would keep building and the next thing I knew I'd be hanging over a basin being sick. I was serious about my two-drink maximum.

I put an elbow on the bar and rested my chin in my hand and gave him a lop-sided grin. "Here I am in my thirties and still trying to figure out what I want to be when I grow up. Turns out you can't do much with a master's in biology. Most good jobs require advanced knowledge and further training to be a forester, a lab tech, microbiologist, pharmacist, whatever. Now that I decided teaching isn't for me, I have yet to see something that excites me enough to pursue additional education. So far."

He studied me seriously. I had the impression he was forming a different opinion about me too and I hoped it was favorable. He said, "Argonne isn't all computers and physics. They also do biological research. Why don't you look for something there?"

"I'll think about it." I would. I had. I'd been to an open house at the national laboratory once and been impressed. It seemed to be mostly computers and nuclear accelerators, though. Biologists? I was skeptical. But then, my mood had been skeptical a lot in the last couple of years.

We turned our stools around and watched the shooters for a while. Little Lindsay had taken over the table, making shot after shot.

"Watch what she's doing," Rusty said. He leaned close, held my arm, and spoke into my ear so as not to disturb the players. "This game she's got solids. The black ball, the 8-ball, has to be left on the table. She has to sink all her solid balls, leaving the 8-ball for last to win. If she sinks it by accident before then, she loses. Sometimes it's hard, sometimes you just get lucky. Lindsay knows how to leave the cue ball somewhere so that it will be easy to make the next shot. It takes a lot of thought and planning. That's called position, and it's position that makes a good player."

Rusty's touch was warm and comforting. It had been a while since I'd felt that warmth. Too long a while.

I had to watch myself. I'd met two men now, Dixon and Rusty, and both were nice guys. I couldn't let loneliness push me before I got my head on straight. This place gave me something to do until I found something better, so long as it didn't become too much of a habit. The last thing I needed at the moment was more complications and bad decisions in my life. I wasn't recovered from my past mistakes yet.

I slid off my stool, picked up my purse and the light jacket I'd worn. "Gotta go," I said.

Chapter 4

DOTTIE LOU CALLED ME AT the beginning of October to tell me that her husband Tom had gotten a promotion. Unfortunately, he was going to be required to work at the branch of his company that was south of Kankakee, an hour and a half south of Lemont. It was a permanent transfer, and too far to commute for any length of time.

My heart sank. I was happy for her, of course, since the promotion, she had told me, came with a considerable raise, and would also involve overtime and extra benefits as a union officer. But a major reason I'd relocated to Lemont myself was to be near her in her Lemont apartment.

"It's a once-in-a-lifetime opportunity!" she said. "This will be a lot of work for Tom, of course. But it will completely change our lifestyle. We won't have to pinch pennies anymore. Having the kids so soon, and me a stay-at-home mom, I never thought we'd get so far so fast."

"When do you think you'll move?" I asked. *Please, not right away!*

"It may take a little while. We're going to look for a house. I can't wait to get the kids into their own rooms, and shop for some new furniture, though. So, the sooner the better, right?"

"You'll be like me. You won't have any friends there. Doesn't that bother you?"

"Not at all. I'm a joiner, remember? I'll get to know people, and if it gets boring, I'll get involved in the PTA or run for the library board."

I knew she'd do just that. She'd be fine without me. But would I be fine without her nearby?

I have no one now!

"You're thinking we won't see each other much, aren't you? I'm not sure my moving will make that much difference. We spend more time on the phone than together anyway. I know it's not the same, but you have friends in town now, right? At Sami's? We'll make it work. I bet you won't even notice."

She was right, at least in part. But I knew I'd miss her.

By mid-fall, with still another reason to feel alone if not downright lonely, I found myself stopping at Sami's not just Wednesdays but two or three nights a week. I avoided weekends, though. I didn't want to admit to anyone, even to myself, that I had nothing better to do on weekends—even though I didn't. Sami's was still the only place I went to be with casual friends.

My life had been too sheltered, but I found the people who patronized Sami's to be surprising and interesting. Surprising for the somewhat wacky things that occurred as well as the fact that I liked them despite what they did. I didn't want to lead their lives, but learning about them fascinated me. Sort of like reading a sexy novel now and then as a break from more serious reading. I could dabble and enjoy the experience outside of my comfort zone, so long as I had the freedom to leave if things got too uncomfortable.

Sami's reminded me of neighborhood bars where I grew up on the South Side of Chicago. These places were populated mostly by men who gathered for a drink with friends after work. My mother used to send me down the street to tell my dad when dinner was ready. The bartender would pull a foot-long pretzel stick from a jar on the bar top and give it to me. My uncle, a hard-core alcoholic, spent days and nights in another, rougher place. Another uncle commuted to his office downtown by train and stopped in a bar near the train station before going home. Sami's was near Lemont's train station and had a similar vibe.

Or maybe I liked doing the unexpected, the unpredictable, now that I didn't have to account to anyone else. But I thought it was more than that. I had little in common with the few women who came there, but I enjoyed talking to the men. They weren't looking for relationships or for sex, which would have been the case at singles bars. Some had wives or girlfriends, some were unattached, but all were generally at a point in their lives when they didn't want the complications or commitments that came with sexual relationships, even casual ones. Some were just more interested in drinking than anything else, including a few hard-core alcoholics. I found even those men easy enough to like most of the time. But the majority of Sami's patrons came to shoot pool or be with friends and enjoy some companionship and conversation.

That was the same thing I wanted. At least that's what I thought. For now.

And I seemed to fit in. I'd always been on the shy side, but I liked the respect I got from the people I met there. That made me feel good and restored some of my faith in myself. They looked happy to see me, they found me easy to talk to and liked to tell me about their lives. Dixon washed my car. Angel helped move some furniture in my apartment. Rusty followed me as I drove home during a rainstorm to be sure I got there okay. One man worked for a major book printer. I mentioned a book I'd liked, and a day or two later he came in smiling with a sack of books by that author for me.

The people at Sami's treated me like a favorite sister, looked forward to seeing me, and took care of me. Since I had never lived alone—and didn't much like it—I was grateful for people nearby I could call on. They made me feel…well, safe.

I developed a habit of arriving after dinner, chatting while nursing drinks—two, I had determined, was my limit, and I stuck to the vodka and grapefruit juice Sami had introduced me to—and I'd leave around nine, before serious drinkers got sloppy. The vibe was welcoming, cheerful, and trouble was rare. If there was any drug use, I didn't see it. It wasn't that kind of place. Not that I'd patronized any of the more troublesome bars for comparison, but I was pleased that Sami's was known as a problem-free place.

Sami encouraged me with a big smile when I entered. "Welcome, pretty lady!" he'd say. "You come visit me often. You give my establishment some class. Good for business!"

Of course, foul language was a given in neighborhood bars. But it was almost never used directly with me and only occasionally in conversation near me, although I could overhear "shit", "piss", and "fuck" and other such profanities in the background.

Then one night a Mexican man tried to hit on me. Angel and Dixon pulled him aside and Angel spoke to him. The man nodded and walked to the other end of the bar.

"What did Angel say to him?" I asked Dixon when he returned.

"Mexican men are very protective of their women," he said. "They don' allow them to go to bars, 'specially not alone. So a Mexican man figures a woman in a bar is lookin' to get laid. That guy thought you were fair game. Angel tol' him he made a mistake—you're a nice lady. Mexican men respect 'nice' women, they just wouldn't expect to find them here."

I felt a surge of warmth. I was so used to fending for myself. How nice it was to have friends to defend me. I smiled at Dixon.

"What?" he said.

"Nothing. Just thinking," I said.

Dixon, a simple, no-nonsense guy who always wore cowboy boots and a small smile on his ruddy face, had become my closest friend at Sami's. I'd been surprised to learn that he drank only Coke. This was unusual for someone who, like many of the regulars, found their sole social life in a bar—except for Saturday morning golf, in Dixon's case. But when I asked him why, he just shrugged his shoulders and said, "I like it."

I learned that Dixon had lived in Kentucky until he was in his mid-twenties, when he came to the Chicago area. His mother had been a McCoy, of Hatfields' and McCoys' fame. He had come to work at a factory on the North Side of Chicago, where he had met and married a Mexican woman, from whom he was now divorced. They had two young daughters in grade school. When his ex-wife moved with the girls to Oak Lawn, he had taken a job at the Union Oil Refinery in Lemont so he could be closer to his daughters.

He told me he spent every Saturday afternoon to Sunday night with his girls, and he adored them. He lived in a very spare one-bedroom apartment with a few second-hand pieces of furniture and a sleeper sofa for his girls. He owned only a single pair of boots, a few shirts and jeans, and a jacket. The only pleasures he allowed himself were his evenings shooting pool before going to work at midnight and Saturday morning golf during the summer. He made a good salary working the night shift at Union Oil, with plenty of overtime available. Regardless, he was always broke.

Dixon drove a battered old car that frequently needed repair. Rusty had told me that Dixon was a poor, but cautious, driver, and that he walked whenever he could and drove only out of necessity, since he couldn't afford gas or insurance.

"You shouldn't drive without insurance, really," I suggested. "You're only asking for trouble."

He shrugged. "What can I do? I don't have the money."

I had previously mentioned to Dixon that I had always managed household money myself and, although it was not always easy, I had somehow avoided going into debt. He asked if I would mind looking over his finances, to see if I could suggest a way he could have more spendable income.

"Of course I'd like to help you, but why me?" I asked him. "I'm not an expert on finances. Sami's wife, Whitney, is an accountant, isn't she, at Argonne? Wouldn't she be a better choice?"

"Naw," Dixon said. "I don't like her much. I don't want her knowin' my business. You tole me you stick to a budget and file your own income tax. I trust you."

Dixon came to my apartment one night and we sat at my kitchen table with a pile of paperwork he had brought. I was surprised at how much money Dixon made. But it all went to his ex-wife.

"Your child support is deducted from your paychecks. It seems a rather large amount. Can you go back to court and get that reduced?"

I suggested, pointing at the amount that was being withheld.

"Elisa needs that money for the girls." His face flushed as he said it. There must be more there. I looked at him and waited.

"I don't want to go back to court." He hesitated again. "I used to give Elisa the support in cash. She said she had trouble gettin' the bank to cash my checks."

"So?"

"Turns out she filed for aid with the state, tellin' the office she didn't know where I was and I wasn't makin' support payments and she needed money for the kids. It was almost two years 'fore they found out she'd lied and they demanded their money back."

"So she got in trouble and then the court ordered the support withheld from *your* paycheck? As if you were the one to blame for cheating the system?"

Dixon only shrugged. "Right."

"What about these large checks to the Department of Public Aid?"

"That's to pay them back for the money she took from them for two years."

I looked him in the eye. "What? Why are *you* paying that? She's the one who lied to them and spent both their money and yours."

He looked at the tabletop. "What can I do? She can't work and take care of the girls too. She ain't got no money 'cept what I gives her."

"The girls are both in school. She can work those hours."

"She says she can't find no work like that."

I shook my head. I wondered why they had divorced but knew Dixon would have told me if he wanted me to know. Out of respect, I squelched my curiosity.

"What about these checks to St. Gerald's Parish? And these large credit card bills? And all these medical bills?"

"I have insurance on the girls from work, but it never covers everything. And there's tuition and stuff Elisa needs to buy for them."

"But isn't the support you're paying supposed to be for that?"

"Elisa says that ain't enough."

It was obvious to me that Dixon didn't want to suspect Elisa's demands and just gave her whatever she asked for.

The rent for his apartment was reasonable. I added up what I saw and deducted it from what he was bringing home.

"Dixon, there's plenty of money left over after all these expenses. You should be able to buy everything you need and have enough for savings or discretionary spending."

"I take the girls out to eat. And I buy their clothes and things they need for school."

"What is the support you're paying going for?"

"Other stuff, she says. And sometimes she gets in debt and I have to help her out, her or her boyfriend. What can I do? If she's got no money, she can't take care of the girls."

Her or her *boyfriend*. Were both of them living off of Dixon? It was clear what was happening here. Now that the woman no longer had double money from support and public aid, she was demanding even more from Dixon. She was bleeding him of everything he had. I wanted to throw my arms in the air in frustration.

He saw the look on my face and blushed. "She's a good mother. She's bringin' my girls up right, they're smart and healthy." He had a point there. I'd met the girls one weekend at a street fair and they were delightful. Polite, smart, happy, and well adjusted—and well dressed. How much of that was due to Dixon and how much to their mother might be hard to tell, but clearly the girls weren't being neglected in any way.

Poor, good-natured Dixon. It never occurred to him that she was taking advantage of him. It wasn't likely I could change his mind.

I couldn't find a way to help Dixon, although I had tried. I wondered if I was the best person to be advising anyone. I was willing enough to help friends, but not able to motivate myself out of my own stagnation. *But then, how can I motivate myself when I can't even decide what direction I want to go?*

Like me, Dixon had few adult friends, just me and Rusty. But at least he had daughters to love and care for. The last thing I wanted to do was mess up the most important thing in his life. Whereas I couldn't pinpoint anything or anyone so important to me, and felt afraid to get close to anybody.

Chapter 5

I ARRIVED AT SAMI'S ONE night in October to find two police cars blocking the street in front. Betts, another of Sami's regular patrons who I'd adopted as a new friend, stood near the door, getting some fresh air. Betts was a severely emaciated man with thinning dark hair that always looked wet plastered over his scalp. No one seemed to know what Betts had done for a living, but he was a smart man with an acerbic sense of humor. His laugh was short, like a bark, and infectious. He would drop his voice, lean toward my ear, and confide witty comments that broke me up. He drank slowly and steadily all day, but never seemed to be drunk, and never lost his wit.

"It's okay—you can go in," Betts said. "They're just here for Adam and Eve again."

A door at the rear of the bar, beyond the restrooms and pool table, led to a small studio apartment, occupied by Adam and Eve. The names sound jokey, but belong to an actually-married couple, Adam and Eve Westgate. Which is ironic, since their tempestuous relationship is about as far from Eden as one can get.

Typically, I would observe the forty-something couple sitting on adjoining stools, cheek to cheek, cozy, whispering in each other's ears and acting as if the world existed only in each other's eyes. Then, with no angry word or warning of any kind, I'd hear a crash and see Eve on the floor, knocked down by a well-practiced swing from Adam. He'd likely reacted to a cruel insult from Eve—that and the cumulative effect of too many beers.

It was not unusual for one or the other, or both of them, to be sporting bruises, as Eve was equally practiced with her swings. To the uninformed, the sweetheart phase or the battling phase was arbitrary and unpredictable, but daily patrons of the bar kept everyone informed of the current status of their relationship. Someone had devised a sign and hung it on the door that led from the bar to Adam and Eve's apartment. One side of the sign showed Cupid with his arrow, the other two boxers in the ring. A number of regulars kept everyone amused and updated by turning the side that faced the bar to denote Adam and Eve's last known disposition.

Both Adam and Eve drank heavily in the evenings, but they had their real binges in private in their apartment. However, there was nothing private about the battles. I'd heard their violent arguments through the door when visiting the restroom. Eve would get dramatic, pretend she was having chest pain, and demand that someone call for an ambulance. Adam invariably fell for it, and she got some sympathy from people in the bar, but little from the police or paramedics, who were tired of being called out for domestics and false alarms.

Adam, on the other hand, just liked to go on binges now and then. He'd drink heavily and alone, usually beer, but anything alcoholic would do. During those episodes he'd remain drunk for a number of days.

Betts filled me in on this evening's battle. Apparently, the fight started because Adam had been on a binge, became almost stuporous and, feeling the call of nature, mistook the refrigerator for a urinal.

"Eve's description left little to the imagination," Betts said. "She said when she came into the kitchen area, Adam had his right arm wrapped around the open refrigerator door, and there he was in the light pouring from the fridge, holding his pecker with his left hand, generously splashing piss over their food."

Betts laughed his typical wry laugh. "First thing we knew, Adam comes busting through the door into the bar, and Eve's right behind, clobbering him with an empty quart beer bottle. She's screaming and ranting and Adam trips on the leg of a bar stool and hits the floor. She leans down all contrite like, and says, 'Oh sweetie, are you all right?' But when Adam stands up, he goes, 'You just shut your fuckin' mouth,' and he hauls back and throws a punch into her face."

"How disgusting," I said, appalled, but at the same time I wanted to laugh. "What did Sami do to stop them?"

"Sami, no. He's not gonna get involved, but he calls the police. Eve stumbles back from the punch and hits her chest against the top of the bar. She's bleedin' from a cut lip, and she's clutching her chest, and she's yelling, 'Call an ambulance, I'm having a heart attack! Oh my God, the pain, what did you fuckin' do to me?' When the police arrive, she's ranting and swinging the beer bottle again."

"She's probably faking a heart attack to make Adam feel responsible. Let's go in and see," I said, and Betts and I entered Sami's.

Eve stood at the far end near the back door that led to their apartment, waving her arms, still holding the beer bottle. Two policemen were nearby with their hands out trying to calm her down. "Fuckin' assholes! Don't you fuckin' touch me!" Eve screamed. "*He's* the one pissing in the fuckin' refrigerator!"

"Hate to admit it," I said in Betts's ear, "but I think I'm with Eve on this one. Physical attack isn't normally my style, but it isn't too hard to see myself grabbing his arm and flinging him into a wall—preferably headfirst!"

"Sweet innocent dignified Janie?" Betts laughed. He was the only one who called me Janie since I'd been a kid.

"You haven't seen me in action," I said. "Anyway, I can't see myself ever living with someone like Adam either. I hope I'm making better choices than that."

"Better choices? Like hanging out here?" Betts said.

"You got a point there," I agreed, laughing. I wondered if I came to Sami's because it was unlikely I'd meet anyone here that would tempt me into a relationship I wasn't ready for.

Although I'd seen Adam and Eve at Sami's many times, I'd never talked to them. There were some regular patrons I preferred to avoid as much as possible. My curiosity went only so far—I had no desire to get involved in their lives. I was learning the ins and outs of spending time in a neighborhood bar.

An ambulance arrived. Apparently, the police had radioed for one. Working together, police and paramedics eventually got Eve calmed down. She refused to go to the hospital so the paramedics left. Adam had agreed to sleep at a friend's house that night, and the police accompanied the couple to their apartment, presumably to be sure the situation stayed under control until he left.

As this was developing, Rusty came in and sat next to me.

Now that the episode was over, the place seemed uncharacteristically quiet. "You missed all the excitement," I told Rusty, and filled him in on the evening's festivities. Like most of the people there, Rusty found the episode amusing.

I pretended to go along, but the more I thought about it, the less funny it was. This was the first time, other than some swearing and raised voices, that anything ugly had happened at Sami's. The incident seemed ominous to me. Background noises were more noticeable tonight, and I found myself looking around watchfully. There was no reason to expect Adam or Eve to return and continue their battle, but I kept thinking it could happen. Did I really want to be making new friends with people who weren't sympathetic about such drama? Or were they sympathetic and just pretending otherwise?

Betts barked his short laugh. "Reminds me of the old Roman story about drunkenness—did you two ever hear that one?"

Rusty and I both shook our heads, ready for one of Betts's tales.

"Since ancient time, the story goes, Satan instructed vineyard owners that to grow grapes that produce the best wine, the owner must pour the blood of four animals upon the vines."

"Any four animals?" Rusty asked, winking at me.

"Oh, no. Satan was very specific. It had to be the blood of a lamb, a lion, a pig, and a monkey, and in that order."

"And what did that prove?" I asked.

"It determines what happens to the one who drinks the wine.

After the first sips, a man is like a lamb. Drink a little more and he becomes a lion, bold enough to risk his life, up for any challenge. If he keeps drinking, he turns into a pig, rolling in the mud and soiling himself. And finally he becomes a monkey, screaming and jumping about with no idea at all of what he is doing."

We laughed. "Sounds like this place," Rusty said.

"I won't argue that." Betts got up and said goodnight to us, a little earlier than usual.

Rusty always came in Wednesday nights, and sometimes other nights as well. He had a long ride to the North Side of Chicago, so he sometimes only stayed for one or two beers and then left. After Saturday golf, he said, he spent his weekends painting the three-story enclosed porch attached to the three-flat rental building he owned and lived in. He was worried about one of his tenants, an old spinster who had rented the first floor for over thirty years and had been diagnosed with cancer. We didn't gossip much but spent time talking about other things we enjoyed. Rusty liked local history, and he had taken some sailing lessons on Lake Michigan. He'd thought about buying a sailboat. He liked to take advantage of doings in the city: Chicago Fest, the Mackinac Race, the Air and Water Show.

"Do you enjoy the city?" he asked.

I laughed. "Suburban girl here. I went to the museums when I was a kid. We lived in Oak Lawn, and my mother used to take me Christmas shopping on the bus and to see the windows at Marshall Field's, but traveling in the city scares me. I don't know how to get around and I'm afraid I won't find a place to park. You make downtown Chicago sound like fun, though."

I would be more inclined to visit the city if someone took me. I thought I'd say yes if Rusty asked me to go with him, but he didn't. Just as well.

I didn't have much to talk about that was interesting, except for telling him about some books I was reading. He wasn't a reader, but he seemed to like listening to me. I talked about how my best friend was about to move to Kankakee and we'd be forced to speak only on the phone now. I told him how she and I laughed over some of the things that happened at Sami's, and she'd enjoy tonight's Adam and Eve story.

I told him I had found Lemont to have a fascinating history, and we chatted about that for a while. "Betts is what people here call a Longtime Lemonter. He was born here and lived here all his life. He'll tell you stories that aren't in the history books," Rusty said, getting up for his turn at pool.

Rusty walked to the pool table with that confident stride I'd noticed before. His demeanor was friendly but at the same time it was clear he took the game seriously and intended to win. When his turn to shoot came up, he positioned himself behind the cue ball, placed his left hand on the table with fingers spread, balanced the cue stick at the base of his thumb, and took careful aim. Then he studied the entire table carefully before lining up his next shot, sometimes walking around the table a number of times with a look of intense concentration. While playing, he seemed different from the relaxed, friendly guy I was getting to know in casual conversation.

Later that evening, when the pool table was quiet and I was humming along to "Elvira" by the Oakridge Boys, which seemed to be the favorite played on the jukebox that night, Rusty asked, "Any thoughts on finding a different job?"

I frowned. "Not really." I should be thinking about that, but I'd procrastinated again. This was a good time to look, after the lazy days of summer and before the bad weather set in. But I hadn't.

"I still think you should consider Argonne," he said. "There's bound to be something there you're suited for."

"But isn't it hard to get in there?"

"Kind of. Unless you know someone who's familiar with the place."

"You, maybe?"

"Maybe." He grinned. "Say the word and I'll see what I can do."

I should have thanked him, but I didn't. I felt a little annoyed, as if he were passing judgement on my current work in the grocery store, pressing me to find a job that matched my education and abilities.

I still had a ways to go to decide what I wanted to do. I was sure I'd figure it out when I was good and ready.

I didn't come here to find a job, I thought, but to stop thinking about it—to ease my guilt about not actively looking. I didn't want to be pushed. Even by a nice guy who meant well. And I sure as hell didn't want any romantic interests either.

After Rusty returned to the pool table, the door opened and a short, elderly, frail-looking man came in wearing an oxygen mask with a portable oxygen tank strapped to his back. He took a seat near John David and ordered a draft beer.

I turned away to take a sip of my drink, wondering what the hell a guy who obviously had bad lungs was doing in a place with so much smoke?

"Hey!" I heard Sami yell. "You can't do that! You'll set my place on fire!"

Looking back, I saw that the man had pushed down his mask and held a cigarette in his mouth. He was holding a lit match to the end of the cigarette. "Don't worry," he said. "I do this all the time. Never had a problem."

Nonetheless, I thought it was a good time to call it a night.

Chapter 6

I WAS SITTING IN MY overstuffed chair, feet pulled up, a blanket over my lap, and a cup of coffee on the table beside me, phone to my ear. Dottie Lou had just told me that she and Tom had taken a drive to Kankakee to look over the neighborhoods and sign up with a real estate agent. Tom would be starting the new job on November 1 and would commute until they found a house. I was happy for her, really. I would miss her, but she was right in that almost all of our contact these days was over the phone, and there would be no need for that to change. Would she get so involved in her new life that there'd be no time for me? That could always happen, of course, but we'd had separations before and we'd always found each other when needed.

After Dottie Lou was talked out about the upcoming move, sensing my hesitancy, she asked, "Are you still worried that I'm leaving you alone in Lemont?"

"It's okay," I said. "I've been better now that I've made a few friends at Sami's." To be truthful, I'd not been sleeping that well. I'd fall asleep easily, but after my bladder woke me up at two in the morning, I just couldn't shut my mind off and tossed, awake, the rest of the night. Probably something in my subconscious kept nagging at me.

Dottie Lou wasn't fooled. "You don't sound enthusiastic. Is there something you're not saying?"

To be honest, what was bothering me wasn't subconscious at all. I knew what was wrong. I just didn't know what to do about it.

"Dottie Lou, after all the hard work to get my degrees, what am I doing with a master's working as a clerk in a grocery store?"

"Yeah, good question. What do you think?"

"My whole life I worked hard to educate myself so I could lead a better life. Then when that didn't work out—the marriage and the teaching job—I thought I needed a break to figure out what to do next." I paused. "Am I wasting all the hard work I did? You and I had similar backgrounds, parents who loved and protected us, gave us everything we wanted, and you're smarter than me. But you never went to college. Doesn't that ever bother you?"

"Not a bit," she said without hesitation. "I didn't want to put myself in a competitive work force. All I ever wanted was my own little family, and I got that. I didn't need college. I can educate myself whenever I want to, in my own good time, when the spirit so moves."

She was as good as her words. Like me, she was an avid reader, but she sought out biographies, history, self-help, and other nonfiction, fitting reading between household chores and children's and spousal demands, while for leisure reading I preferred mysteries, historical novels, and gothic romances.

"Besides," she reminded me. "You and me, we're not like everyone else. We're better, right?"

Our old joke since high school days. I chuckled. "So here we are, two top-of-our-class brainiacs, you talking to kids all day and me a cashier and blue-collar bar hanger-outer."

"You're hinting that you're superior to the people you're hanging around with."

"Maybe I am—hinting, that is," I said, feeling both defensive and ashamed. At myself. I knew Dottie Lou would understand. She'd been around enough to watch how easily my degrees had come to me. I didn't have to work as hard as most of my classmates, probably because I processed information intuitively. Instead of taking detailed written notes, memorizing and storing facts, my brain put things together into relationships that allowed me to infer facts and solve problems. While others searched their memories, I looked at the information in front of me and came up with the only answer that made sense to me. I was almost always right. It was a gift. So now, with the learning plus the gift, what was I doing?

Dottie Lou was the one to put it into words. "Well, what do you expect? You're doing a job any high school student could master. You're hanging around with factory workers and manual laborers with high school diplomas. This wasn't how you saw yourself when you were getting your degrees. It isn't how you see yourself now."

But here I was. I couldn't explain it. If I thought my job and my new friends were beneath me, why didn't I do something about it? Find a job that challenged me, make friends that were intellectual equals?

I was silent too long. Dottie Lou asked," "Do you feel like a failure? After quitting both your job and your marriage?"

I thought about how to explain. "Disappointed that it didn't work out the way I expected. I think I can do better if I make better choices. I just need to spend enough time considering the choices before jumping back too soon and making more mistakes."

"And you're not ready yet?"

I sighed and pulled my blanket up to my chin. "As Rusty might say, not even close. I'm not even doing the menial shit right, Dottie Lou. Take the time I spend at Sami's. I'm not really comfortable there, not completely. Truth is, I feel like an outsider. Probably because I *am* an outsider. And why, I ask myself, if I look down on these new friends of mine, then why is it that I'm trying so hard to make them accept me? When I'm with them, I feel like I don't measure up. I don't shoot pool, and I don't drink to the point of intoxication, and I don't cuss. And they only talk about things that aren't important—sports and gossip, and they crack jokes and play loud music on the jukebox. Those aren't things I value. I'm a misfit. But nonetheless I want them to like me."

"Sounds like a dichotomy," Dottie Lou said.

"Yes, exactly. Part of me thinks I'm better than the people I'm spending time with, and part of me is a combo of envious and ashamed. What makes me better than any other person? And as I get to know them, I see them in a different light and give them more respect. I want them to like me, so I pretend to be the different person they see me as, the not-me person. And at the same time, part of me wants to fit in. I'm better than them, but I'm not as good as they are. It doesn't make any sense, but I can't stop how I feel."

"Maybe instead of asking yourself what you want, you should ask how you'd feel if nothing changed. Or what it is you're trying to escape by going to Sami's."

I sighed. "You're too smart for me, Dottie Lou. I might need to start drinking at home to figure that out."

"Don't you dare!" She chuckled. "It'll come when you're ready. Just hang in there."

"And call you when I'm too mixed up, right?"

After we hung up, I reheated my coffee, which had sat untouched while Dottie Lou and I talked. Then I returned to my chair and pulled up the blanket again.

Why did I care? About Sami's? About my job? About life? About men? What if nothing changed and I continued to live my life as I was living it now? Would I be satisfied with that? Why didn't I know myself well enough to answer these questions?

I was in some kind of limbo, marking time until my real life began again. Something was holding me back, like trying to drag myself out of quicksand.

Instead of looking for my real life, my real career, the friends I would have for a lifetime, I got up every day, put on my work clothes, walked the half mile to Ordman's, and stepped behind the desk to check the schedule. The days were effortless, just smile and answer whatever anyone wants, then move on to the next person. That cashier needs help, step over and fill a few bags. Get a bagger to run out for carts. Explain to a customer that their coupon is expired. Relieve for lunches.

And when the day is over, instead of reading want ads or contacting old friends from school who have more productive lives by now, I walk over to Sami's and I watch, and I listen, and I smile, and I act like I'm enjoying myself, when in truth I'm like a fish out of water who above all else wants to be one of the boys.

And then I go to a home that doesn't feel like home, but like some strange, temporary place. When was the last time I felt the peace and security of home? Not when I was married. Not since then. Not since I first left my parents' house after college.

And then I don't think some more.

I don't think about what I should be doing because I don't know what I want to do or what's keeping me from doing it. I just go to bed, and I wake up the next morning, and I do the same things the next day. And the day after that.

Will tomorrow be the day I wake up and chart a new path? Maybe. Not likely, though.

Chapter 7

AS FALL WORE ON, LITTLE Lindsay switched to a league that played on Tuesday nights. Most of the time I went to watch her play. I hoped it gave her a little sense of friendship, but developing a close relationship with Lindsay wasn't easy. At Ordman's she still went quietly about her work, not sharing confidences with anyone, even me. I still didn't know much about her, but she often appeared preoccupied. Instead of her usual routine, competent task performance, she was making frequent mistakes.

One night, something was obviously bothering her. Except for Little Lindsay, all the pool leagues were composed of men. I guessed that some members of her team were giving her a cold shoulder, humiliated or even jealous because a tiny woman shot better pool than they did a good part of the time. Common sense said they should be happy that her skill moved them up in the league standings, but some men might feel their ego threatened. With that in mind, I watched her not just when she was shooting, but between her turns at the table. I also observed the other players to see how they interacted with her.

My observations were largely unrevealing, until I realized that Lindsay was in turn surreptitiously watching someone—not another player, but someone sitting at the bar: John David Christopher. She glanced his way repeatedly when she wasn't shooting, during which time he stared at the bar top, as was customary for John David. Conversely, when Lindsay was shooting, she concentrated on her game, but John David's gaze stayed focused on her. Something was going on.

Since I'd been hanging out at Sami's, I had rarely seen Lindsay talk to John David. He was always sitting on his usual stool near the middle of the long bar when she arrived, and she'd say hello and give him a small smile. John David would drop his head and mumble hello, and then his eyes would follow her to the pool table. Tonight, he seemed to be watching every move she made. I was worried that I saw some malice in his eyes, but maybe he was just shy. Or maybe I was mistaking his look of longing. The few times Lindsay caught him looking at her, she gave a fleeting smile and turned away.

Betts seemed to be in a bad mood. He was ignoring everyone. Angel had his head down on the bar already. Pizza Bob stopped in and set down three free pizzas for everyone in the bar, one on each of the side tables. Sami handed Pizza Bob a draft beer and he took a stool. I had met Pizza Bob a few weeks ago, and with no one else to talk to at the moment, it looked like a good opportunity to get to know him better. I left my friends around the pool table, slid a slice of sausage and mushroom pizza onto a bar napkin, and eased myself onto a stool next to Pizza Bob.

A number of Sami's regular customers had been tagged with nicknames that reflected something characteristic about them—like Little Lindsay and Dirty Wally. Pizza Bob owned a pizza place directly across the street from the bar. Rather than letting food go to waste, when an order was undeliverable for some reason, he would generate good will for his business by bringing free pizza to Sami's. Pizza Bob was a pleasant-looking young man in his late twenties, average height, a little stocky, with a full head of curly dark hair. I had been told he had a lot of smarts and a good business sense. As one might expect, many of Sami's patrons weren't inclined to go very far when hungry, so most were regular customers of Bob's Pizza. Bob would stop in for a beer now and then, but not more than one and he never stayed long.

I filled my mouth and chewed. I'd not had Bob's pizza before, and it was surprisingly good.

"This is great!" I told Bob. "Thanks for treating us."

"No problem," he said. "I'd rather it go into my friends' bellies than the garbage bins. It wouldn't have been fit to eat a couple of hours from now."

I swallowed and said, "I beg to differ. I love cold pizza."

He laughed. "Try *delivering* it cold. See how many loyal customers you get that way."

I took another large bite and worked on it, then asked, "Have you been busy?"

"At the pizza place? Yeah, but it's about to get worse. Election time is upon us. I won't get a break until late November."

"Why is that? What does the election have to do with pizza?"

"I'm not expecting to slave in a single pizza restaurant in Lemont all my life. If you want to get ahead in Cook County, you have to know the people who get things done. It's all about favors. You do favors, you get favors in return. You bring free pizza to campaign headquarters, and people get to like you. Then when you need a license, or to pass an inspection, or something else, someone puts in a word in the right place. Schmoozing is not an option. You get to know people, you campaign for them, you deliver subpoenas for the sheriff's office, things like that."

"You do all that?"

"Yeah. Neil Hartigan wants me to manage his campaign for governor this year. He's offered me free use of his box tickets to Cubs games in return. I can use those to earn more favors."

"Isn't this White Sox territory?" I asked, grinning.

"Yeah, but Neil is from Rogers Park. I'll find takers, don't worry."

I knew little about Chicago neighborhoods, especially the North Side, but I thought I remembered that Rusty said his building was in Rogers Park. A coincidence?

When Pizza Bob left, I moved back to my customary stool in the rear to watch Little Lindsay and the pool games.

I found myself feeling more warmly than usual about the friends I'd made at Sami's. For some reason the camaraderie of the place seemed enhanced. Maybe the single drink I'd consumed, or the pleasant chat with Pizza Bob, was responsible. When Little Lindsay finished her game, she sat on the stool next to me and reached for her drink. She was drinking something dark reddish-brown in a cocktail glass tonight, not her usual tall glass of rum and Coke.

"You're having something different tonight," I commented.

"Southern Comfort on the rocks. I don't usually like straight alcohol, but I can sip this real slow. It's a change of pace."

I still wondered why the change, but she hadn't picked up on my hint, so I dropped it.

The familiar refrain from the jukebox, "Take this job and shove it," rang through the bar. Rusty and Dixon were playing against each other. Neither seemed too happy. The ball Rusty had played bounced off the rail and the cue ball went into the pocket. "Shit! Piss!" he said. Dixon leaned over the table, pumping his pool cue as he lined up his shot. When I turned back, Lindsay was staring into her drink, oblivious of the game. That wasn't like her.

"I know it's not my business, but…is something bothering you lately? You don't seem yourself," I said. I was as curious as I was concerned, but I wanted her to know I cared enough to notice.

"I'm fine," she said.

We watched Rusty and Dixon for a while, sipping at our drinks, not saying anything.

"How much do you know about John David?" I asked, thinking about their behavior this evening. Lindsay seemed to go rigid for a moment, her expression guarded.

Nonetheless, I went on. "It seems like no matter when I come in, he's always here. Do you know if he has a job?"

"Nah, he's on disability. He was in Nam, you know. He wasn't quite right in the head when he got back. The VA's got him on permanent disability. It's not much, but enough for a cheap flat and it pays his bar tab. He doesn't need much. Why do you ask?"

Instead of answering her question, I said, "How do you know all that? Did he tell you?" I was a little surprised she knew so much about such a secretive man.

"How does anyone know anything about people in here? Someone knew him way back, knew his sister, knew somebody who knew somebody who said something, and it got around. Maybe he had a good night, someone asked him, and he told someone. Maybe someone saw him cashing a check, or someone at the currency exchange told someone. Maybe somebody just made it up." She took a sip, then went on. "People think they're smarter after a few beers, you know. They make something up, it gets around, and after a while people believe it." It was a long speech for Lindsay. She sounded a bit defensive. I must have touched a hot button.

As if to prove what I was thinking, Lindsay said, "Maybe that's why I keep things to myself, to make 'em keep guessin' about me."

"Ah. You know, talking about John David though, I couldn't help noticing that he seems to watch you a lot. I wondered if that bothered you."

Little Lindsay stuck out her jaw, took another sip of her drink through a short red plastic straw, and then returned to watching the pool game. After a bit she turned back to me, seeming to be more relaxed.

"He's really a sweet guy, you know," she said softly after a while. "Very harmless. Everyone pokes fun at him because they think he's strange, or simple. He isn't either—just very shy and doesn't know how to make friends or act around people." She was quiet again. Then, "I guess they probably say that about me too."

"Oh, no!" I said. "They don't say anything like that about you."

"What *do* they say?" She looked up and watched my face.

Okay, I told myself. *You started this, now you have to finish.*

I took a deep breath. "Okay. People say you're very private, very serious, don't seem to have much fun, and keep to yourself. Maybe they wonder about you, because no one knows what you're like. At Ordman's they only know you do a good job, and here at Sami's they only know you shoot a hell of a game of pool." I paused. "They probably think that's unusual."

Lindsay said nothing, just stared at her drink.

"Look," I said after a moment. "I work with you all day, sit here and watch you at night, and *I* don't know what you like or dislike, where you came from or how you live, if you have any family— anything personal. Let alone what seems to be bothering you now. I can't make small talk with you, because I don't know what you want to talk *about*."

Lindsay gave me a small smile. "Maybe that's the way I want it," she said quietly, then paused again. "Or maybe there just isn't anything more to me than what you see."

"That can't be true. You obviously have some feelings, and that shows you must have some interests too. I know that because you just got through saying some kind things about John David, and no one else seems to care enough to do that. So, *does* it bother you when he stares at you all night? Or do you two have something going?"

"You don't want to drop that business about John David, huh?"

"Look, Lindsay, I'm trying to be your friend here." I tried to catch her eye, but she avoided me. "Correct me if I'm wrong, but you don't seem to have a lot of female friends. Lady friends talk to each other, they share their problems, and it helps. Something goes wrong, we talk about it. We don't always find solutions, but it still helps."

"And if there's *nothing* wrong?" She still gazed at the wall behind the bar, refusing to meet my eyes.

"Then why is your mind someplace else lately? Why do you jump every time someone tries to get your attention? Why are you making mistakes at work you never used to make?"

Lindsay sighed. Finally, she looked in my direction. "Okay. So maybe I *am* worried about something, but that's my business, and I'll handle it," she said in a defiant tone.

I thought the conversation was over, but some moments later Lindsay said unexpectedly, "Okay, maybe you're right about John David."

"His staring does bother you?"

"In a sense. You know, I don't know *how* to feel about this. I never had a boyfriend, you know?"

"So, he's your boyfriend?" I asked. I hadn't expected her to say that.

"Oh, no! No!" she said, something like alarm on her face. "Not like that. I mean…if I *had* had boyfriends, then I'd know how to act, what to do. I'd know how to handle the situation."

"Explain."

We were interrupted by Sami, wanting to know if we were ready for refills. We weren't. He seemed annoyed, probably because we were taking up bar space while nursing a single drink. Sami didn't make much money from us. After he walked, Lindsay continued to stare at her whiskey for a while, probably trying to decide how much to tell me. In the interim I fished my hankie, which I'd remembered this time, out of my purse and removed my glasses to clean them. I wouldn't need to borrow Rusty's hankie tonight.

As I placed my glasses back on, Lindsay said, "You want to know about me, okay. It's not a pretty story. My mother was a druggie and fed her habit by prostitution. She loved me and tried her best but just wasn't capable of handling a child. We lived on the South Side, in a poor area—almost what you'd call the slums. I never knew my father—I don't think Mom even knew who he was. I never did well in school, was held back a couple of times, and quit high school after only two years when I turned sixteen. I pretty much raised myself. I never fit in and there was no one I wanted to hang with, so I had no friends either."

I moved my hand next to hers, just making contact as she held her glass on the bar. Lindsay jumped and then stared at my hand, but didn't pull away. "I don't know what to say. I'm sorry. I mean…I'm sorry that's what your life was like," I said.

"I know." She glanced at me. "You can understand why I don't want people to know that?"

I nodded sympathetically. "It's bad enough for you without people having preconceived notions. That would only make your life harder."

"That's about it. I'm not a very positive person and I'm not very good at anything."

I grinned at her. "Except for pool."

"Yeah," she said. "After I quit school, I hung out in South Side bars where they shot pool. This black, grandfatherly guy—he felt sorry for me and taught me the game. Turns out I had a knack for it."

"How'd you end up in Lemont?"

"After Mom died, I had to find work to support myself. I wanted a change of pace—a fresh start. Someone told me Lemont was a nice place to live and Ordman's was looking for help. I guess they were desperate because they hired me. I'm not well educated, but I learn quick and I work hard." She sounded defensive.

"Yes, you do," I said with a smile. In a way Lindsay wasn't much different than me, two lonely women looking for a fresh start in Lemont, hanging out in a local bar to avoid sitting home alone. Would life ever change for either of us? Shooting pool might be satisfying for Lindsay, but was there anything here that would make me feel good about myself again? I hoped that Lindsay's lack of ambition wouldn't rub off on me. I didn't see this place being my forever scene, but Lindsay probably did.

"They're lucky to have you." I moved my hand to her arm. She looked down at my hand as if the contact was strange to her.

I removed my hand. "So, you aren't comfortable around people, and you've never had a boyfriend. Now John David, who has problems of his own, seems to have a crush on you. And you don't know if you want to encourage that or shut him down."

"He's a really sweet guy," she began and giggled. "I said that already, didn't I? Well, I like him, really, but more like a kid brother or something, if I had a kid brother, which I never had, or knew my father either, so I'm clueless about guys, right? I don't feel any *attraction*, you know…nothing, just sorta…kindly towards him. Maybe I'm reading him wrong, but he just seems so *obsessive* about me!"

"You're probably not wrong," I said. "I caught him watching you too."

"I don't want to treat him mean or anything, because he doesn't deserve that, and if I make him happy, then that's good, because it doesn't seem like he has much that makes him happy. But I can't make him happy the way he dreams about, so am I leading him on, then? I don't want to encourage him either. That would only make things worse for him later on, wouldn't it? So, what do I do?" She watched my face.

"You're both sensitive people. You both have lousy communication skills." I grinned at her. "Sorry, but you can't argue that. So how do you communicate with each other...well, I guess that *is* a problem. Surely you've talked a little. What have you told him?"

Lindsay smiled sadly. "Nothing. We don't talk much. We say hello, we smile, we say goodbye."

"Do you want someone else to tell him? Is that an answer?"

She shook her head. "I couldn't do that."

We sipped our drinks silently for a while, mulling on the problem.

"I guess it does feel better that someone else knows. Thank you for making me talk," Lindsay said.

"Any time. Do you want me to talk to him?" I suggested again. "I wouldn't look forward to it, but I will if you want me to."

"No, let's leave it a while. Let me see what happens," said Lindsay.

Rusty came over to order another beer. He wasn't in a very good mood, probably because he was having a bad night on the table. After he left, I asked Lindsay, "So what about the ears? Is that story true, or what?"

"How do I know?" Lindsay said. "We don't talk, remember?"

We laughed. Then Lindsay got serious. "If the rumors are true, it would just make it all the sadder, you know? If it were true?"

"Yes, it would. I have more empathy for him after talking to you. He's not just that quiet strange guy anymore; he's a real person." I looked at her face. "And you've seen that all along."

"Does that make things better or worse?" Lindsay asked. Dixon motioned to her. She shrugged and walked away to start her game. I hoped our conversation had helped her in some way. I wanted her to be happy, but I was afraid to encourage her relationship with John

David. The man just made me uneasy.

John David is Lindsay's business, I thought. Yet the mysteries that surrounded him fascinated me.

A customer I didn't know dropped some coins into the jukebox and Kim Carnes's "Bette Davis Eyes" began to play. I couldn't help but wonder if John David thought the words of the song pertained to how he felt about Little Lindsay.

SAMI CAME OVER. "YOU WANT in the football pool? There's a few squares left."

"Sure, give me one," Dirty Wally called. The sheet Sami set in front of Wally was divided into one hundred squares, ten columns of ten rows across, with space left along the top and the left margin. Most of the squares had names in them. Wally signed his name in one of the empty squares and handed Sami a five-dollar bill.

The football pool, usually just called "squares," was another kind of pool played at Sami's. Every week during football season, bar patrons bet on the Chicago Bears' football games. Winning at squares was sheer luck, since no one knew what numbers he had until all one hundred squares were sold. Then Sami brought out a deck of cards and picked a few customers as witnesses to keep the process honest. Depending on the number and color of the card that came up, all numbers from zero to nine were placed in sequence across the top and down the left side until all numbers were used.

Players could then consult the grid for their "square numbers." For example, if the player's numbers were visitor three, Bears nine and the score at the end of a quarter ended with the visiting team having three, or thirteen, or twenty-three, etc., and the Bears had nine, or nineteen, or twenty-nine, etc., the player would win a hundred twenty-five dollars for that quarter. It was possible, on those occasions when all scoring was done in the first quarter, or when the ending number remained the same, for a single player to win more than a single quarter, even all four quarters, and thus potentially the entire five hundred dollars.

Sometimes there were multiple pools, with squares costing lower or higher amounts. The biggest pools were for the Super Bowl. Sami could have taken a cut of the winnings, but he didn't. Pool squares kept people coming in and buying drinks when they picked their squares, checked their numbers, or collected their winnings. Many customers came to watch games that were only seen on cable television, or just to feel part of the action with a crowd instead of watching alone at home. Big winners were expected to buy a round for the house. It was all good for business.

"How about you, pretty lady," Sami asked me.

I shook my head. "I don't gamble." I turned to Rusty, who was reaching for his wallet. "Good luck."

Waiting his turn behind Rusty was Poker Dan. In addition to Pizza Bob and Dirty Wally—I had since learned that Wally's dirty face, clothes, and hands were from his work on furnaces and air conditioners—Poker Dan was another regular with an identifying nickname.

Poker Dan was a pleasant-appearing guy, mid-thirties, average height but a little stocky with a receding hairline. He popped into Sami's at any odd time throughout the day or night and rarely stayed long. Although friendly, he always seemed restless, as if he needed to be somewhere else.

In addition to minor bets on the pool tournaments, the poker machine, and the sports pools, Poker Dan introduced still another element of gambling to Sami's, although only tangentially. When I asked Betts about this, he filled me in. Poker Dan rented the apartment upstairs from Sami's bar and had no known source of income. Everyone assumed that his sole income came from the poker games he hosted in his apartment.

"Is he that good of a gambler?" I asked Betts.

"He doesn't actually gamble himself. He provides a place for the games to be held and takes a fee from every hand played. Usually there's more than one game going on. Sometimes there's up to four tables playing, and the games can go for two to three days. It must be pretty steady money for him, since he doesn't seem to be hurting."

"Two or three days! Who plays that long?"

Betts laugh-snorted. "They play day and night. Players go in and out. Some bring food, from Bob's Pizza or wherever, and it's BYOB. When a player gets tired, he either falls asleep somewhere in the apartment or goes home and comes back after a nap." He barked his unique laugh again. "Sometimes, despite the stakes and action, a novice player or wannabe will drink too much and fall asleep right at the table. Other players will help him get to a sofa or chair until he wakes up and gets back into the game again."

According to Betts, the stakes varied as much as the players did. When a player didn't want to lose any more money, or had won enough, or had to be somewhere else, he'd leave and different people came in with new money to take his place. Although everyone was there to win, the players did watch out for each other to some extent and cautioned players who were too drunk to play wisely; most of the guys knew each other and didn't want to take advantage of their friends. Everyone intended to engage in a friendly game of poker with reasonable rather than high stakes, but players could still have pretty good winnings or go home having lost a week's pay. The players lived nearby and most of them walked from their homes.

"How many people know about this?" I asked. "Is it even legal? I mean, what do the police think?"

"I wouldn't say the games are commonly known, but most of the people at Sami's know about them. They keep that knowledge to themselves. The games are for neighborhood people. No one wants to attract ringers, people that would raise the stakes too high. As for the police…well, let's just say they haven't bothered. They have more important things to do than break up friendly games so long as there's no incidents or no one complains."

I remembered reading that in the infamous Smokey Row days

in Lemont, back in the early 1900s, the police were pretty lax about gambling and the town even used the gambling establishments as a source of income to build the town hall, schools, infrastructure, and of course, put some money into certain pockets. I was sure that was no longer the situation, and presumed Poker Dan took pains to follow whatever guidelines had been agreed upon.

Poker Dan was also one of the better pool players and won some money himself from small bets on the pool games. Since he needed to stay alert, he generally drank only a few beers, but I soon discovered that he loved to socialize and was an amusing conversationalist.

Poker Dan often bragged about his Sicilian heritage, and was reputed to be mob connected, but no one knew if it was just talk. Among the regulars at the bar, Pizza Bob, who was also Sicilian, seemed to know Dan the best. "How do I know if he's mobbed up? He's Poker Dan, right? No one calls him Poker Vito. Now that would be another story," Pizza Bob would joke.

After buying pool squares for himself and on behalf of a couple of poker players, Poker Dan came to say hello.

"Did you catch the launch of the Columbia this morning?" he asked.

"I did, actually. It wasn't as thrilling as the first walk on the moon, but still, it's amazing. We're still leading the space race!"

"True. The last launch sent a man into space and landed him on dry ground using the same shuttle. This one will prove we can use the same spacecraft again."

"My mom and dad got to see the landing of the first launch at Edwards when they were visiting my brother in California," I said. "Dad said it was much more impressive than seeing an airplane land. There's knowing where the shuttle's been for the last couple of days, of course. Then, before you can see anything from the ground, there's this sonic boom. Then the shuttle comes in sight, glowing from the heat shield. Dad said what made it so awesome was how quiet it was. This big, heavy thing, no engine to stop it, just the wheel brakes, and then it touches down and just moves slower and slower, seeming like forever."

"You must be psyched to see this one land on Saturday, if only on television."

I smiled. "I wouldn't miss it. Think we'll ever see a woman on the shuttle?"

"I imagine we will. One of the announcers this morning said the Columbia was named for a female figure that represented the United States at some point in time, like 'Lady Liberty' does now."

"I missed that," I said.

Poker Dan gave a sign to some of his friends, and they left. I knew where they were going and why, of course. Tonight, all my friends seemed to be missing. Dixon and Lindsay hadn't come in at all, Rusty called it a night early, and Angel was already dozing, head on the bar. Even John David was absent. I thought I'd finish my single drink and head home too, unless someone showed up before then. I was the only woman in the bar, but I'd gotten comfortable with that.

A dignified-appearing man I didn't know sat down on the stool next to me, pulled out a thick roll of bills, peeled off a twenty, and placed it on the bar in front of him. In a cultured voice he ordered Wild Turkey Reserve on the rocks. Sami, who seemed to recognize him, grinned and took a bottle from the top shelf, where Betts told me the rare and expensive bottles were kept. Most of Sami's customers were more interested in quantity than quality. When the drink was served, the stranger told Sami, "And give this lady whatever she's drinking."

I looked more closely at him. He was well-dressed in what appeared to be an expensive pinstripe gray suit and vest, his deep red tie quietly professional but loose around the neck of his crisp white shirt. On his left hand he wore a pinkie ring with a large green stone. He looked to be in his late fifties or early sixties, slender, tall, with almost black eyes and close-cropped kinky gray hair, and appeared to be of mixed race, or perhaps a light-skinned Black man.

I didn't want another drink, but I knew by now Sami would be angry if I turned down the offer, so I said, "Thank you," figuring I'd just leave it on the bar if I decided to go home. But now bar etiquette obligated me to talk to this stranger.

Sami set down my drink, took the twenty from the bar, and laid down change in front of the man.

The stranger smiled at me. "Do you come here a lot?"

"A couple of times a week," I replied. "I haven't seen you here before."

"I probably haven't been here for six months or more. You seem uncomfortable sitting alone. Are you waiting for your husband?"

"No, I'm not married, and I'm not uncomfortable here. Why do you say that?" I asked, glancing his way.

"Maybe it's wishful thinking." He glanced at a heavy gold watch that looked pricey. "Would you like to go somewhere else?" he asked.

I was puzzled by the abrupt question. I wrinkled my brow and frowned at him. "No, I wouldn't. Why would I want to leave?"

Was he hitting on me? Maybe I was misjudging him. I looked up and he winked. No, he was hitting on me. Protected child that I was, I had no experience with how to handle it.

"I have a BMW with a nice big, comfortable back seat. I also know a luxury hotel nearby. I bet you're not used to that." He placed a hand on my arm.

I pulled my arm away, at a loss for words. *Slam! Bam! Who is this guy? Isn't there some sort of seduction rule or pick-up routine to follow? And who does he think I am?* Eventually I said, "Look, this is a mistake. I just come here to be with friends."

"Ah. But it seems like your friends aren't here, but I *am* here, and *we* are now friends." He pointed at the drink I had yet to touch, hinting that I now owed him something, I supposed. "I'm also a wealthy man. I can afford to do more for you than any friend you're likely to meet in *here.* Come with me." He placed his hand back on my arm. His cologne was cloyingly sweet and much too strong, making me feel a little dizzy.

What gave this man the idea he could just buy me a drink and I'd follow him anywhere? He mustn't come here often if he expected to find prostitutes at Sami's—it wasn't that kind of place. What would make him think *I* was a prostitute? Maybe I just looked destitute and vulnerable to him.

I pulled away again, trying to escape both him and his dizzying odor. "I'm serious. I don't want to leave with you."

He gestured to Sami. "Bring her another drink."

"Sami, I don't want another drink, okay?" I said, forgetting how Sami would react.

"He buys you a drink, here is the drink. Why you want to make me a problem? If it just sits there, I don't care, but you have a drink." Sami quickly mixed another vodka and grapefruit, set it next to the partially empty glass and full glass in front of me, took some bills from the bar, and walked away.

After Sami left, the man grasped my elbow. It was almost painful. He spoke in a low voice near my ear. "You're insulting me." His face had taken on an angry appearance. "You sit here alone, waiting for action. But you won't leave with me, and now you refuse my drink? Why shouldn't you want another drink if you don't want to leave here? What's wrong with me? Are you prejudiced? Have you ever tried a man of color? I can guarantee you don't know what you're missing. We are good lovers."

I had always avoided situations where things like this happened; I didn't know what to do. I pulled out my hankie, a blue-flowered one today, and used it to hide my discomfort, blotting my eyes and dabbing at a nose that wasn't running. I shouldn't have been worried about offending the man, but for some reason I was. I only knew how to be polite. How could I get out of this without causing a scene?

"Please," I said. "Can't you just drop this? I don't want to be picked up by anyone. It has nothing to do with your color."

"I can't believe that. Why would you come here if you didn't want to be picked up?" He looked furious and still held my arm firmly. "You're just a bitch that's giving me a hard time and I don't like it," he said, between closed teeth.

I looked around for someone to help me. Sami obviously wouldn't.

Angel was there but would be useless if I woke him up. Dirty Wally was, as usual, absorbed by the poker machine. I'd never had an actual conversation with him anyway—why would he help? I was the only woman in the bar. I glanced hopefully at the door, thinking a friend might come in, but it stayed firmly shut. I saw a couple of slightly familiar men near the doorway, looking at us, poking each other and laughing, as if I was the butt of some joke.

I said, "I'm sorry," pulled my arm away, got up and went into the restroom.

I stayed in the restroom a long time, rubbing my arm, which would probably develop a bruise. I was safe for now, I thought. But what if he broke in? I had locked the door, but could he force it open? Was this escape or had I made myself a sitting duck? If he barged in, I would scream. I'd never screamed, though. The most I'd ever managed was a startled cry or a giggling protest. Could I scream or would I be too embarrassed to let it out? For now, all I could do was cower in this small space. Fortunately, with no other women in the bar, no one else needed the room.

What would happen when I came out? I would refuse to go with him, of course. He wouldn't physically drag me out, would he? Sami didn't seem to want to help, but surely other customers, even if they didn't know me, wouldn't let me be carried away. I couldn't walk out, because he might follow me. I had to gather my courage to face the man again and make him look elsewhere. God help the poor woman he found!

Surely a half hour was long enough to wait it out. I glanced at my watch repeatedly. I'd just walk right past him and sit by the men near the door who seemed so amused by my situation. If he came up to me again, I'd turn to them and tell them this man was bothering me and ask for their help. It would be humiliating, but they'd have to help me then, wouldn't they? It wouldn't be pretty, but I could do that.

I nervously opened the door and peeked through. The man was no longer in the bar. I waited a bit longer to be sure he hadn't gone into the men's restroom, then returned to the bar to settle my tab.

Sami grinned and laughed. "So, the judge was giving you a hard time?"

"Sami, why didn't you help me? You saw what was going on! Why did you take his side?"

"I did not take his side," said Sami. "I take the business side. I do not offend my customers; he was a customer. He buys expensive drinks; he buys you a drink. It is business, and that is what I do—I sell drinks and I treat my customers well."

"Sami, you didn't treat *me* well, and I'm your customer. I needed you to help *me*."

"Ah, but you will still be my customer. You will not stay away because I did not help you. It turned out well, you are okay, your friends come here, so you will come. So, you see, I sell my expensive drinks to my wealthy customer and I keep my regular customers. See, no problem. I make good business."

"Sami, tonight I'm angry with you, and I'm going home. But first tell me, why did you call that man 'the judge'?"

"Because that is what he *is*, a judge. He is famous man in Chicago, surely you must have heard of him? He is Judge Stratton Thornberry. He is in news all the time, very controversial. Lets criminals go free and issues long time sentences for minor offenses. Very wealthy, is said because he takes bribes—but he is smart and no one proves. A real problem guy for the city. He has big house on North Side, but he drives out here to find a girl for the evening. He thinks no one this far away will recognize him, no one will find out he picks up girls if he goes away from the courts and from his home. They say he wants 'kinky' sex—that is the word they use. Bad for his image if it gets out, you know, the kinky business. He goes to different bars all the time. No one gets to know him, he thinks, comes here maybe once or twice a year. But all the bartenders, we know him, and we talk, so it does not work, people know him after all."

Yeah, and the guys that were laughing must have known him too, I realized. I wonder if they would have stepped in if I needed them. After they had their laughs at my expense, of course. I hadn't heard of the judge, but then, I rarely followed Chicago politics.

"Sami, you just told me you knew what was going on, and you still didn't help me? You know that was a bad man. He could have hurt me. I am very mad at you, Sami! I'm going home."

Sami only shrugged and turned away to serve another customer. I adjusted my opinion about what Sami's priorities were. Clearly, I wasn't one of them.

As I was leaving the bar, I walked past a man I didn't know who was plugging coins into the jukebox. Eddie Rabbit's "I Love a Rainy Night," blared into the room. I opened the door to discover that a cold drizzle had started. *How appropriate...the music, and the weather, and the outcome of the whole evening.* I was not only angry but disillusioned. I hoped the judge wasn't lurking outside to approach me again or follow me home. Thankfully, he wasn't.

I came to Sami's to have a good time with friends, but now I wondered what kind of place Sami's was. I had met people with problems they couldn't handle, and people who were troubled, but they weren't cruel. Tonight, I felt the people at Sami's were selfish and cowardly. I felt like I'd brushed evil. I hadn't bargained for that.

If tonight had happened sooner, I probably would have quit Sami's right away. But I'd gotten dependent on the social life. Where else did I have to go? My friends were here and this was where I had to be if I wanted to see them. I felt attached to Sami's, warts and all. So, from now on I'd look for my friends when I arrived, and I'd leave if none of them were in the bar. That was the way to stay safe here.

I felt alone again. And I didn't like it.

"THIS YOUR QUARTER, DIXON?" CALLED one of the pool players, a man who looked familiar, but I didn't know by name.

"Yeah, it's mine," Dixon replied, then turned to me. "Gotta go. I'm up." He walked away, leaving me sitting at the bar to watch the game and nurse my drink.

I was learning the game of pool. When a player pockets a ball, it falls into a rail under the table until the balls are released by putting a quarter in the slot. On non-league nights, if someone wanted to challenge the last winner, he'd put a quarter in line on the edge of the table to pay for his game, then either watch or sit at the bar until his turn came up. The challenger always paid for the next game and released the balls. Most nights there were a number of quarters in line placed by people waiting to play. Although all quarters looked alike, somehow the players knew whose was next, even though waiting players could be found anywhere in the bar, laughing and talking with friends, often paying little attention to the game being played. I had never heard an argument over whose quarter was next. Most of the pool players knew each other and were courteous.

I was determined to view the episode with Judge Stratton Thornberry as an unpleasant memory, but now I glanced around suspiciously whenever I wasn't in conversation. Some might say I desired companionship more than I valued safety, but I also had a stubborn streak. I decided not to let one jerk keep me from my only current social life. Surrounded by friends again, unlike earlier in the week, I felt comfortable at the moment.

Dixon's game was over in short order. His opponent sank the cue ball on the break, relinquishing his turn to Dixon, who missed his first shot, turning the game back to his opponent, who then ran the table. Dixon put another quarter in line and came to sit next to me again.

"Tough break," I said, then laughed. "I didn't mean when you broke the balls..." I blushed and stopped again when he grinned. I tried a third time. "I meant, your first shot was unlucky. That guy seems to have written the book on position. He's got a really smooth stroke, too."

"Yeah. Well, I'll get another chance at him." He laughed. "You're getting pretty good with pool lingo."

Betts, on the other side of me, said, "Maybe that guy's the Masked Marvel, reincarnated and without his mask."

"What's that mean?" I said.

"I don't know that one either," said Dixon, leaning closer to hear over the bar noise.

"I heard stories from some real old-time Lemonters," Betts said. "Guys who were here even before I grew up in this town. Lemont's always been a big saloon town and these buildings date back to the eighteen hundreds, some of them, when this part of town was known as Smokey Row. Course, this wasn't always Sami's, since owners changed over the years, but there's always been plenty of them— saloons, that is. This building is from that era. It was probably always a bar."

I'd heard about Smokey Row before, but liked to let Betts tell things in his own unique way. He drank some beer and wiped his mouth on his sleeve. I made room for Dixon, propped my elbow on the bar, and rested my chin on my hand, ready for a long story. Betts had a way of dragging stories out but was always entertaining.

"The old-timers say the Masked Marvel used to come in here, back in the 1930s or thereabouts. There was more than one Masked Marvel, actually. The guys wore black masks that covered their whole head except their eyes. They'd drop unannounced into pool halls around the country to play the local champions and give exhibitions of trick shots. The idea started with a billiards company as a promotional gimmick, but then later on the Coca-Cola Company hired a whole stable of top players and pool sharks for publicity. I was told Andrew St. Jean and Ralph Greenleaf, famous pool champions, came to Lemont, to this very saloon—whatever it was called at that time—and more than once. Word would get out on the street and everyone would crowd in to watch. Of course, that's all anecdotal history."

Betts suddenly closed his eyes, screwed up his face, and doubled over on his stool with his hands over his belly.

"What's the matter, Betts?" I asked, alarmed. "Are you okay?"

He took a few, obviously painful, breaths. Then he straightened and slipped off his stool. "I'm good. Just got to visit the men's room for a little while." He limped away, still holding his stomach.

Dixon frowned and shook his head. "Poor Betts. Must be havin' a flare of his pancreatitis. He knows the drink's killin' him, but he just don't seem to care."

"He's got pancreatitis? I didn't know."

"You see how skinny he is. He's in and out the hospital since I known him. They give him some IVs, he gets better and comes out, he's good for a while, and then he's back in again. One of these days he's not gonna make it, though."

I liked Betts. This was a blow.

Dixon changed the subject. "Hear you got to meet the Judge a few days ago."

"Yeah, what a treat that was! You know, everybody around here, they all usually treat me with respect. No one hits on me or tries anything, they watch their language around me, apologize if something slips out. Then here comes this guy in an expensive suit, a professional of all things—you don't expect *him* to be the guy to give you trouble. And no one in the place was any help at all, especially Sami. He just thought it was funny. I was *so* pissed at him!"

Dixon smiled at my uncharacteristic profanity. "I kin see that. But the people here, they know about the Judge. They hear him talked about in the news and in the papers, about his bad calls and he's corrupt and all. He ought to be removed, but he knows how to work the system. So he comes in here, all fancy-dressed and important—makes him feel good, and people sorta enjoy seeing a demonstration right here—him sitting there thinkin' he's like God Almighty, gets away with whatever he wants, no one knows who he is or what he's up to, and the guys in the bar seeing right through him and laughing up their sleeves at him. Havin' a good time, ya see?"

Dixon sipped his Coke and continued. "So he hits on you. He's looking for some tough gal who hangs around gettin' high, up for some casual sex. But surprise, you're not what he expects. You're high-class, but he thinks you're still game. He don't expect to get turned down. That's different for him, and so he don't believe it, don't know when to stop, and you bein' a challenge for him. And then you, like I heard the story—you sittin' there blushin' and all innocent-like. But you put him down real good. I mean, everybody in the bar watchin'—it was great entertainment. Sami's not about to step in and spoil the fun. Everyone's having a good time, and that's good for business."

"Everyone but me having a good time, at my expense," I said, resting my chin on my hand, elbow on the bar again. "But you know, Dixon," I went on with a chuckle, "for a backwoods boy, you're half smart. I guess I can see the humor."

Dixon grinned and waved to Sami for fresh drinks. We watched the pool table for a while. The games were dragging on and it would be a while before Dixon's quarter came up.

"Say, didn't you tell me you used to work for a doctor?" Dixon asked.

"Yeah. I worked in medical clinics summers and medical typing pools during the school year to pay my way through college and grad school. Thought about going into medicine myself for a while, but it's almost impossible for women to get into med school, even if you have top grades."

He paused, sipped his Coke, then asked, "You know anythin' about the high blood pressure?"

"A bit. Why do you ask?"

"They give me a physical at work this week. Doctor says I have the high blood pressure and wants me to take pills." His eyes searched mine. "You think I have to do that? I don't trust doctors. There's always somethin' in it for them."

I sighed. "God, I wish people didn't distrust doctors so much. In my experience it's rare that a doctor isn't always trying to give the best advice he can to his patients. Why are people so suspicious of their doctors?"

"Doctors are all in it with the drug companies. They get people to take things they don't need, and the drug companies pay them under the table."

I shook my head. "You really believe that, Dixon? I guess that happens, but it's really rare. I'm sorry—I won't get started, but obviously you've hit one of my hot buttons." I tried a different approach. "Look, high blood pressure is nothing to mess around with. How high did the doctor say it was?"

"He give me some numbers, but I can't remember them. Didn't know what it meant. And he give me a prescription—said I had to start taking pills right away, see my regular doctor and get 'under control.' I don't have a regular doctor. I never get sick. I feel fine." He paused and then looked me in the eye. "I don't think I need to take no pills."

"Did you fill the prescription?"

"I took it to the drugstore. The pharmacist said my insurance won't pay for this pill, so it would cost me over two hundred dollars for one month. I can't pay that—you know I don't have that kind of money. The girls need braces, and I got to pay for that now."

Never mind Dixon's own mouth full of crooked teeth. But there was no point having that discussion again.

I put my hand on his arm. "Dixon, you need to be treated for this. There are other things you can do. You need to find a regular doctor, and you can ask him to give you a different prescription for another pill—something that won't cost as much."

"Can't you get me somethin'? You know people, don't you?"

"Dixon, it doesn't work that way. I can't write a prescription just because I once worked for a doctor. And no doctor is going to write something for someone he's never seen. They have to examine you first, then decide what the best thing for you is. Can you go back to the work doctor?"

"Well, I'll think about it. I don't think I need pills, though. I feel just like I always did. There's nothing wrong with me."

"Dixon, that's what high blood pressure is like—you don't feel any different. That doesn't mean you don't need the pills. This is important, Dixon. Please tell me you'll talk to a doctor."

"I'll think about it," he said again, looking away. But Dixon still appeared doubtful. I was afraid he'd put it off or forget about it.

I'd started the evening expecting to have a pleasant time with friends, and now I was worried to find out that one was seriously ill, probably related to drinking, and another had a common medical problem that in most cases was easy to treat, but he was indicating he wasn't going to follow his doctor's orders. How far, as their friend, should I go to help them? Did they even want my help?

As I was considering the question, Betts came back to his stool, looking considerably better, and nodding toward the door. "Damn! What are those two doin' in here?" He was looking at two men who had just entered the bar, men I'd never seen before.

Both were large, over six feet tall, strongly built, muscular, and they were loud and boisterous from the moment they walked in. They were laughing and red in the face, elbowing each other and stumbling. It was obvious they'd had a fair amount to drink already but weren't about to call it a night yet. Other customers were looking away from them and frowning. A few people greeted them briefly, but most appeared disturbed by their presence.

"Who are they?" I asked.

"The Czacki brothers," Dixon said, leaning close. "The one in the blue shirt's Logan, and his brother is Warner. You don't want to have anythin' to do with them, Jane. They're mean bullies who make trouble wherever they go. Just 'bout every bar in town's banned them. You *don't* want to be in the bars they hang out in now. Don't know no reason they'd be comin' in here, 'less they got kicked out of their regular bars too. Sami's not gonna like this, their being here—it's bad for his business."

"What will he do?" I asked.

"Not much he *can* do, 'less they start makin' trouble. He can refuse to serve them, but he prob'ly won't do that 'til they give him a reason. He won't want to tell 'em he won't serve them because they're bad for business. But if they start somethin' then he can ban them. They'll stay away a while, then come back and try agin." He drained his Coke, pulled some bills out of his pocket and set his empty glass on top. "Sure they'll make trouble sooner or later. Meanwhile, let's just hope they don't come around too much or stay too long. They start out okay, just noisy. The more they drink, the rowdier they get."

"Are they really brothers?"

"Yeah, they are," Betts said. "I heard there's a sister too. She never comes in here, but word is she's so mean she makes her brothers seem tame. Just you stay away from them, the whole bunch, keep an eye on what's going on, and leave when the time's right. From what I see already, this isn't a good night."

He reached for his jacket on the back of his stool, leaving his unfinished drink on the bar. "I'm gonna head on out, and I think you should too, before trouble starts."

"Don't have to tell me twice," Dixon said. He slid off his stool, walked over to retrieve his quarter from the pool table rail, and strolled out the door, avoiding looking in the Czacki brothers' direction.

I took Betts at his word, gulped the remainder of my drink, and headed for home.

I WAS HEADING FOR ORDMAN'S break room for lunch when I spotted Rusty in the checkout lane. I stopped and changed direction, not sure if I felt comfortable talking to him at work. No one at Ordman's knew Lindsay and I hung out at Sami's. For some reason I couldn't define, seeing him outside of Sami's seemed awkward.

Shit! Too late—he's already waving at me.

I waited near the service desk for him to finish paying and pick up his single bag.

"I hoped I might run into you," he said, walking over to me with his confident stride and warm smile. "Are you free for lunch?"

Well, why not? I enjoyed talking with Rusty at the bar, didn't I? *What harm would lunch be? It's not like we're starting a thing—we're just buddies, right?*

I glanced around. The service manager must have overheard Rusty's invitation, but everyone else was busy. She might talk about it, but who would care? *I'm entitled to a life.*

"I can get away, but only for forty-five minutes. Then I need to relieve the front desk. It'll have to be fast food, I'm afraid."

"McDonald's okay?"

"Sure." There were few fast-food choices in Lemont, and only McDonald's and Lemon Tree were nearby. I really liked Big Macs and hadn't had one for a while.

As we sat at a table a few minutes later with Big Macs and Cokes,

Rusty handed me a napkin and said, "Well, I wasn't expecting this to be such a cheap date." He took off his wire-rimmed glasses and cleaned them with his handkerchief before picking up his burger and taking a bite, stirring a memory of when he lent me his handkerchief shortly after we met.

I laughed. "I'm a simple girl. My tastes are modest."

"I can get used to simple." He looked into my eyes—like a puppy. *Just what I was afraid of.*

I swallowed, picked up the napkin to wipe my mouth, and changed the subject. "Dixon and you are pretty tight. Did he tell you about his high blood pressure?"

"He mentioned it. Also said you gave him a hard time about taking his pills. Said you acted like a mom, wanting to take care of him. I think he was rather pleased by that, actually. Said no one ever wanted to take care of him, only take *from* him."

"I *am* worried about him. He needs to be on medication. Is he taking the pills, then?"

"Not exactly. You know Oscar, from Sami's? No? Well, he's from Haiti, where he says they know about herbs and things like that." Rusty wrinkled his nose. "Voodoo stuff, in my opinion. Anyway, he gave Dixon some leaves and a recipe to make tea with them. Swears it'll take care of his blood pressure. Dixon says he's been drinking it every day—or at least most days."

I shook my head sadly. "Why does he do that? I mean, maybe it works, I don't know—but why mess around? He should see a real doctor, then ask him if the tea is okay or if he has to be on pills. This is important."

"He swears he can't afford it. The herb only cost him $10 and it'll last him months. Says he feels fine."

"I worry about him, Rusty. Please, do me a favor. *You* tell Dixon to see a doctor and do what the doctor says. Maybe if you tell him too, he'll listen."

"I'll try. But speaking of Dixon, he tells me you're learning the game of pool pretty fast. Says next thing you know, you'll be challenging one of us to a game." He winked.

I laughed. "Not hardly. I can't even hold a cue stick comfortably, let alone line up a shot. But I *am* catching on to the strategy. I can predict what ball the shooter will play and how he plans to leave position for his next shot."

"Listen to you, using the lingo! I told you, what you need is just to get out there and play."

"We'll see. I'm happy watching right now. Before I came to Sami's, the only thing I knew about pool was from one of my favorite movies, *The Music Man*. I can still see Robert Preston dancing around the town square, fluttering his fingers in the air and singing, 'Trouble, with a capital T and that rhymes with P and that stands for pool.' I laughed and Rusty laughed with me.

"As it happens, I actually know that movie. Also a favorite of mine."

I set my partially eaten hamburger down and leaned forward a little, smiling. "I loved that movie so much. Had a crush on Robert Preston at the time. I went to see it lots of times."

Rusty relaxed, leaning back into his chair. "You said one of your favorite movies. What others?"

"My favorite of all time is *The King and I*. I had a crush on Yul Brynner too." I laughed.

Rusty ran his fingers through his thick curly hair. "I guess I don't stand a chance then, do I?"

I laughed again. Rusty was easy to talk to. What had I been worried about? "Oh, I don't know," I said, with a sideways glance.

Rusty grinned. I took a sip of my Coke, looked off in the distance, and sighed. "Maybe that's one of the reasons I failed at marriage and I'm so reluctant to get involved in another relationship. I'm looking for some dream movie star that doesn't exist in my world."

"Tell me about your world." He crossed his arms over his chest.

"It's pretty dull. I grew up in Oak Lawn. I was a chubby, shy girl with very straitlaced staunch Catholic parents. I did well at school, though. Had good friends but wasn't part of the popular crowd. I was too much of a prude." I laughed. "Got that master's degree in biology now but I can't find a way to use it…something I *want* to do with it, that is."

Rusty looked at me. "You're not chubby now. What do you *like* to do? Other than work and hang out in pool bars?"

I put the last bit of burger in my mouth, chewed, wadded up the wrapper, and dipped a French fry in ketchup. "I'm pretty boring there too. I like to read. In undergrad I took a minor in creative writing, and I may be the only person in the world who actually loves English grammar and diagramming sentences."

"Family?"

"My mother and father still live in the same house I grew up in. They're doing fine, taking vacations and enjoying retirement. I see them every second weekend, unless they're away. Brother lives in California. Rarely see him."

"Friends?"

"I lost most of them after the divorce." I paused. He was probably curious about my divorce, but I didn't feel like getting into that. "Two of my best friends moved away even before my marriage, one to Arkansas, the other to Iowa. My only remaining best friend, Dottie Lou…she lives in Lemont now, which is one of the reasons I relocated here. But she just recently told me she'll be moving soon, over an hour away."

"She's good for you? You'll miss her when she moves?"

"We're good for each other. She's busy raising her kids and I rarely see her anyway, but we talk on the phone whenever we can. That shouldn't change too much after she leaves Lemont."

I took a sip of Coke through my straw. "Dottie Lou is always there when I'm lonely. I can tell her anything and she understands. Never tries to tell me what to do, just listens. I do the same for her, which gives her an opportunity to talk to an adult. Her husband isn't good about listening—he just likes to talk, mostly brag about himself and give orders." I paused, deciding not to further explain my opinions about Dottie Lou's husband. Instead, I said, "We always make each other laugh. We need that."

"So now you're living alone. Gives you a lot of freedom. How's that working?"

How *was* that working? Freedom was what I'd wanted, but I'd never been a loner. Never lived alone before, as a matter of fact. It was fine enough during the day, but the bumps in the night got to me. Probably one of the reasons I was so reluctant to stay home nights. But how much of this did I want Rusty to know?

I looked in his eyes. "Still getting used to it. What about you?"

"Pretty dull too. I grew up living behind a dry-cleaning business in the city. My mother and father were workaholics and taught me to be the same, I guess. I keep thinking there's more for me in life if I only work harder. So that's what I do—I work. My off time I shoot pool—as you well know. And play golf on Saturday. I've been thinking about joining a bowling league, but with this traveling from the North Side to Lemont every day it's probably not a good idea."

"Friends?"

"Casual friends, not close, like Dixon. I was close to childhood friends but we don't see much of each other anymore. Men don't depend on each other on a day-to-day basis as much as women do, I think." He paused. "Or share their troubles." I had the impression he was reluctant to say more. And then he did.

"I was married for a short time. My wife couldn't accept the situation with my mother. That and the demands of my job, I guess. Anyway, it didn't work out and we called it quits. So I'm not involved with anyone. Probably never will be."

"The situation with your mother?"

"Mother's a bitch."

"Ouch."

"Yeah. After my father died—I was in high school at the time—she was real bitter. Lost their business, started drinking, hanging around the wrong men. I got drafted, spent a tour in Vietnam. After discharge I came back to find out she'd stopped drinking and whoring but turned into a recluse, an alley-picker and a pack rat."

He chuckled. "I guess the polite term is hoarder. Anyway, she was a little less trouble than before, but still not right in the head. She lives alone, isn't any danger to anyone, but she's certifiable. She owns an income property—from the dry-cleaning business she started with my father. Three stores downstairs are rented out now and she lives in the second-floor apartment. I manage the property for her, collect the rents, see that she gets food and money to live on."

He drained his Coke and piled the remains of lunch on a tray. Then he leaned back in his chair again and went on.

"She thinks I stole her property from her, but I'm only trying to keep her from losing it, which she was about to do when I returned from Nam. Neglecting tenant complaints, not paying bills or taxes, that sort of thing. Now when I have to see her for some reason, I borrow a ladder from a friend down the block, climb up to the flat roof outside her apartment, and break a window to get in."

He snorted. "I know, pretty far-fetched, isn't it? You can't make this stuff up, right? Anyway, she screams at me for a while, then I do what I came for and patch everything up again. No woman's going to want to live with a man with that kind of burden, and I don't blame them." He snorted again. "Women in my family live a long time."

"How sad—for you, but also for your mom. Was she always like that?" Rusty's situation seemed so much worse than mine. I felt my respect for him growing.

"I didn't notice when I was a kid." He shook his head. "Not sure a kid *would* notice. Her sister—my aunt—told me she was outgoing when she was young. A fun-loving, sort of life-of-the-party girl. But I never saw her like that. She was always working. She was a fantastic tailor. She could sew anything. She might have dreamed about being a fashion designer, but she never talked about that. She gave my dad a hard time, always nagging about the business. They fought a lot. And she never wanted visitors. Even if her sister came to visit, she'd have me hide behind the curtains and pretend no one was home. I guess the signs were always there."

"Should she be...well...in a psych hospital or something?"

"What good would that do? Every thirty days she'd have to be re-certified, unless she signed herself in. She'll never do that. She'd fight it every step of the way. She's happier where she is. Not happy, but…." He shrugged.

"Wow. That is tough." I was shocked, but I was also impressed. This was a really good man.

"How about you? Do you mind my asking how your marriage broke up?"

I took a deep breath. My story was mild compared to his. How to tell it without portraying myself as a spoiled princess…but he'd been so forthcoming, I felt I owed him an explanation.

"I guess we just grew apart. Maybe we were both too innocent and inexperienced to know what to expect from marriage. Maybe we didn't realize we had so little in common, or that different things were important to us. I wanted to plan for the future, go out and have fun, be with friends, take vacations, have a family. He wanted to put money in the bank, stay home and watch television. We couldn't talk about anything meaningful. He'd just listen to me and I never knew if he agreed or disagreed with me because he never shared his thoughts, just said nothing."

I looked into the distance, not wanting to see what Rusty thought about my words, feeling teary-eyed, wondering if he noticed. "I was bored silly and started spending time with friends instead of going home. One day I realized I had no feelings left for him and that was never going to change."

I found my handkerchief in my purse and brushed at my eyes. I laughed. "Sorry, I don't usually get emotional." We sat in silence for a minute.

Rusty ended the awkwardness by changing the subject. "How's the job hunting going?"

I frowned. "It's not. I'm still procrastinating—haven't even looked. Like I explained before, I need a life, and I'm still trying to figure out what that is. The only thing I know for sure is that it's not the life I left behind."

He finished clearing up the mess we'd made. "Got to get you back to Ordman's."

I stood up, realizing I was sorry the lunch was over. He'd been nice, and I liked how easy it had been to share with him. For some reason, compared to talking to Dottie Lou, going over things with a man made me see things in a different perspective. Instead of feeling like a poor, troubled divorcée, I felt relieved that I wasn't the only person going through a rough spell. Sharing confidences with someone who didn't know my past seemed to make my burden a little lighter.

As we neared the door, Rusty turned to me with a grin. "I heard *The King and I* is coming to the Arie Crown Theatre at McCormick Place in April. Yul Brynner is scheduled to do a farewell performance. How about if I get tickets and take you?"

April was a long way off, but how could I say no to that? If either of us was still around....

Chapter 11

RUSTY WAS SHOOTING AGAINST DIXON when I arrived. Rusty racked and Dixon broke, then gave up the table after he didn't pocket any balls. Rusty walked completely around the table, studying it carefully while chalking his cue stick. Finally, he stopped, leaned far over, weight on his left leg, and took aim. He called his shot, "Nine ball off the side rail, off the twelve, into the corner pocket." The cue ball struck the nine ball which hit the side rail, bounced off, traveled across and down the table where it glanced off the striped, purple number twelve ball, and dropped into the left side pocket. The cue ball settled inches from the red eleven ball, in perfect position to ease eleven into the corner pocket.

"Shot!" Lindsay yelled, sitting on the stool next to mine and thumping her stick on the floor. I applauded, then the watchers all fell silent to let Rusty concentrate. Sitting on stools adjacent to the pool table, Lindsay and I continued to watch the game.

John David sat in his usual place, six stools away from us, with his head down. He appeared even more despondent than usual.

I caught Lindsay's eye and nodded toward him. "What's with John David tonight?"

"I'm not sure. He said something about his sister, and then he clammed up. He's pretty dependent on her, you know. She and her husband are helping him pay for his studio apartment and she keeps an eye on him. Sees that he eats some decent food, keeps his apartment and himself clean, stuff like that."

"I didn't know he had a sister. That's good, I guess." We watched the game for a minute. Dixon was up now. He was a slow, cautious player. "You and John David work things out?" I asked.

"We just talk a little. Sometimes he walks me home. Nothing physical going on or anything like that. Just…I think I'm the only one he talks to, except maybe his sister. She's always telling him what to do. He needs that, I suppose. But he talks to me about a few other things. As I told you, he's a nice guy. You'd never know it to see him. Just because he's so quiet doesn't mean he's not really smart. He says he spends a lot of time in the library—reading and stuff. They have a computer there for the public to use." Lindsay laughed. "He told me the librarian has to kick him off so other people can get a turn."

I smiled, knowing that the Lemont Library shared space with Lemont High School. The students must find John David rather curious in many respects. "I read somewhere that it won't be long before people have computers in their homes," I said. "It's hard to imagine. Reminds me of *The Jetsons*. Do you remember that show?"

"Barely. A cartoon about a family that lived in the future, wasn't it?"

"You got it. So, what about the crush thing. Did you ever talk to John David about that?"

She nodded and took a sip of her drink. Southern Comfort instead of rum and Coke tonight, I noticed. "I told him I was flattered he liked me, but as far as I was concerned, we were just good friends. If he wanted me to stay his good friend, he had to cool it."

"Good for you. And he said…?"

She smiled "He said he needed a friend more than anything else."

"So you're good?"

"For now, at least. The pressure is off and I'm not uncomfortable around him anymore. In fact, we're doing a few things outside of Sami's. We both like to take long walks, along the canal or in the Palos Woods. This weekend we're going to some fall festival nearby."

"So maybe if you take it slow, something more will develop?"

She shook her head. "I don't know. I'm good with 'just friends' too." That pretty much described me and Rusty as well, I thought.

Lindsay paused. "Maybe you noticed. I don't have much ambition."

"Why not? You're bright. People like you if you give them a chance." I squeezed her arm. "I like you!" She grinned.

I went on. "The world is your oyster, as they say. You've got no one to interfere, you can make whatever you want of your life. You don't have to spend it all picking bruised fruit off the shelves at Ordman's."

She looked down into her Southern Comfort. "What if all I want to do is pick out bruised fruit?"

I looked at her. "You're serious?"

She nodded. "I'm not like you, Jane. I'm content with what I do and who I am. I work at my own pace doing something that gives me a sense of accomplishment. I come here knowing I'm really good at something. It makes me feel important. I have friends now…two at least, you and John David. I make enough money to pay for my food and apartment. What else do I need?"

I couldn't agree with Lindsay, but when I tried to see things through her eyes, I understood her. From her point of view, she was happy. Was she wrong for not wanting more out of life? Perhaps I was wrong, and should be content like Lindsay. Who was I to criticize? What had ambition done for me? Was I happy? I couldn't put my finger on what was wrong or what was holding me back, but I knew the life I was living now wasn't the life I wanted to live forever. I thought in a rather snarky way that my ambition was for something more worthwhile than shooting pool.

Looking around, I realized that except for Rusty, the majority of people sitting around me had little ambition. Dixon didn't. Neither did Betts. Adam and Eve had apparently patched things up again and were sitting shoulder to shoulder and thigh to thigh. I noticed Eve's hand moving in Adam's lap and looked away. *Get a room*, I thought. Certainly, Adam and Eve didn't have ambition, nor did Angel or Poker Dan or Dirty Wally. The exceptions were Pizza Bob and Sami and his wife, Whitney. But I didn't visualize myself like them either.

Which made me wonder again why I was hanging out here. And yet I didn't seem to be able to help myself. Sami's seemed to have become an addiction, not to alcohol, but…what? A character addiction? There were certainly enough characters at Sami's for a lifetime.

I wondered if, now that she knew John David better than most of us, Lindsay had found out the truth about his ears, but I didn't think it was the right time to ask, so I didn't. I also wondered what sort of action John David had seen in Vietnam, to have apparently scarred him to the point of disability. There was my incurable curiosity again. There didn't seem to be a way to find out.

Adam and Eve stood up and walked toward their apartment, still clinging to each other. Eve's hand must have moved things along to the point that they wanted more privacy. Thank God for little favors.

Rusty had won the lag shot and the next player, a man I didn't know, was racking. Dixon came over to join Lindsay and me. He held up his hand and motioned for a refill of his Coke, but Sami just nodded and kept drawing drafts and fixing drinks at the front end of the bar, which was unusually busy.

Dixon sat down. "He'll get to me sooner or later."

A little scene seemed to be developing near mid-bar. Two men, one short and plump, the other tall and thin, were standing behind their stools, facing each other and waving their arms. They looked familiar but I didn't know their names.

"It's not voodoo economics, asshole! It's Reaganomics!" the tall one said.

"It's voodoo to me," the short one insisted. "I'm tired of the middleman paying ridiculous taxes while this idiot has rich businesses paying next to nothing. No wonder that Hinckley guy tried to shoot him down as soon as he found out what he was up to."

"That wasn't why he tried to shoot him. It was about that actress, Jodie Foster."

"Yeah, right. Tell me another one."

"I'll tell ya that when Reagan took over from Jimmy Carter, we had double-digit inflation, twenty percent interest rates, and ten percent unemployment. Those numbers are coming down and his plan is working, whether you like him or not!"

The two men were shouting in each other's faces, hands balled into fists at their sides.

Sami interrupted. "Gentlemen please! You are upsetting to my customers. Please sit down and stop your loud voices. My bar is no place for politics."

The men glared at each other. Then the tall man picked up his jacket and headed for the door. The short man sat down at the bar. Sami picked up the tall man's unfinished mug of beer, took two bills from the short man's pile, and walked away. The man opened his mouth to protest, then closed it again and rolled his eyes.

Dixon winked at me. "Show me a bar where no one talks about politics," he said. "Sort of goes with the territory, don't you think, Jane?"

I hadn't followed politics too much on the news in recent years due to being involved solely by my personal problems. I had been raised by strict Democratic parents. I had cried when John Kennedy was assassinated, and later for his brother Bobby, but I'd gotten more conservative during my college years when I had been turned off by evidence of what I viewed as the unreasonable power wielded by unions. Currently, much like the malaise that infected my personal life, my views on politics were weak and indecisive. I called myself an independent and voted for the man rather than the party. I hadn't voted for Reagan, who I didn't see as more than a pretty actor.

I heard the door open and looked up to see two newcomers in the open doorway.

"Oh, no!" Dixon's jaw dropped and he stared as two large, burly men walked in.

"Shit," said Lindsay. "The Czacki brothers again. Just what we need."

As they moved into the room, Logan and Warner Czacki were laughing loudly, staggering a little, whether from laughter or drink I couldn't tell, but my bet was on the latter.

"Did you see the look on his face?" Logan managed between laughs. "Priceless! All gray and collapsed like, his jaw all loose and shit."

"Yeah, and then he goes, like, 'You guys ruined me! I got nothin' left, no savings, no job. What about my wife? Who's gonna pay for my kids?'" Warner imitated in a whiney voice. "Like some poor slob in a movie, pleading for his life. Like he thought we'd give a fuck!" They both laughed boisterously, elbowing each other.

"You'd think he would of got crazy mad, tried to punch us out or somethin'. No, just kept whinin' like a fuckin' baby. Stupid prick, no guts at all," said Logan. The brothers both roared again.

With the bar so full, they pushed between two stools at the front corner, carrying on loudly.

"Boss, our usual," Warner demanded. He tipped his cap at Sami, then let out another peal of laughter. "That wife he was talkin' about— should be no big deal to him anyhow. She wasn't even worth the fuck, just laid there not getting into it, worst fuck I ever had. Least it was a good thing you were there to take your turn and liven things up."

Logan slapped Warner on the shoulder. "Yeah, then her gettin' all teary-eyes, actin' like we should feel sorry for her or somethin', poor little stupid fuckin' bitch! Thinkin' she's helpin' her old man keep the business goin' by makin' *us* happy. Fuckin' fools, the both of them."

Warner said, "Well, that's what you told her we'd do, and she fell for it, didn't she?"

"Yeah, well, the fuck wasn't worth a damn, but the look on his face when we told him we screwed his fuckin' wife, that was fuckin' worth the effort!"

"Yeah, an' then you tell him, 'It's not me, it's my fuckin' brother here. He'll screw anythin' that walks, crawls, or ain't been dead too long.'" Laughing uncontrollably now, jostling the adjacent customers.

Having just stopped a fight, Sami had had enough. "Can't you boys tone it down?"

"Whatza matta, camel jockey, our language too rough for this *refined* establishment?" asked Warner, pointing to his chest, feigning insult. "Maybe you want us to take our business down the street?"

"Maybe you should come back another day," suggested Sami.

"And maybe you should kiss our fuckin' ass," said Logan. But they were apparently in too good a mood to take serious offense. They left, still laughing heartily.

Watching them leave, I caught sight of John David's face, which was bright red, his eyebrows low, glaring through squinted eyes with a clenched jaw. A vein jumped wildly in his neck. A look of hate I'd never seen before on his face. If I didn't know better from Lindsay, I'd think the simple, gentle guy was ready to kill. Apparently the Czacki brothers had even gotten to him. John David drank his remaining beer in two swallows, got up, put on his jacket, and left.

Strange. Is he following them? I quickly dismissed the thought. Surely John David, a small and meek man, was smart enough to avoid men with such a dangerous reputation.

Relieved that the Czackis were gone, I turned to Dixon, looking over the top of my glasses. "Well, that was a treat! Their language was really overboard, even for bar talk. Do you have any idea what that was all about? It sounded really nasty."

Pizza Bob was standing nearby and overheard my question. He squeezed in between me and Dixon. "Sorry about the language, which *was* overboard, as you say, but classic Czacki brothers. As for what they were talking about, the story on the street *is* nasty," He paused and motioned to Sami for a beer. "You know, you see 'em in here, behaving like the lowlifes they really are. But like lots of people in bars, they don't act the same way in their daytime lives. Doesn't make them different people, of course, but during the day, some guys pretend, playact so they can make a living, and some are pretty good at it and fool a lot of people. The Czackis are like that."

"So what's their day job?" I asked.

"Whatever they think they can make money at. Usually manual construction, mostly concrete work but in cold weather light carpentry, masonry, roofing, things like that. But they're always on the lookout for something more lucrative. And they're smart, street-smart I should say. But they're also ruthless. They get what they can, move on and leave some other guy with the pieces."

Sami set a draft beer on the bar in front of Pizza Bob and finally brought Dixon's Coke. Pizza Bob took a couple of swallows of his beer, wiped the foam from his mouth with a sleeve, and went on. "Eventually they screw up too much and get themselves canned, then move from contractor to contractor. But they're always on the lookout for a mark, you know, a way to take some poor slob's money for themselves."

"That sounds like them," Lindsay said.

Bob nodded. "Some time ago, they ran across this guy, a factory worker, a young guy with a wife and two kids and a little money in the bank, and a dream to make that money into something else, maybe open his own business someday. They tell this guy there's an opportunity to buy a neighborhood bar. It's a popular place, near 63rd and Pulaski in the city, no trouble, a lot of regular patrons, makes a lot of money, but the owner, he's sick, he needs to sell it right away, and it's goin' real cheap. The Czackis convince this young guy that they know everything there is to know about the bar business. Yeah, they know how to operate the place, it's a gold mine, but they don't have the start-up money. They talk this guy into puttin' up the money—he can keep his day job, and they'll operate the business as their part of the partnership."

"How do you know all this?" Dixon asked.

"A close friend of the poor sap is one of my part-time drivers." Pizza Bob sipped, put his drink down. "So, the Czackis tell a convincing story. They're very charming to him. They lay out exactly how the business will be run—they really sound like they know what they're doing. The buyer checks out the details, finds out the opportunity is pretty much as they've described. What he doesn't do is check out the background of his 'partners,' or if he tried, he didn't get the right story. We know, of course, that those two know a lot about bars, and they're quick to recognize a deal that works to their advantage. But we also know to stay away from them. This guy didn't."

"I can guess where this is going," I said, shaking my head.

"The guy didn't have enough money saved, had to borrow some, incur some debt. Well, surprisingly, it started out okay. Maybe the Czackis even tried to make a go of the business for a while. But being Czackis, and being in a bar all day, their true nature eventually took over, and between drinking up their profits and offending their patrons, it didn't take long before they ruined the business. Customers stopped coming in, but the bills still did."

"When did the partner catch on—or did he?" Dixon asked.

Pizza Bob repositioned himself on his stool, drank some more beer, and cleared his throat before continuing.

"The poor guy who put up the money, he didn't believe it at first. This business was a good thing, right? It had always been a popular place. The money poured in when they first opened. Surely the downturn was temporary, and the business would turn around. The Czackis, riding a good thing on someone else's money, hid everything from him. They even ordered extra inventory, charged it to the debt, sold the goods on the side, and pocketed the sales. When their partner eventually found out what was going on, the place was so far in debt there was no way out. The brothers had made sure that he appeared as the sole person responsible for the debt. He talked to a lawyer but there was no legal recourse against them, since the 'partnership' turned out to be a sham. The Czackis had taken whatever profits there were initially, but there was no bookkeeping to trace what had happened, and only one name appeared on all the paperwork. Not a Czacki name, of course."

"So that's why the brothers didn't come in for so long. It wasn't because they were persona non grata, but because they had their own place to drink," I said.

"You got it," Pizza Bob said, and drank some more beer. "But it gets worse. Because they're the Czacki brothers, knowing the business was a goner, they milked it for what it was worth. The more desperate their 'partner' got, the more fun they had at his expense. They didn't need him anymore—he was the fall guy, but he was good for some laughs. So they went to his wife and convinced her they had another guy who was willing to take over the debt, and that they would make that arrangement and step out of the picture if she went to bed with them. She was desperate as well, so she did it. You heard from their mouths tonight how that turned out."

"And they got away with it?" I shook my head. *How disgusting.*

"Apparently so."

"And the guy? What happened to him?" Dixon asked, his frowning face full of sympathy.

"Well, he missed a lot of time from his day job when this was going on, the stress affected his performance, and then the bill collectors started calling his job. He was screwing up so much his company had to let him go. He lost his house and his wife took the kids and moved in with her parents in Indianapolis."

"Those poor people," I said. I glanced at Lindsay, who was staring into space, blinking rapidly.

"Yeah. The wife felt bad for her husband, but she was also a victim. Word is he's not the same guy anymore, and they don't have much of a marriage left. They may get back together. Or not." Pizza Bob rested his elbow on the bar top, his chin in his hand.

"That's all so sad," I said. "And these guys, they come in here laughing and bragging. This must have happened over some months, didn't it? Wonder what made them talk about it today."

"Who knows. Maybe they bumped into a former customer or someone reminded them. The wife moved just a few days ago. Maybe the brothers just got word and were reliving the whole thing tonight," Pizza Bob said.

I closed my eyes and shook my head again. It was hard for me to believe the Czacki brothers could be so cruel. I'd seen things like this happen in movies and read about it in books but never encountered such meanness in real life.

Now the bar din seemed sharp and rude, like one would expect if a prison brawl were about to take place, not the friendly place I thought it was. Maybe I ought to look elsewhere for companionship. And then

I swept my gaze around my circle of friends—Dixon, Lindsay, and Pizza Bob—and felt a fondness for them. I remembered how lonely I had been the months I'd lived in Lemont before I met them. Did I really want to start over? Like everything in life, places had their pros and cons.

"Monsters," I finally said.

"Monsters, you said it. There are totally amoral people out there. Life is all about them and it's all a big joke. The Czackis are the top of that food chain, but there are more like them."

"You said the wife went back to her hometown of Indianapolis. Funny. That's where John David's family lived," said Lindsay, her voice weak and breaking.

Bob slapped himself on his forehead. "I didn't tell you. Strange twist of fate, small world, whatever you want to call it. The wife is John David's sister."

Chapter 12

THE NEXT FEW TIMES I visited Sami's, I was alert for more problems. For whatever reason, the Czackis hadn't returned, and Sami's also remained unchanged.

I also kept an eye on John David. I expected he would stop coming in, at least for a while, or that he would act differently in some way after what the Czacki brothers had done to his sister. However, he remained the same quiet, shy guy, staring at the bar top or watching Little Lindsay, just like he had always done. I thought perhaps this was because the whole story had developed over time and wasn't new to John David, only to those of us who heard it for the first time when the Czacki brothers demonstrated their nastiness.

Not long after Thanksgiving, I was sitting with Betts near the front door when Rusty arrived and slid onto the stool next to mine. He didn't even glance at the pool table, I noticed. There was a big grin on his face.

"Can you get away from Ordman's tomorrow afternoon?" he asked.

"I'm working until four. Why?"

"Can you get someone to cover a couple of hours?"

"I repeat, why?"

"I arranged an interview for you. I think you're going to want to make it."

An interview! I was stunned. A stab of fear struck my chest, stopping my breath for a moment. *I'm not ready yet! Whatever possessed him?* I glanced at Betts, who shrugged his shoulders, then turned back to Rusty. "What's this all about?"

"Wait." He motioned to Sami, who brought him a draft beer. "Let's go in the back, where it's quieter." He picked up my drink too. I rolled my eyes at Betts and followed Rusty to a small table for two near the rear door.

Quieter? I thought as we walked past the jukebox, which was blaring Kim Carnes's "Bette Davis Eyes."

"I repeat," I said, draping my jacket over the back of a chair and sitting. "What's this all about?" I placed my arms on the table and leaned across it so I didn't have to shout.

Rusty leaned forward too. He normally spoke in a louder voice than I was accustomed to. I wondered if he had developed that habit from being in noisy places, like Sami's, a good deal of the time.

"I told you there were things you could do at Argonne. Things you'd like…that don't require further education. Get your foot in the door, see what's going on. Sooner or later, something will make sense, and you'll follow that path. But you got to get started."

"You say."

He grinned, reached over and squeezed my arm. "I say. And I know what's good for you. A good thing when I see it." His words were cheerful, teasing, and sounded confident, but he appeared apprehensive, as if he'd acted rashly, butting in where he wasn't wanted. His face fell as he watched mine. My reaction clearly wasn't what he had hoped for.

"Will you listen at least? I'll cancel the interview if you don't want to go."

I sighed. I didn't want to think about starting over yet. But if something fell in my lap….

I leaned back in my chair, arms across my chest. "Talk," I said.

"It's in the biology division. That's your master's."

I shook my head. "But I'd need a doctorate. Otherwise, I'd be a lab assistant, a flunky. That's not much better than what I'm doing now."

"No, it's in the transcription pool."

"The transcription pool? They have a transcription pool?"

"Sure they do. The scientists need to get their reports typed up, most for publication. You don't think they're going to do that themselves, do you?"

"I hadn't thought about that."

"I know the director of the department, and she told me she's looking for someone. I told her about you, and she asked to meet you."

I narrowed my eyes. "What did you tell her?"

"That you've done it before, you know biology, you know the lingo, you can type—"

"Not very fast, but I'm accurate," I interrupted. He must have remembered that I'd done medical transcription part-time while in college. But was I good enough for Argonne?

"And…ta da!…you're a grammar expert. The same department edits and proofreads the scientific reports. You love to read, you love grammar, and you'd be using your degree—to some extent. But no stress, right up your alley, and you don't have to work long hours or bring work home. Perfect, right?" He pushed up his glasses with a forefinger. His eyes searched mine hopefully. "It's not your forever job by any means, but a chance to get your foot in the door to a new career, perhaps. Right place at the right time and all that."

"And all that nonsense, you mean," I said. But I had to agree it sounded interesting. An opportunity I should find out more about, at any rate.

He looked disappointed by my lack of enthusiasm. "So, you're not interested? You want me to cancel the interview?"

"Wait. I never thought of using those particular skills to get a job. Let me think." It wasn't a forever job, like Rusty said, but Argonne had loads of potential. And it did sound not only interesting but without the pressure I'd been trying to avoid. I couldn't come up with a good reason not to at least go to the interview. Bad reasons—*I can't get off work, I need a haircut, I haven't got anything to wear—I'm scared to death!*—were plentiful. My heart raced.

Rusty could be right. The job sounded like it could be a fit, provided the people were okay. Even if they weren't, I thought I could do this work, and I thought I'd like it. The possibilities started to seem attractive. Maybe there'd be some project going on that I'd fit right into. I could get more training, work my way up, use that degree I'd wasted so far....

This could be the future I've been looking for. But what if I screw it up again?

I'll never know if I don't try.

I leaned forward and smiled. "Where do I have to go and who will I be seeing?"

Rusty beamed and grabbed my jacket off the back of my chair. "Let's go talk about the details over a Big Mac."

Chapter 13

THE NEXT DAY, THE ORDMAN'S store manager was a little annoyed when I told him I needed the afternoon off for a personal matter that had just come up.

"Couldn't you have given me more notice? I need time to get a fill-in," he complained.

"I'm sorry," I said. "I didn't know until last night. But it's important."

He eyed me suspiciously. "More important than your job?"

Swell. Now I need to worry about keeping this job. I need the income!

He looked at me closely when I didn't answer and let out a long breath. "I'll find someone. I have to start calling right away." He walked away.

At Argonne, a security guard found my name on the visitor list. I answered a few questions to clear security and was given directions to the building my appointment was in and told where to park. There was no receptionist in the large workroom, only work cubicles with a private office at the side. I told the typist in the first cubicle that I was there for an interview and handed her the resume I'd prepared. She asked me to sit in a chair near her desk and took my resume into the private office. After a few nervous minutes, during which time I assumed my resume was being read, the typist's phone rang.

"Julia's ready for you now," she said. "Good luck."

Julia McCarthy, the director of the Department of Writing and Editing, was a grandmotherly type, tiny and skinny with short-cropped gray hair and lots of energy. Kindness radiated from the chatty woman.

"I understand you're a friend of Rusty Dineff," she began.

"Yes, I met Rusty soon after I moved to Lemont," I told her, meeting her eyes but hoping she wouldn't ask how we knew each other. *What will she think if she knows we met at a bar? Or will she want to know more about our friendship?*

Fortunately, she only said, "I like Rusty. He's good people." She looked down at my resume, turning pages. I'd been up half the night typing up my education, job experience, qualifications, and achievements, as well as contact information for references I could provide. Her finger stopped near the top of the first page.

"You have a master's degree in biology, I see. And taught high school biology for...um, six years?"

"That's right." I nodded, rubbing the fingers of one hand through the other on my lap.

"But you've applied for a position as a transcriptionist, not a teaching position."

"I like transcription. I did medical transcription at St. Francis Hospital for over three years while I earned my degree. I haven't worked at a research laboratory, but I believe my skills are transferrable, and I was a good transcriptionist." Ms. McCarthy looked at me as if she wanted more information. "I didn't like teaching and I wasn't using my education to advantage," I admitted.

She drew her eyebrows together. "Why go back to transcription? That's not moving forward from teaching."

This was the hard question I'd dreaded. I looked her in the eye. "I left my teaching job and my husband at the same time. I moved to Lemont to start fresh." I gave her a wry smile. "And lick my wounds, you might say. I took a job at a grocery store because I needed income while I was preparing for a new career—not teaching. I think that career can be at Argonne. I know biology, I know terminology, my typing skills are pretty good, and I'm a hard worker."

I paused. "I have to be honest," I said. "When Rusty and I talked yesterday, he told me about the research Argonne does. It seems the concentration is on computer science and physics. I'm not familiar with those sciences. My degrees are in biology, with a minor in chemistry."

"Let me reassure you. First of all, we do a *lot* of biological research. We were one of the first facilities in the country with an electron microscope, and we still have one of the most powerful. We do a lot of medical and pharmaceutical research, especially in the field of genetics. Second, you'd be taking Shirley's place. Shirley is our principal biological research transcriptionist. But do you see this job as a stepping-stone?"

I met her eyes again. "Yes. And no. I'm loyal, and if I like something I tend to stick to it. I'm determined and I'm not a selfish worker. You will get all of me from day one and spend very little time in training. I'll be equaling your other workers in very short time. I have no plans to go elsewhere, but if I'm offered advancement, I'll take it if it's right for me. But I'll never leave you in the lurch." I paused. Was I trying to convince Julia McCarthy or myself? Despite my present lack of confidence, I knew that everything I said was true when I was on my game. I planned to try as hard as I could.

"Isn't that the kind of workers you want?" I added.

She gathered the pages of my resume together and stood up. "Let me show you around."

I sat stunned for a moment before leaping to my feet. *Was it this easy? Was she going to offer me the job?*

"Call me Julia," she said, as she linked her arm through mine and took me into the department. Three women and two men were sitting in office cubicles, leaving five of the ten cubicles open. I supposed, if I got the job, I'd be occupying one of them.

Each cubicle was the same size and layout, containing a word processor, a transcription machine with headphones, a telephone, and ample desk space, with closed shelving above and file drawers under the desktops. The six-foot by eight-foot workstations had cushioned, tan-fabric walls five feet tall that allowed workers easy access to the whole department yet gave each typist a reasonable amount of privacy. As we walked through the area, I noticed that each worker had customized their space, some desktops bare, some cluttered with photos, plants, and office tchotchkes, others messy with stacks of paper, notes, and writing tools that left no room to set anything down. Evidence the staff here would have a lot of freedom, I thought. Yet I'd be able to concentrate here.

A woman about my age in a late stage of pregnancy was standing near the entrance to her cubicle. She leaned on crutches, and I was surprised to see that she had only one leg. She caught my eye and smiled at me as we walked by. She must have known I was applying to be a co-worker. The desk behind her was uncluttered and a photograph of two little girls who appeared to be about three and five years old sat beside a word processor.

Julia smiled at each worker we passed, and each in turn looked up from his or her screen, grinned, or nodded pleasantly. One woman was busy on the telephone. I didn't get the impression that any worker was rushed or annoyed.

A short, somewhat pudgy man jumped up and stopped us.

"I'm sorry to interrupt, but could I just ask if you'll have some time to spend with me tomorrow morning? I really need to go over some issues with Dr. Stephen's manuscript."

"Absolutely," Julia said. "Make it nine a.m. And bring coffee for both of us." She winked at me.

After she'd shown me around, I was excited by what I'd seen: the working conditions, the staff I'd met, and especially Julia. When we returned to her private office, instead of sitting behind her desk, she turned one of the guest chairs so we could sit facing each other.

"We're here to help the scientists in any way we can," Julia said. "We call ourselves the Department of Writing and Editing, and the staff are referred to as scientific transcriptionists. We not only transcribe the researchers' dictation, but we also do everything we can to make our publications professional, including proofing the spelling, grammar, and punctuation, giving some developmental editing guidance, line editing, and setting up top notch manuscripts. Argonne is a world-class facility with a reputation to keep, you know. We do in-house reports, studies that appear in scientific journals and for professional societies, and we publish a fair number of books. Some of the scientists consult with us from the beginning of the process. It's exciting to see everything Argonne does and know we're on the cutting edge of scientific knowledge. What you do makes a difference, not only here but to the world."

Make a difference to the world! I want this job. What if she doesn't want me? Am I good enough?

"I counted ten workstations," I said, nervously. "But I saw only five people. Are you that short-staffed?"

"Not at all. The people here not only have a variety of skills, but their schedules vary. Some work days, some nights, most full-time, but some part-time. We even get temporary staff when the workload demands. Most of our proofreaders work from home. Occasionally a scientist wants to bring in someone with special knowledge for a particular project. We have to be flexible.

"I mentioned that you'd be taking Shirley's place. She's taking maternity leave soon. She'll be out at least six months, and to be honest, I'm concerned that she might not return. She has two little girls at home now, and I don't know how she'll be able to manage three young children and job, especially on one leg."

Pregnancy leave? She'll be returning? An empty feeling of disappointment filled me.

"So, this is a temporary position then?"

"Not if I have anything to say about it. Someone does a good job, we keep them. There always seems to be a place for people who like their work and it's up to me to keep my staff happy. I like your background, your skill and knowledge level. Rusty thinks highly of you, and I trust his judgment. After meeting you, I like you too. I understand you may not always stay in this department. If you find something better for you, that's fine with me. My people are like my kids. I want my kids to do well and to grab their dreams. If they move on, I share their happiness."

This is too good to be true. I've got to get this job!

"If I took the job, when would you like me to start?"

She grinned. "I've been here a long time, and I can get you through the red tape in Personnel on *my* schedule. I want you to have as much time as possible to work with Shirley. She leaves in a little less than two months, so you'll work together until then. Of course, you'll start out doing the biology transcription, then take on some proofing if the proofreaders get backed up—which happens a lot, so it won't be long before you're called on, I suspect. We'll see what you can do and move you wherever it works out."

She put her hand on mine. "Sleep on it overnight and call me in the morning with your decision, and then we'll discuss the details. But I'm sure you can do this. You'll be working independently for the most part, but you'll find your co-workers to be friendly, knowledgeable, and willing to help. I won't keep anyone on who doesn't fit that description." Her eyes searched mine. "Is that clear?"

Despite my fears about failure, I knew I was going to accept her offer, no matter what the salary and benefits were.

Chapter 14

I LAY IN BED THAT night, tossing and turning, not sleeping much for the second night in a row. As Julia suggested, I took overnight to think over her offer, but I had no doubt I would accept it.

Not without qualms, though. Was Julia's confidence in me misplaced? Working at Ordman's, all I had to do was show up on time and respond to customer requests. If I worked at Argonne, exciting as the new opportunity was, I'd have responsibilities again. I kind of liked my life the way it was at the moment. Without stress, except for that nagging feeling of "I can do better." I originally intended to work on cruise control at Ordman's for only a short time and then move on to something more commensurate with my education and abilities. Now, I'd been there since March, close to ten months. Was I going to keep procrastinating until it was too late?

I knew myself well enough to realize that things would be very different if I worked at Argonne. I wouldn't be satisfied with just showing up and sitting at an electric typewriter or word processor all day. I'd be challenged by the people I worked with. I'd want to work the hardest, be as good as their best transcriptionist, learn more skills, impress the professional staff. I'd want to look good in everyone's eyes so I would look good to myself. I didn't face challenges lightly.

I also knew I wasn't at the top of my game yet, although I was confident I could measure up quickly. My typing skills were, as I'd told Julia, slow but accurate. I thought I'd soon be putting out the same amount of work as others because I'd spend less time fixing errors. But there was going to be a significant learning curve—learning the equipment, the routines, the details of the research projects, new terminology. Not to mention the people involved.

Could I do it?

Hell yes!

Did I want to? I was less sure of that. But I did know I'd feel like a failure once again if I didn't try. After the double failure of marriage and teaching career, still another failure would be devastating.

I started my job at Argonne the following Monday, two weeks before Christmas, after agreeing to work evenings and weekends at Ordman's until my replacement was hired. From the beginning, the days went pretty much as I'd expected. My coworkers were smart, helpful, pleasant. Soon I had a handle on the workload and produced as many pages as the other workers. Julia was great to work for, very understanding, and if she ever had bad moods, she hid them successfully.

The scientists...well...they were scientists. Some were lovely, friendly, understanding, respectful. Others clearly thought we were beneath them. Some were classic absentminded professionals with their heads somewhere else who were surprised when we couldn't read their scribbled notes or their minds. Julia, always kind and respectful to her staff, rode supreme over the researchers and wouldn't allow anyone to be rude or bully us.

The atmosphere, and the work, were exciting!

Argonne had just launched the first spallation neutron source, sparking a new era of neutron science. This science, among other scientific areas, offered methods for advanced biological research, making it possible to determine the structure of biological molecules and understand how they worked. This would aid in the development of drugs and vaccines to combat disease. Researchers were flocking to use the new resource to prove or disprove their theories.

In my position, I got to meet these pioneers and recognize the importance of their discoveries before their findings were announced to the world. I was sure some of these scientists would be the next Nobel Prize winners. More than once, I picked up the phone and dialed my father, who was always impressed by contact with important people, to say, "Dad, guess who I met at work today?"

One of my favorite new friends was Stephen Cass. Stephen taught biology and biochemistry at a local college, but also worked at Argonne, where he had taken on the role of writing coach for undergraduate students working internships at Argonne. He taught them methods to improve their research reports and presentations. As I worked with Stephen and his students, I had the benefit of witnessing an inspiring man who was creating an ideal environment for learning, while working with students who were driven by their passion to learn. It was the teaching experience I had hoped for and given up on when I stopped teaching. Maybe someday....

Almost immediately after starting work at Argonne, my personal life also began to change.

Once I was trusted with doing some proofreading, I began to bring work home on a regular basis. Since Rusty and I now worked at the same place, we started having lunch together every Friday. I also saw him on Tuesday nights at Sami's when he showed up for the pool league.

Starting my job in December, I had soon discovered that Argonne had a chorus that was preparing for a concert of holiday music. I'd loved singing in high school and relished the opportunity to sing once more. Once I started singing again, the Argonne chorus wasn't enough. Although there were four Catholic churches to pick from in the small village of Lemont, I joined St. Alphonsus because of their large choir, led by a director who wasn't afraid to select challenging pieces for the group. These obligations made every Wednesday night and Sunday morning permanent commitments.

With the work I brought home, starting my days early, and my changing, more professional interests, gradually I spent less time at Sami's. I still went there on Tuesday nights to watch Lindsay, Dixon, and Rusty play, and perhaps Thursday night if I wasn't too tired. I'd never been to Sami's on weekends. I'd gone from having nothing to do to driving myself to the limit of my physical ability.

Even my calls to Dottie Lou were limited by all these new activities, although I always knew where to find her if I needed her, and that she would similarly find me if the shoe was on the other foot. Real friends knew such neglect was temporary, necessary, and they wouldn't go away.

Dottie Lou and Tom had purchased a three-bedroom brick ranch home in a newer subdivision south of Kankakee, and had closed on it right before Christmas. I made time to help her pack and lent a hand on moving day. The home had a big fenced backyard and a garden. I was happy for her.

"I've got bunk beds coming for the boys' room and a twin bed and crib for the girls. It's a little crowded still, but we have a full basement for play room." Her voice was alive with plans. Not for the first time, I admired her energy and her ability to find pleasure in family life.

Although I saw Rusty for our weekly lunch and on pool nights, he was busy too, driving to his three-flat on the North Side of Chicago and the upkeep on the buildings he and his mother owned. He also worked long hours, pushing himself to complete a project that was nearing the end of its budget. He didn't know if the project would be extended. If it wasn't, he would be placed elsewhere by Sargent & Lundy. I began to worry about that. The time I spent with him had become comfortable and important to me. If he left Argonne, I'd miss him. He'd still shoot pool, at least for a while, but I worried that he might join a North Side league and not come to Lemont anymore. I began to fantasize ways I might entice him back to Lemont if that should happen.

But what if he gets transferred to the East or West Coast? I pushed the thought out of my mind.

I thought of Rusty as a sort of bridge between Argonne and Sami's. No one at Argonne except Rusty knew that my social hangout was a neighborhood bar, and for the time being I didn't want them to. In my early days at Argonne, I had once overheard a random comment as I walked down a hall. A man I didn't know, wearing a suit, was saying to a professionally dressed woman, "I heard she spent a lot of time in bars. I didn't think she'd be the right person for the job." I had no reason to think he meant me, but I decided it might be a good idea to keep my social life private. Others might not look down on a man like Rusty shooting pool in a bar, but it could change their opinions about me.

My new work environment was pleasant, but I couldn't deny that Argonne stressed excellence and an element of competition. I still needed a comfortable place for my social life, and that was still pretty much limited to Sami's.

While my new job was changing my life in many ways, from what I observed during my less frequent visits and talking to my friends at Sami's, their lives seemed to stay the same.

Dixon continued to stop at Sami's weekday evenings and spend Saturday afternoon through Sunday night with his daughters. His ex-wife continued to bleed him dry.

Betts still sipped slowly all day and entertained everyone with his wit. Incredibly, he had lost even more weight. His pants hung on him and his belt flapped below his waist from the additional holes he'd had to punch in it. He spent more and more time in the men's room, and we wondered how he kept going. But his personality was unchanged.

Pizza Bob came in and out, and his business thrived.

Poker Dan ran his games most nights and spent off nights playing pool.

Angel drank himself to oblivion every night and somehow got up fresh and friendly the next morning. His wife hadn't sent for him since I'd known him, which made me wonder if the story about them was even true.

Dirty Wally was Dirty Wally, slapping and cussing at the poker machine.

Adam and Eve alternately shmoozed and battled, requiring occasional visits from Lemont police or ambulance drivers.

Now that I wasn't going to Sami's as often, others told me that

Lindsay spent more time talking quietly to John David. Although no one knew for sure, the word was that they had become a thing. Of course, I no longer saw Lindsay at work.

And, once again, the time never seemed right to ask Lindsay about John David's ears. Curious as I was, it felt like an imposition. If John David didn't want to talk about it, that was his business. He would expect Lindsay to keep his secret, and, no matter how badly I wanted to know, I didn't want to get in the way of that.

The Czacki brothers had disappeared again. No one had seen them for months.

Sami continued to fill drink orders, pushing himself to near exhaustion, smoking too much, and getting drunk by the end of the night. Whitney continued to sit at the end of the bar, alternately going over accounts and glaring at her husband.

The Judge had never been seen again after that night he'd insulted me.

Rusty had given me a little gift for Christmas. He pressed a small flat box into my hand, wrapped in silver paper with a blue ribbon and bow.

I felt my face grow hot. "For me? I didn't know we were exchanging gifts."

"It's just a little gift. Saw it when I was shopping for the secretaries, and it made me think of you."

"Do you want me to open it here?"

"Sure."

I unwrapped it slowly, untying the ribbon and wrapping it around the bow, then carefully peeling back the tape to remove and fold the paper. In a small box were three beautiful white handkerchiefs embroidered with my name in blue thread.

I laughed. "Got tired of me using yours, right?"

One new regular customer joined us soon after the holidays, or I should say returned. He had been part of a biker gang who occasionally met at the bar when it was under previous ownership some years ago, so Lemont old-timers knew him from those days. He had gone to California to join the Hell's Angels, and then after some time got religion, quit biking, and became an ordained minister in some faith none of us had ever heard of. We suspected it was some sort of self-styled, washed-in-the-blood-of-a-lamb cultist thing that wasn't seriously recognized by most religions and required little formal education. He refused to discuss what had brought him back to Lemont. The rumor was that he was running away from something.

He was trim and healthy-looking, with longish, slicked-back dark hair, and a goatee. He always wore black pants, a black button-down shirt, a thick leather belt with a large brass buckle, and a well-worn black leather jacket. He was pleasant to talk to, drank slowly and moderately, and was popular with everyone. He didn't use profane language himself, but didn't seem to mind the bar language spoken around him. He never pushed his religious convictions on anyone. He was known only as Preacher John. I didn't know him well, but he seemed nice enough.

It all seemed to be too good to be true. Now that I had found rewarding work and activities, life was good. I still had friends at Sami's I enjoyed being with, and now that it wasn't my only personal life, I felt more relaxed about being there. The stigma and sometimes crude behavior no longer bothered me, and the unpleasant incidents seemed to have stopped.

But could it last? Despite job, success, friends, music and church activities, I still fell asleep alone each night, yearning for someone to be with.

Chapter 15

DURING THE WINTER OF 1982, I was consumed by my newfound career at Argonne and singing with my choirs. My new friends at work were more casual than close. I didn't spend as much time at Sami's, but I kept up with what was happening there. When I found time to visit, I chatted casually with my friends, especially Dixon, Rusty, Angel and Betts, who all kept me informed about events there.

At Argonne I felt I had become part of a team of like-minded workers who functioned well together, as Julia demanded. We didn't socialize, though. All my coworkers except Julia, who was a widow, had families and homes to take care of. Nor had I formed any close friendships at the choral groups, although I hoped that would change with time. At work, I looked forward to my Friday lunches with Rusty, where we fell into a habit of talking not about what was happening at Sami's, but what was going on in our personal lives.

"I know you're not a big family man, especially with your mother and all. But didn't you ever think about having your own family?" I asked him one day.

"You mean wife and kids? Well, you already know about the wife thing, and kids pretty much go along with that. I'm sure having kids would be nice. I'd be a good father and love them if I had any. But knowing how I feel about marriage, I don't see that happening. I'm more of a bachelor. How about you?"

"I'm not sure. I think I want a family, though. Life seems rather pointless if you don't have kids to love and work for. I don't see life as being just about me. There has to be more."

"Lofty ideas, nicely said. I can believe that about you."

We didn't pursue that discussion at the time, but it seemed pretty clear that Rusty and I didn't want the same things out of life. Up to my divorce, I'd always thought there was plenty of time to start a family. Now that the divorce had interrupted that ticking clock, with my mid-thirties approaching, I hoped I wouldn't miss my opportunity.

One lunch hour late in February, Rusty reached across the table and placed his hand over mine. "I've been trying to find a way to talk to you about this," he began.

I looked in his face. I saw apprehension, but also that dreamy-eyed hopeful look I remembered from past relationships. *Oh, no! He's going to say he's attracted to me! Shit! And things were going so well!*

"This is hard for me, but you've become more than a friend. More than just someone to share words with and the only other person in the room that carries a hankie." He grinned, but it looked forced. "I sit here across from you but what I want to be doing is holding you. I want to take you places. I want to see you on the weekends, and…I don't know…more."

I pulled my hand away and held it up, palm forward, to stop whatever he was going to say next. Then I rubbed my face with my hands while I thought of what to tell him. I wondered if the idea came to him because we'd both spent Valentine's Day alone. Despite my lonely evenings and desire for a partner to share my life, I feared intimacy with any man, especially one I depended on for friendship. I was afraid to lose Rusty to a cheap affair. Finally, I looked into his eyes.

"Rusty, you're a good friend. A valuable friend. And very important to me. What you're suggesting…here's what I'm afraid of. Things get complicated. One or the other of us gets more needy than the other. We have a good time for a while, and then we break up." I placed my hand over his. "I don't want to lose you as a friend. I can't take that chance. You're too important to me just the way things are."

His jaw was clenched and a muscle on the right side of his face jumped. He eased his hand back and placed it over his mouth, looking down at the table. "I'd hoped you'd say something else. Well…at least I'm important to you." He looked up, searching my eyes with his. "I don't know if I can continue to spend time with you and not want something more. But I'll give it a try. For now. We'll see what happens."

He gathered up the remains of his lunch and stood, although it wasn't time to return to work yet. He gave me a weak smile, squeezed my shoulder, and walked away, leaving me with troubled thoughts.

His words both reassured and frightened me. I was relieved our relationship would continue unchanged for now, but what if he tried and it didn't work for him? Or for me, now that I knew his feelings? I didn't want this man to remove himself from my life. Didn't want our lunchtime sharing sessions to end. Didn't want to go into Sami's and see him there, sitting with other people—I wanted him to sit with me. I wanted to know he'd be there if I needed advice or just to talk about something.

But I wanted a husband and a family eventually. I did have a mild physical attraction to Rusty, but I'd intentionally squelched those feelings. Even if I allowed myself to be physically attracted, this was a man who was intent on remaining unmarried. I didn't want to tie myself to another man yet. Nor was I ready to put Rusty in that picture.

We were very compatible in a social way, but really, we had very little else in common. I'd never even been on a golf course, and pool just gave us an excuse to go to Sami's as far as I was concerned. Rusty didn't like choral music, and he didn't read. His property was on the North Side, which was totally foreign to me, like another part of the world. In the future, even if I didn't stay at Argonne, I wanted to be near my family on the South Side that I knew and loved. So, if we started a relationship, I couldn't see it lasting very long. And after we broke up, the likelihood of staying friends seemed slim.

I hoped we'd be able to continue a platonic relationship, but I feared that whichever path we took, it would end before long.

Chapter 16

THE FIRST TIME RUSTY AND I had lunch after his "confession" started out uncomfortable. But with what I'm sure was effort on his part, he made comments that made me laugh, and before we finished lunch that day, I felt relieved. It seemed there had been little change to our friendship.

Spring of 1982 came, and golf season was approaching. One afternoon in late April Rusty stopped by my office cubicle and stood beside my desk. "Did you remember that Yul Brynner is playing in *The King and I* at Arie Crown Theater?"

Up until then I had forgotten that he had suggested getting tickets and taking me. I hadn't thought he'd really do it.

"No! Really? I thought he was done playing The King."

"Might be his final tour. Who knows? You should go."

Oh. He wasn't taking me, just informing me. Disappointed, I said, "I'd love to. But Arie Crown…I don't drive in the city much. I'm a suburban girl, remember? I wouldn't know how to park or any of that. I'm afraid I'll have to miss it."

"What about if I took you? If I can get tickets? Next Friday night? We could go downtown after work, have something to eat, and I'll bring you home."

"Really?" I grinned, but a wave of apprehension came over me. Wasn't I determined to have only platonic relationships? This would be the first time I'd be on a real date with Rusty. Would it encourage him in ways I wasn't prepared for? But Yul Brynner!

And so we went. In addition to the play, Rusty had made plans for after the show. Friends of his had invited him on a sailboat ride the same night. They would bring their twenty-seven-foot sailboat to Burnham Harbor, arriving when they expected the play to be over, and wait for us there. The harbor was only a short walk from Arie Crown and McCormick Place. We could leave Rusty's car in McCormick Place's parking lot, and they'd drop us off there after sailing. I'd never met his friends, but I'd also never been on a sailboat, and it sounded exciting.

The play was everything I'd imagined. The King was, of course, The King, and I was captivated. As we exited the theater after the show, I linked my arm through Rusty's, on a high, forgetting in my enthusiasm to remain platonic.

"Wish we could meet him," I said, grinning and hugging Rusty's arm.

Rusty stopped and looked down at me. "Why not? Let's try to go backstage."

"Oh, no. I'm sure he's tired, or people will be flocking around him, or he needs to be somewhere. Too bad, though. We could invite him for a sailboat ride. Wouldn't your friends be surprised if we showed up with Yul Brynner?" I chuckled.

"Should we?" Rusty said again.

I started walking again, pulling Rusty with me. "Nah. It's just me dreaming. Your friends will be wondering where we are, after so many curtain calls. I hope they're patient."

The night was pleasantly warm with a gentle breeze. A bright moon seemed to accentuate the twinkling lights of the city behind us. When we arrived at the harbor, we saw a light flicker from a boat moored in the first row of piers. The occupants waved at us, and Rusty waved back. The sailboat was one of the smaller boats tied to the slips, a white boat with blue trim, the masts bare. It bobbed gently, as did all the boats tied in the harbor, emitting clanking noises from their masts that were somehow not annoying but created a peaceful atmosphere.

"Where are the sails?" I asked Rusty.

"No sails in the harbor. They run under engine power. Sails don't go up until we're out on the lake," he said. I felt a bit dumb.

Rusty's friends, Bill and Kathy, welcomed us warmly. It was readily apparent that they were quite fond of Rusty. They were a fun-loving couple who bickered playfully with each other. Bill pretended to know what he was doing, but Kathy confided that they hadn't had the boat for long, and didn't know all that much about sailing. Most of the evening we sat tied up in the harbor, ate snacks and sipped wine.

"You two should join us for the Fourth of July fireworks at Monroe Harbor," Kathy said. "That's where our slip is. They'll have three barges out in the harbor and the fireworks will explode right above us, the best seat in the house. We're having a party on the boat that night."

"Since Jane Byrne's been mayor of Chicago, she's expanded the city's special events, ChicagoFest, Taste of Chicago, neighborhood festivals. She's promised this year's fireworks on the Fourth will be spectacular," Bill said.

It sounded exciting. Even suburban girls like me knew, of course, that Jane Byrne was the first woman to be elected mayor of Chicago. I also knew she'd been taking a lot of flak from politicians who thought she changed her mind too much and didn't have what it took to do the job.

"Only mayor who ever had the guts to live at Cabrini-Green to prove her point," Rusty said.

I remembered the big deal it was when she'd moved temporarily into a high-rise housing project to show the city cared about people in public housing. From what I knew of her, she seemed like someone who seriously wanted to help people and hoped that everyone knew she was doing her best. I respected her.

I found myself wondering why I had been so afraid to spend time in Chicago. This night it seemed that I was missing a lot. I'd have to reconsider my reluctance—starting with accepting my invitation for the Fourth of July. Which, I now realized, meant another date with Rusty.

It was a calm, balmy night, so after some hesitation Bill decided to chance a short run under sail outside the breakwater.

We motored around the breakwater and into Lake Michigan. Bill turned off the engine and some confusion ensued as Bill, Kathy, and Rusty argued over how to raise the sails while I sat at some distance, sipped wine, and watched. Eventually the sails were up. They filled with a gentle breeze and the boat started to move once again, traveling north parallel to the lakeshore.

Other times I'd been in boats there'd been a lot of noise from motors or crowds of people. Kathy had said it was the quiet that had hooked her and Bill on sailing. Out on Lake Michigan under sail, there was only a faint swooshing sound as the boat pushed through the water. I was amazed at how peaceful it was, especially at night. Looking west, traffic flowed along Lake Shore Drive backed by the entire skyline of Chicago against the nearly silent night.

Kathy and Bill navigated the boat from the rear, and Rusty and I sat at the front—the prow, I was told. He sat behind me and wrapped both arms around me. I didn't push him away. Despite my fear of falling for him, tonight it felt right. I leaned my head back against his chest. The night was so calm I felt his breath stir my hair. It was magical and I wanted the evening to go on forever.

When Rusty drove me home, we engaged in very little conversation for most of the forty-minute drive. I don't think either of us wanted to break the spell. I told Rusty how lovely the whole evening had been, and how much I liked his friends, and I asked if he thought we'd be invited again. And he answered, "I agree," and "I'm glad," and "Maybe." He reached over and placed his hand on my leg. I liked how it felt and didn't want him to move it.

"It's so late. I wish you didn't have to drive all the way to the North Side. Are you sure you won't fall asleep?" I asked.

"I'm sure. I'm wide awake. Not even tired," he said. I believed him. I was wide awake myself.

When we reached my apartment, he found a spot in a dark corner of the lot and parked. Although it was three o'clock in the morning by then, neither of us wanted the evening to end. Rusty slid closer to me on the bench seat and stroked my cheek. I closed my eyes and let him. When he took me in his arms, I shivered in anticipation. And when he kissed me, I felt lightheaded. Then I knew. My world was changed in an instant and I was lost.

I pulled away, opened my eyes and stared into his. He said, "Go on in. If anything is going to happen between us, it's not going to happen in the front seat of my car. Sleep on it, and I'll call you tomorrow."

"No," I said. "Come in."

He touched my cheek again tenderly. "Are you sure?"

I'd never been so sure of anything in my life.

Chapter 17

IT WAS UNHURRIED, WITH A few quiet words, and it was wonderful. The bedroom lit only by a soft nightlight, I sat on the edge of the bed, hesitantly peeking as Rusty slowly removed his shirt and pants. Once he stood in his V-neck T-shirt and jockey shorts, he insisted on taking my clothes off himself. As he removed each item, a gesture of intimacy took its place. When my blouse came off, he nuzzled and then kissed my neck and ran his hands up and down my back and the sides of my chest. Trembling at his feather-light touch, I alternately closed my eyes or searched his face. I wanted him to kiss my lips again, but he took his time. My skirt came next, and then he slowly peeled my pantyhose down and gently sat me on the side of the bed.

Kneeling in front of me, he stroked my bare legs. *Did I shave close enough?* He ran his hands over the soles of my feet. I'd never realized how sensitive, and how seductive, my feet could be.

I reached out to pull him to me, but he said, "Not yet."

With me still wearing my bra and panties, he rolled me onto my stomach on the bed. Eyes closed, my face against the pillow, I heard him removing his underwear. He moved alongside me, and then over me, and kissed each of my ears, then my neck, moving my hair carefully to one side, then my shoulders. He loosened my bra and kissed where the straps had been and down my back to below my waist. *Does he find my body attractive?* He kissed behind my knees, and my feet once again, lingering on my toes. I'd never thought of myself as sensual before, but Rusty was finding spots I'd never realized existed—all the right spots. He aroused the sleeping hungers I had never felt before.

For a moment I wondered how he had learned to please a woman so fully. I felt a stab of jealousy that was quickly replaced by gratitude. I was filled with intense yearning, a need to wrap myself completely around him, to have every part of me in contact with him. I seemed to be an extension of him, no longer a separate person. When I thought I could stand it no longer, he turned me over gently and we truly became one. I stopped fighting the insecurities of a lifetime and gave myself up completely to sensuality.

And then we slept.

Chapter 18

IN THE MORNING, WE KISSED and cuddled after waking. Then I fixed eggs, toast, and coffee for breakfast. Rusty was sorry he had to leave, but he had an appointment to meet one of the store tenants at his mother's building.

"He says water is dripping through the ceiling from her apartment. I have to find out what the problem is and fix it. She probably left the water running in the bathroom sink again, but it could be a plumbing issue. You never know. I'm going to have to get into her apartment, and you wouldn't want to be a part of that," he said. I remembered about his having to climb a ladder to see her, and he was right—I didn't want to be part of that. And so, in midmorning, he left.

He was barely out of the house when I dialed Dottie Lou.

"Everything's changed!" I said. "I can't believe it!"

"Wait a minute," she said. "We're in luck, Tom's taken Bobby, Karen, and Timmy to visit his mother. Let me put Betsy down and then I'll be free to talk. I'll call you right back." And she rang off.

Dottie Lou's fourth child, Betsy, a chubby and cheerful infant with a full head of dark curls, had been born in March. Dottie Lou could spend hours just watching and marveling over every kick, wave, or grimace her new baby made.

I waited impatiently, aimlessly walking around my kitchen, putting away the washed dishes from breakfast, looking through the refrigerator to see if I needed to grocery shop. I checked the time. It had been all of five minutes. How long did it take to get Betsy to sleep? As I recalled, my kid brother, who hated to nap, sometimes never did fall asleep. More likely Dottie Lou was finding it hard to stop smooching and hugging. I wandered into the sitting room, moved a lamp on the table that had been off center, wiped some dust off the lamp base with my fingers—smiled when I remembered Dottie Lou once telling me her dust cloth was broken. I straightened a picture on the wall and the phone rang! It had been seven whole minutes. A really long seven minutes.

"So, what's happened that's so earth-shattering?" Dottie Lou asked.

"You know Rusty, from Sami's and Argonne?"

"Of course I know Rusty! You've talked about him enough."

"We had sex last night."

"No! I thought you said you weren't attracted to him? You were just friends?"

"Yeah, that's what I thought too. I didn't want to wreck a good friendship over casual sex. Maybe I should start at the beginning."

"Yeah. Maybe you should. So what changed?"

"Way back last fall, I told him how much I liked Yul Brynner and he remembered all this time, so he invited me to see *The King and I* at Arie Crown Theater."

"Yeah. I heard he was in town. Maybe his last time."

"Well, Rusty was able to get tickets, and we went last night. After the play some friends of his took us out on Lake Michigan for a sailboat ride."

Dottie Lou whooped. "Setting the stage, yes. Do you think he planned it that way?"

I hadn't thought of that. "I doubt it. We'd been going along fine as friends, I thought. But maybe…." Did it make a difference if he planned it? Perhaps a little, but nothing that would change how I felt now, I decided.

"And so? How did he get you into bed? And where?"

I giggled. "I got him into bed, actually."

"No!"

"I mean, think about it. He takes me to see Yul Brynner, who I had a crush on. And then his friends were so nice and fun, and the sailboat was magical, swishing soundlessly through the lake at night. Watching the stars and the skyline, all lit up and twinkling, slide by. With Kathy and Bill sailing from the back of the boat, and Rusty and I in the front, it felt like he and I were alone out there. It was so romantic! He had his arms around me—it felt like a dream."

She hooted. "So you were primed. What happened next?"

"Well, he drove me home after. It was really late. Too late for him to be driving all the way back to the North Side to his building, especially after the wine we drank on the boat. I felt a little guilty about that, but it's what we'd expected."

"Stop stalling! Get to the good part."

I giggled. "Then when we got to my apartment and he parked the car, we didn't want to get out. At least I didn't, and I assume he didn't either. And then he slid across the seat and kissed me. I was so thrilled it was all I could do to keep myself from jumping him right there."

Dottie Lou hooted again. "But you didn't?"

"I didn't. And he said he wasn't going to have sex with me for the first time in the front seat of a car, and that he should go home and we should think about it. But I didn't want him to go home. So I invited him in."

"You didn't have to talk him into it, I bet."

"I did, actually. A little. He pulled away and asked me if I was sure that's what I wanted."

"You've never been a sleep-around sort of girl. I'm sure he knew that. So how was the sex?"

"Amazing. I was putty in his hands. He was so tender. It was like he was playing me, caressing me, like mastering a favorite instrument. I felt loved." I laughed. "I felt sexy, and you know that's not me! I felt like we were a single thing, not separate people."

I closed my eyes and felt the warm sensations once again. I couldn't tell Dottie Lou about the toes. Some things seemed too intimate, even for best friends. I dropped my voice to a whisper, knowing it was silly with no one else to hear. "I had a climax, Dottie Lou, for the first time ever. I never knew how amazing that could be."

"The first time? What about Dick?"

"Never. I faked it."

"Go on! I'm loving this! You never told me that!"

"Yeah, well, I'm a prude, remember? I didn't even tell these things to myself." I paused. "I was ashamed, I guess. I thought there was something wrong with *me*. Whatever. I'm telling you now." Another pause. "I guess Rusty—and Sami's—have changed me in some kind of way."

"For the better?"

"That remains to be seen." We laughed.

"So why did you marry Dick anyway?"

"I shouldn't have to tell you—you and I shared everything that was going on back then—not only before we got married but leading up to the divorce."

"True. Well then, I guess you're going to say the problem was because you were a virgin."

"We both were. Things were different in those days. We thought we'd go to hell if we had sex before marriage. Dick and I did, anyway. Not you. Now it looks like you were smarter than me."

"Finally admitting that, college girl?"

I laughed. I always suspected Dottie Lou *was* smarter than me, but she'd married right out of high school and started a family instead of going to college like I had.

"We didn't know any better in those days. We thought we made a good couple because we were a lot alike: similar education, religion, friends. It seemed the thing to do. We did laugh a lot, as you recall."

"I always liked Dick. But I didn't think he was right for you. Sorry I never told you that when you first started dating him." This was a surprise, but it shouldn't have been. I never told Dottie Lou I wasn't too crazy about her husband either. She was so smitten with him, she would have married him no matter what I said. I couldn't let her down then. Even now I believe it could harm our friendship if I was truthful. She had probably kept her opinions from me for the same reason. Tom treated her like a slave, but she never complained about it. I had a feeling Dottie Lou wasn't sharing some things with me now either. I just let her tell me what she wanted to. That's what friends do, right?

I sighed. "Maybe we were too *much* alike and that was the heart of the problem. Neither one of us was willing to yield when we disagreed. Dick wouldn't even explain himself, just stubbornly kept doing whatever he wanted, no matter if I told him something was important to me. It was more important to *him* that he was right, and my feelings never entered into the equation. I felt like every minute with him was a competition, not a partnership. He never cared enough about me to bend. And that hurt. Not that I was much better."

"He was a nice enough guy."

"He was. But one day I just realized that I deserved a man who put me first, or at least considered it. Dick wasn't going to change, and I wasn't happy."

"I know you weren't. And after you told him, he started to get nasty. I remember the blow by blow."

"Thank goodness for you!"

"I always had an urge, though, when I talked about my friends Dick and Jane, to follow it up with 'See Spot run.'"

We laughed. "I actually had that same thought more than once," I said.

"So Rusty—is he different?"

"I think so. I mean, the sex part, for sure. He wants to please me, not himself, and he knows how to do it." I felt my cheeks grow warm again. "I'm not used to a man putting me first. Isn't that what sex is supposed to be? But even at work, and when we're at lunch or at Sami's, he treats me like I'm special, always asks what I want. He's affectionate, and we have deep, serious discussions, he listens to me and respects my opinions. He respects *me*. Dick didn't respect me. Dick made everything a joke, and I never knew what he was really thinking."

"And you and Rusty have a lot in common?"

I hesitated. "No. Not really. He shoots pool, plays golf, and works around the house. Doesn't read at all, except newspapers. Doesn't like classical music. Yeah. We're not alike at all. Maybe that's why the sex was so good!"

We both laughed.

"So what's going to happen next?" Dottie Lou asked.

"A lot, I hope. He said he'd call."

"Yeah, right. They say that."

"I think he meant it. I hope he meant it. Oh my God, what if he didn't mean it? This whole thing was so sudden. A huge surprise, and now it's all I can think about. I don't know what I'll do if I lose him now. That happens after sex, sometimes, right? That's what I've heard. That's what I was afraid would happen. What if I'm wrong? What if that's all he wanted me for? Now that I'm putty in his hands, like I said…."

Dottie Lou tried to reassure me, but I was frightened now. Suddenly my life depended desperately on Rusty being part of it. I didn't want to imagine a world without him in it.

"What the heck got into me, Dottie Lou? One minute I'm insisting that the last thing I want is a man in my life, and the next minute I'm terrified Rusty might leave me."

At the end of our call, Dottie Lou finished with a little story our talk had reminded her of. "One of my neighbors is a lot like you, recently divorced and trying to make a new life on her own. Also like you, she told me she had a crush on Yul Brynner and went to see *The King and I* last week by herself. On a whim she thought she'd try to meet him. What was the worst that could happen? They'd turn her away, she figured. So, she went backstage after the show and knocked, and he opened the door, and they talked. He always has dinner after the show, it turns out. And he was tired of eating alone, and he asked her to dinner."

"And she went?"

"She did. And she'll never forget it, of course."

"Did he hit on her?" That would wreck my image of him.

"Nope. He was a perfect gentleman. Even a little boring, she said."

"Still…."

"Still."

As soon as I hung up the phone it rang again.

"It's Rusty Dineff," he said, as if I needed him to identify himself. "I've been trying to call you for the last hour, but your line's been busy. I can't think about anything but you."

BY THE MIDDLE OF THE summer, Rusty and I were living mostly in my apartment. Every Monday after work he came home with me and stayed until Saturday morning. Since Argonne and Sami's were in Lemont, this arrangement was much more convenient for him than driving some forty miles to Rogers Park in Chicago every night. Weather permitting, Rusty and Dixon played Saturday morning golf. After golf, Rusty would check on his mother's place on the South Side and then drive to his three-flat on the North Side to keep up the building. I'd see him again at lunchtime on Monday.

Of course, we didn't do this just for convenience. The main thing was we wanted to be together.

I liked the arrangement because it gave me the weekend to spend with my parents, catch up on personal and work matters, and sing at Sunday Mass. Among our different interests, Rusty wasn't a churchgoer either. I usually went to Sami's only on pool league nights now. Rusty went to Sami's more often than I did. I'd stay in the apartment alone, except on choir practice night. I felt less need for a social outlet anymore, and I often had work projects or just wanted to read or have some alone time. You know how it is—you get busy with a new job; it takes all your time. In your mind you can always go out and socialize tomorrow, so you put it off, and you fool yourself, all the good intentions just never happen.

Rusty and I were happy. And the sex continued to be amazing.

Every time.

I felt very different from the person who had first stepped through Sami's door almost a year ago. I was confident now. My work was fulfilling, my casual friends at Sami's thought well of me, and I had a man in my life. That brief period when I worked at Ordman's and before Rusty and I became intimate was the only time I'd ever lived alone. It was long enough for me to realize that I much preferred having someone around. I thought the new life I'd so desired was starting to happen. Now and then I feared that our happiness was only temporary, but I pushed those worries from my mind. I'd enjoy the moment as long as it lasted.

When I did go to Sami's, I watched the pool games from a different perspective. I could recognize now that Rusty was a really good player, not just because of the number of games he won but because of how the other players treated him—he was the guy to beat. I could see this was important to him, and it made me feel good to see him happy.

I preferred to go with Rusty on league nights, because we knew the leagues would finish at a regular time. On open pool nights, it was a different story. Rusty might say, "We can't leave yet because I'm winning." Otherwise, he might say, "We can't leave yet because I'm losing." Since those were obviously the only two choices, those nights tended to run later than I wanted to be out.

Rusty and I had taken a ten-day vacation in July, touring through Washington, D.C. and the East Coast. Returning on a Friday night, after a quick fast-food dinner, we decided to make a quick stop at Sami's. I smiled as Rusty expertly maneuvered his car into a tight spot on the street. I'd never been any good at parallel parking, but it was a skill North Siders soon developed. Since we'd been living together not-quite-full-time, Rusty cheerfully took care of little details that were challenging for me or that I didn't like to do myself. I loved that about him. That's right—I used the *love* word in my mind now, although neither of us had been comfortable enough to say it aloud yet.

I had changed during the year since I'd first set foot in Sami's Saloon, but the place still looked the same. The same jukebox, the same poker machine, the same bar, the same pool table, and for the most part the same crowd.

"It's good to see you back, and on a Friday night for a change," Sami called out as we walked in. "You two, my classy friends, good for business."

Which of course we'd heard before. "I thought I was more like a fish out of water," I said, laughing, although I was pleased he thought of us that way.

When had Sami's face gotten so thin? His eyes so sunken? And his skin, always a rich brown, had taken on a grayish tone. I thought he seemed exhausted, but his voice remained as welcoming as ever. We'd only been away a couple of weeks. Perhaps this had been going on for a while and I just hadn't noticed before. Perhaps I'd been too concerned with my personal life.

Betts, who sat near the door, gave us his crooked smile and waved weakly. He looked even worse than usual too, his face appearing shrunken and yellowish. I squeezed his shoulder, wanting to talk, but Rusty pulled me away, whispering, "He doesn't look well. When he gets like this, it's best to just leave him be. I don't think he wants to be on stage for you tonight."

Neither Dixon nor Lindsay was there, but then it wasn't a league night. John David was sitting on his customary stool, staring at the bar top as usual. I wondered again about his ears, about what had really happened to him in Vietnam, and whether I would ever find out that story.

Because my curiosity wouldn't die, I had tried to talk to Rusty about PTSD, since he'd also served in Vietnam. His answer had been surprising to me.

"Bullshit! You do what the army tells you to do, and then you come home and forget about it. There's nothing more to it than that."

His seemingly unsympathetic response had been both unrevealing and revealing. Obviously, he didn't want to talk much about his time in Vietnam. That would seem to indicate there were things he didn't want to remember. Yet, from what little he'd told me on previous occasions, he spent almost all his time on the base at a communications desk and saw very little action. Perhaps he was just one of the lucky ones who came back unscarred, even a little proud.

On the other hand, Rusty had been through tough situations at home that would leave many people scarred and he'd just accepted fate and moved on. Perhaps he had little patience for men who had more trouble facing the unpleasant times in life.

As we took stools near the far end of the bar next to Angel, Survivor's "Eye of the Tiger" blared from the jukebox. Angel looked reasonably sober—so far. A surge of warmth flooded through me when I saw his loose-jointed lanky frame and widely smiling face. He hopped off his stool to greet us enthusiastically, the way he always did.

"Hey boss," Angel said, high-fiving Rusty. He gave me a smile and a wink. "Señorita, you have good time away?"

"We did, thank you. Anything exciting happen here while we were gone?"

"Sì! You notice something missing this night?"

I looked around. "Adam and Eve," I said. "They're not here." Friendly or battering away at each other, they were not on their usual stools. Not only that, but the sign that graced the door to their flat was missing.

"Sì. Adam, he mucho bad, is bender, really bad. Even Eve, she no can control him. He at Hines now, the VA. He serve in Nam, so they take him. No one know when—if—he come out again. Some say he die there, not long."

"How awful! What about Eve? Is she spending all her time there now?"

"She…maybe…is good thing for her. She never say nobody, but have hombre, mucho dinero hombre Sami say. She go to him right away. Same day Adam go away, she move out, say no-ting to no-body. Adam move out, Eve move out, no more Adam and Eve make trouble for Sami no more. Sami have enough Adam and Eve."

My interpretation of this long, broken rendition was that Eve had left Adam and found a new "daddy."

"Eve is making some other guy's life a living hell, then," said Rusty.

We chuckled, but then I felt ashamed. It was a sad situation, but I wasn't really sorry Adam and Eve were gone. I wouldn't miss them.

"So is their flat up for rent?"

"No, no...no rent. Pizza Bob expand bar."

Maybe Angel was more inebriated than I thought. "You mean Sami, right? He's going to expand the bar?"

"No, no...Pizza Bob." Angel glanced at Sami at the other end of the bar and lowered his voice. "Sami, he sell bar to Pizza Bob. Fin de ano."

Rusty and I stared at each other. Sami was selling the bar to Pizza Bob? By the end of the year? It couldn't be that sudden. They must have been planning it for a while, but news just got out when the flat became available.

"Isn't the business doing well? Why is Sami selling?" Rusty asked.

"You know Sami have all the time cigarette. He sit them on bar, burning from one end to the other, so he can take drag wherever he go? Keep him energy, he say. Almost ever' body smoke here. So, Sami find out he have cancer in lung. Is from smoke." As Angel said this, he reached for a pack of cigarettes next to his beer glass, shook out a cigarette and lit it.

"Oh, no!" I said, ignoring the irony. "How bad is it?"

Angel's news explained my observations when we came in. The smoke-eaters never did a good job in here. My father had been a smoker but gave up the habit after having a heart attack, and I'd never hung around heavy smokers. Of course, ashtrays were plentiful throughout Sami's, as they were in most public places. But it had still been hard for me to get used to the smoke, and I was only here for a few hours a couple of times a week. Sami was here from opening at one in the afternoon until closing at two in the morning, seven days a week. And he probably had a four-pack-a-day habit, if not more. I was glad Rusty had stopped smoking, at least around me.

"I think is not so good. He going for operation soon, very soon. But no matter, even if he better, no work in bar so much anymore. Too dangerous, he say."

"There's been some talk about making all public places smoke-free, but that's very controversial for places like this," said Rusty.

"But that's so sad," I said. "He worked so hard and never got to really enjoy life. I wonder what Whitney thinks about all of this."

"I doubt she's very happy. Sami was her cash cow. I bet she doesn't stay around long to take care of him," Rusty said.

"That's not a very kind thing to say," I said.

"No. But I doubt you can argue about it. Wait and see," Rusty said.

Angel got up to use the restroom. There were some strangers at the pool table and Rusty turned to watch. After a short time, he got up and put a quarter on the table. I sighed. He'd challenged the newcomers. We'd be here a while.

I glanced around. No one was sitting near Betts. He looked distracted and lonely. I decided to talk to him, despite Rusty's warning. If he didn't want company, I'd come back. I picked up my drink, walked to the front end of the bar, and sat on the empty stool next to Betts.

He looked up and gave me a half-hearted smile.

"Is something wrong, Betts?" I asked.

"Nothing that a chat with my favorite little lady won't fix," he said, but he sounded like his heart wasn't in it.

He sipped his beer and I sipped my drink. We just sat quietly for a few minutes. Clearly, he didn't want to tell me what was bothering him.

In the background I heard a couple of men talking about the Chicago Bears, discussing what the season would look like this year. I'd never been a football fan and knew as little about the game as I'd known about pool the first time I'd entered Sami's. Since this was primarily a men's bar, though, televisions were always tuned in to whatever sport was in season.

One man said in a loud, almost angry voice, "I certainly hope the new coach will manage Walter Payton better this year. It's about time we had a season and Payton's the key. Neill Armstrong never knew what he was doing. Best thing Halas ever did was get rid of him at the end of last season."

"You're only saying that to remind us all that you met Payton once," another man commented.

"Yeah, well, you're jealous. Mark my words, he's going to go down as one of the best running backs in football."

I looked at Betts with a wrinkled forehead. "Doesn't football season start in the fall? Why are they talking about this now?"

"Training camp is starting. These fans can talk about football any time of the year," Betts said.

I bit my lip. "And Neil Armstrong? I thought he was an astronaut, not a coach."

Betts snorted. "Same name, different guys. The astronaut spells Neil with one 'L' but the coach uses two."

I chuckled, feeling stupid. "Sort of like the Ogden Nash poem—did you ever hear it? The one-l lama, He's a priest: The two-l llama, He's a beast."

"Ogden Nash was my kind of poet, for people who don't much like poetry but want to give the impression that they do," Betts said.

Betts motioned to Sami to refill his glass.

"We had a good time on vacation," I said. "You ever go to Virginia? It's really pretty, hilly and bright green. I didn't expect that."

"Never was much for traveling. Glad you two had a good time, though." He turned to look at me. "It's good to see you. You don't come in here so much these days."

"Yeah, I know. The new job is great, the people are great, and Rusty is great. I'm getting to be quite the homebody, enjoying reading and even cooking again. It's almost like I'm reverting back to the prig I was when I first came in here, before I made friends and got comfortable."

He gave his bark of laughter. "Yeah, you had a stick up your butt all right. It was fun to tease you. Are you glad to be back from vacation?"

"I am, I guess. Something seems off in here tonight, though. Maybe it's just because I don't usually come here on Fridays. We were only away ten days, but the place seems different in that short time.

Some different people." I checked to be sure Sami wasn't in earshot. "And I heard about Sami's cancer and selling the place to Pizza Bob. Too bad about Sami. I hope it turns out all right for him. But how's Pizza Bob going to manage two places?"

"Oh, Pizza Bob will do just fine. He knows a lot of people and he's a good businessman. His place is practically next door. He'll just have other people doing the work and run back and forth, don't you think?"

"I suppose so."

We sat and sipped some more.

"Something else I bet you don't know. Did you hear about Poker Dan?"

I hadn't. "No. More bad news?"

"Depends on how you look at things." He chuckled. "He's got himself a girlfriend and they're planning to get hitched. It's been going on for a while, but he just brought her in last week and made his big announcement."

"Really? Does she play poker? Or shoot pool?"

He let out a short burst of laughter. "Not hardly! You'd think he'd of picked someone from the neighborhood, maybe a tough kinda gal who'd been around a bit. But no, somehow he got himself hooked up with an innocent little farm girl type, comes from some little town southwest of here about seventy miles. Young girl too, not long out of high school, twenty if that. Dan's totally whipped, just nuts about her."

"How'd he meet a farm girl?"

"Her brother sat in on one of the poker games when the two of them were visiting a friend here—one of Poker Dan's regulars, I understand. He's talking about moving to where she's from, so she can be near her family. I got no idea what he'll do for income there, can't imagine he'd find many jobs in some farm town. He might find some pool players but I don't expect there'd be enough farm boys around to make much off of poker. But he's happy as a clam."

I was delighted, but wondered, not for the first time, what it was about clams that made them especially happy. "Did you meet her?"

"Hell yeah, I met her. They invited me to their wedding. I bet Poker Dan will invite you and Rusty too. No fancy invitations or nothing, he'll just ask ya."

"He's really going to get married and probably find a real job, then. Will wonders never cease! And move to farm country. I guess the flat upstairs is gonna be available—something else for Pizza Bob to figure out. But sure, we'll go to the wedding. You know anything about the plans?"

"Yeah, I do. You know Preacher John?"

"Sure. We all do." I saw Betts wince. I tried not to stare but started watching him out of the side of my eye. "Preacher John's that hippie guy who used to ride with the Hell's Angels until he got religion, whatever religion it was—or something he made up—and started dressing in black and wearing a collar. I guess he could be legit. Didn't you tell me he'd been going around the bars in town looking for alcoholics he can help to lead a better life?"

"You got him—described him to a tee. Couldn't be two like that. Anyway, seems he and Poker Dan were buddies when the preacher lived in Lemont before goin' to California. He's gonna perform the weddin'. Guess he's preacher enough to have the authority to marry people, and Poker Dan wants him to do it. Says it's gonna be a traditional bash, white dress, bridesmaids and reception and all that. They rented the old Methodist church where the historical society is now for the ceremony. Poker Dan says it's gonna be a nice, dignified affair."

He barked another laugh. "Just you imagine. Everybody he knows from here, and some of his poker guys, plan to show up. There'll be free drinks at the reception, so nobody's about to pass that up! What kind of ruckus you think there's gonna be when they refuse the guys who drink too much and when they shut the bar down for the night? Can't imagine what that poor girl's family's gonna think."

"Well, I want to go. I like Poker Dan."

"You got to decide first who you gonna sit with. The straitlaced relatives or us nutcases."

We chuckled. *Wow,* I found myself thinking. *We're only gone a couple of weeks and Sami's is starting to feel like a different place. Sami getting cancer, Adam and Eve gone, Pizza Bob taking over the bar, Poker Dan getting married. What's going to happen next?*

Suddenly Betts groaned, wrapped his arms around his stomach, closed his eyes, and started to slide sideways off his stool. I threw my arms around him to break his fall. He felt light, like a scarecrow.

"Betts! Are you okay?"

But he wasn't. In fact, he didn't react at all as I guided him to the floor. He wasn't conscious.

Shit. People in this bar are all dropping like flies.

"Somebody help me! Call an ambulance!"

Chapter 20

THAT WEEKEND, AS USUAL, RUSTY had to check on his mother and run to the North Side to mow the grass and take care of two weeks of maintenance neglect, but Monday night I made him take me to see Betts at Silver Cross Hospital. I hadn't sorted out how I felt about all the changes at Sami's, but I wanted to support my friend.

Betts was in a private room, and to enter we had to put on gowns and wear masks. I'd never seen Betts look worse, lying there with a blanket pulled up to his chin. His skin looked sallow and his eyes yellow. An IV ran into his arm. A tube ran down the side of the bed into a clear plastic bag full of dark, orange-brown fluid I assumed was urine. I looked away because it made me a little queasy. But Betts spoke with the same wry tone of voice.

"Did you bring a six-pack?" he said and barked his familiar single laugh.

"You kidding?" Rusty said. "Gestapo lady at the door did a strip-search and then made us put these gowns and masks on. We had to 'cause she's bigger than me."

"She's on to you," Betts said. "You look like troublemakers, especially Janie here."

He reached for a control device and raised the head of his bed. When he was almost upright, he started to cough, deep, hard, and long. He finally controlled himself, wiped his face with a towel from the over-bed table next to him and then fussed with his bedding until it was to his liking.

"They tell me coughin' is good, helps clear out my lungs, but damn! It sure takes a lot out of a guy," he said, in a weak voice.

"You look better than you did when I last saw you," I told him. I was lying, of course. He still looked like death warmed over, as Rusty would say. "Are you *feeling* any better?"

"This hose runnin' into my arm, it's full of painkillers and other stuff, so yeah, I'm feeling better. Gonna be here a while, though."

"What are your doctors saying?"

"Chronic pancreatitis gone acute again. Affecting my liver now. Can't eat nothing, it just comes right back up and then the belly pain cuts right through the painkillers they're giving me." He lifted his arm to expose the site of his IV attachment. "So they're feeding me through this thing, too. They say the inflammation is real bad this time. I got peritonitis, infection in my belly. The doc wants to operate, but I told him to try antibiotics a bit longer. The IVs fixed me up before so I'd like to stay with 'em if I can. I got some pneumonia this time, too. That's why you gotta wear the masks. Sorry about that."

"Don't *you* be sorry, Betts," I said. "*We're* the ones who are sorry to see you in here."

"Ah, damn! I been here before. I'm a pretty tough guy, you'll see. Couple more days to clear out my lungs, the antibiotics will do the job and I'll be out of here. You'll see me back at my regular place at Sami's."

"Well, I hope so," said Rusty.

I couldn't stop myself. "You're a smart man, Betts. You know all this is from your drinking. It's not our place tell you what to do, but we care about you. Did you ever think about stopping?"

"Drinking? You crazy? I'd never do that." His lips were compressed, his eyes hard, and it was clear he wasn't open to discussing the matter further. I opened my mouth to apologize for bringing up the idea and then thought better of it. Betts was smart enough to know what he was doing, make his own decisions, and he knew we would help him if he asked.

"Say, Betts," Rusty said, "ever been to Colonial Williamsburg? You like history so much. We had a beer in an old tavern that dated back to George Washington's day—served in a pewter mug, no less."

"You'll get a kick out of this, Betts," I said. "One night we stayed outside of this little town of maybe two thousand people and Rusty and I stopped in a local bar. Wouldn't you know, they had a pool table, and of course Rusty had to put his quarter up. He ended up beating all the best players in the bar, and toward the end of the evening some locals were calling friends to 'Come play this guy from Chicago.'"

I caught Rusty's eye as I finished the story, smiling and feeling again the admiration I'd felt that night. It had been such a pleasure to see him succeeding in his element.

Betts grinned weakly. I could tell he was tiring rapidly. We gossiped a little while longer, told him we hoped he'd be out of the hospital soon. Then we wished him well and left. I was glad we'd visited. Betts had seemed happy to see us and sorry when we had to leave.

"He looks terrible, but you were right to make us come. We're probably his only visitors," Rusty said as we were walking to the parking lot.

"I hate that," I said. "I wish there was more we could do. I bet he doesn't get the operation and he's back at Sami's soon. But how many times can the doctors keep patching him up? One of these times he's not going to make it. Does he have a death wish?"

"Apparently so. I think he just knows himself too well. When he said he'd never give up drinking, I think what he meant is he *can't* give up drinking. I think he's tried it before and he knows it won't work, so he's just stopped trying."

I was silent for the rest of the drive. I couldn't justify what Betts was doing to himself. It was hard for me to accept alcoholism as a disease, harder still to face the idea that someone I truly cared about had tried, failed, and given up. Part of me was angry with myself for making Sami's my social outlet, a place that by its very essence facilitated Betts's addiction. I almost wanted to never walk through that door again. Now that I had gotten past the first hurdles of finding work that was satisfying, engaging in activities I enjoyed, and being with a man I cared for, why did I need Sami's anymore?

Deep down, something was still missing, and I had to keep searching for whatever that was. Clearly, I still had some sort of attachment to the place. I wasn't ready to give up my friends, Dixon and Lindsay and Angel and Pizza Bob, and others. And I didn't want to be away from Rusty on the nights he spent there. But I didn't want any of us to end up like Betts, either.

And so, the writing was on the wall as far as how the evening ended. When Rusty suggested we stop at Sami's on the way home to tell everyone we had visited Betts and how he was doing, I just smiled and said, "Sure."

Pizza Bob was behind the bar instead of Sami. We hadn't seen Pizza Bob since before our vacation, of course.

"Congratulations!" said Rusty. "Too bad about Sami, but looks like things are going your way. I thought you weren't taking over until the end of the year."

"I'm not. But now that Sami's cancer treatment has started, he can't work so many hours. I'm relieving him and learning on the job, so to speak. It's a good arrangement for both of us. Just a minute. I'll be right back with your drinks, and we can talk some more. It's not too busy for a Friday night."

I thought about how convenient it was going to be for Pizza Bob to run two places that were practically next door to each other. Bob's Pizza had become a Lemont favorite with good reason—I'd never had a better pizza. He was never stingy, not with the ingredients, not about the price, and free pizzas were always present where things were happening around town. As a result, he was well known and popular with local businesses and politicians—everyone important. When he needed a favor for himself or a friend, people remembered. Owning a bar made sense. Not only was the location convenient, but, like peanut butter and jelly, booze and pizza went together very well. Bob was young, energetic, smart, and going places.

Pizza Bob came back with our drinks. "Try the vodka-grapefruit juice," he said. "First time I've made that—not that it's much of a challenge, but tell me."

I sipped. "It's just right," I said. Yeah—it was a drink that was hard to mess up, though.

"Isn't it going to be hard to run the bar and the pizza place?" Rusty asked.

Bob leaned over the bar and dropped his voice. "No one knows yet, and I don't want it to get around, but I know I can trust you two," he said.

We both nodded. "I could run both places, probably, because I have good staff. But actually, I'm selling the pizza business right about the same time I take over ownership of the bar."

Rusty and I both looked at Pizza Bob in surprise. "Why?" I asked.

"I thought you loved the pizza business. It's still doing great, isn't it?" Rusty said.

"Yeah, well, that's why, actually. I got bought out by this large chain—I'm not going to tell you their name yet. They want to corner the Lemont business, and they thought my competition was too strong for them. The price they offered was so good I would have been a fool to turn it down. It was time to get out anyway, with the business at its peak. I already knew I was buying Sami's, and if I want, I can open another place after the non-compete clause runs out."

"How will owning this place fit in with the side work you've been doing, delivering summonses and political campaign work?" Rusty asked.

"Quite well, actually. In the bar business, it's always helpful to know the right people when you need a favor. And in Cook County, it's likely the need for favors is going to come up more than once."

"Crook County, you mean," said Rusty. It was an old joke, but we chuckled anyway.

"Do you think it's going to be hard to make the change?" I asked.

"I don't think so. Both places have a lot of evening hours. I'll need to be a bit more involved in the operation, especially at first, to build the business back up again. And keep out riffraff."

I wondered what he'd do about people like Betts. Would Bob continue to serve him? Was it a bartender's job to stop people who were destroying themselves with drink?

"Sami had gotten a bit lax on that end," Pizza Bob went on. "He never wanted to toss out someone who was willing to spend money. I don't know if you noticed, but the police have had a bit more presence around here lately. Sami's is starting to get a reputation as a problem place, especially late in the evening."

I hadn't noticed. But then, I usually left no later than nine in the evening, too early for troublemakers.

"I did notice that Sami was drinking more himself. By the end of the night he was probably pretty wasted," Rusty said.

"You're right, that didn't help," Pizza Bob said.

"I bet his wife had a lot to do with that," I said. "Whitney was always keeping an eye on him, being sure he pushed drinks. He probably didn't do much drinking until she left."

Bob shook his head. "That one! We almost didn't make a deal. Whitney wanted way more than the place was worth, and then she wanted to stay on as part owner. I thought we had come to a friendly agreement—Sami and I had it all worked out. But I had to get a lawyer to talk reason into her. Eventually we got it done."

"Well, we wish you the best," Rusty said. "I just hope the new owner of Bob's Pizza doesn't tamper with the recipe. Best pizza for miles."

"Thanks for the compliment, but I'm sure the chain will use their own recipe. You'll have to wait for the non-compete to be up. Meanwhile, I'll be busy enough here. It'll take a little doing, but I'm learning already."

He lowered his voice again. "If you're gonna be in this business, you really have to be disciplined about your own drinking. Customers— they always want to get on the owner's good side, and they buy him drinks. An owner wants to encourage that, since it helps his profits. But he better be pouring something like Coke or water for himself. If he spends twelve hours a day in a bar and doesn't keep a clear head, it's not going to be long before the business suffers, and his health as well."

Pizza Bob saw a customer hold up his glass for a refill. He stepped away for a moment but came right back.

"I don't want to speak badly about a friend, but like I said, a couple hours before last call, Sami might have some drinks. And when Sami drinks too liberally himself, he lets customers drink too much, then doesn't know how to deal with the result. He's a nice guy, but he's too driven, too jumpy, takes offense too easily. That doesn't make for good business. Eventually customers will start going elsewhere."

He picked up a bar rag and wiped the area in front of us, shaking his head. "I'm more laid back, but I don't let people get away with shit, and I think I have pretty good judgment, especially as to cutting off drinkers who've had too much, even friends. And I think I can keep troublemakers out. I hope I'm getting the place before too many people drift away, though."

"People like the Czacki brothers, you mean?" I said.

Bob shuddered. "God protect me from the Czacki brothers. It's been a while since they've been in here. But the other day I bumped into Milan, you know, who runs Tom's Place? He said they were in there last week and he tossed them out. I hope they stay away from here."

"When do we stop calling you Pizza Bob and call you just plain Bob instead?" I joked.

He laughed. "Don't care if the old name sticks. I kind of like it."

Chapter 21

BETTS HAD BEEN RIGHT IN his prediction. He did recover and less than a month later, by the middle of October, Rusty and I stopped at Sami's and there was Betts sitting in his usual place near the front door. We were glad to see him, but worried that he'd not heeded advice to give up drinking. Rusty and I went over to make a little fuss over his return. Rusty squeezed his shoulder and I pecked his cheek fondly.

There were two glasses on the bar in front of him. One glass was beer, the other filled with an opaque white liquid. I pointed at the second glass.

"What is that?" I asked.

Betts put his forefinger to his lips, leaned close to us and whispered, "It's my new secret weapon. It's called 'milk.'"

I blinked and caught Rusty's eye. "Milk. And beer," I said.

"After every glass of beer, I have a glass of milk. Makes the beer go down easier," Betts said.

I knew milk was commonly used to calm stomach ulcers. I hadn't heard it helped pancreatitis, but I guessed there was some logic there. Absence of alcohol was part of that program too, though.

"What's that taste like?" Rusty said, wrinkling his nose.

Betts gave his barking laugh. "You don't want to know."

I was relieved that he was feeling better and making some changes by drinking less beer and eating more healthy food. It was a step in the right direction that I hoped would help.

Meanwhile, it had become difficult for me to find time for long, leisurely phone calls to Dottie Lou. I was at work in the daytime when she was free to talk, and evenings she was involved with her husband and her children, and I wanted to focus on Rusty.

That left weekends, when Rusty was away and Tom was frequently taking advantage of available overtime. But I found it frustrating trying to have a deep conversation while Dottie Lou was juggling constant interruptions from her squabbling kids.

Even with the infrequent calls circumstances forced on us, our friendship was never threatened. We both knew we would drop everything if the other was in need. We both knew we could pick up where we left off, even if years had passed. But it never got that bad; a month was about as long as we ever went without a heart-to-heart.

After one of those longer non-contact periods, Dottie Lou and I finally connected late one Saturday morning in mid-October. We spent twenty minutes or so catching up on what was happening in each other's lives.

"Hope you haven't bought any Tylenol recently," Dottie Lou said. That was the big news lately. Seven people throughout the Chicago area had been poisoned by someone who tampered with Tylenol bottles, putting cyanide in the capsules and then returning them to the shelves. A nationwide search for the poisoner had so far not had any results.

"I'm sticking to aspirin," I said. "No capsules for me."

"And making sure the seals are tight, I hope. But say," Dottie Lou said, "did you happen to catch that new sitcom called "Cheers"?

"Not yet. Is it good?"

"It's pretty funny, but it reminds me of Sami's, at least from what you describe. It all takes place in this bar in Boston where the same bunch of characters hang out. The words to the theme song made me laugh. Something about how you want to go where people know you and are glad to see you. That's Jane and Sami's, I said to myself."

"I'll have to catch it. Sounds like us. We all lead personal lives, but we know that if someone doesn't show up there are people who will notice and care."

Dottie Lou and I usually shared random updates for a few minutes—sometimes it was politics or events in the news—before delving into matters that were affecting our lives. That was the important conversation—the time when we thought deeply and faced things we didn't talk about with anyone else. It wasn't all serious. In fact, we resolved most matters by finding ways to laugh at ourselves and put worries in perspective.

"Does it ever bother you that you spend virtually all of your weekends away from Rusty?" Dottie Lou asked.

Did it bother me? "I see plenty of Rusty and he's there when I need him, but I like having my freedom on weekends. In many ways, it's the best of both worlds," I said, sounding defensive, even to myself.

"You are good together, and you go to Sami's together, and you see each other at work. But you're not involved together in other parts of your life."

"What do you mean?"

"You've never met his mother. You don't go to the North Side, where his three-flat is, or spend any time with his family or friends, other than those two times on Kathy and Bill's boat. You don't bring him places. *I've* never met him, and you've been living together, albeit part-time, for three or four months now."

"I haven't seen *you* since Rusty and I started living together either."

"Yeah, but you could have if you really wanted to. Has he met your mom and dad?"

I spoke defensively again. "I've gone with him to do a little work on the North Side building a few times. He doesn't talk to his sister, and you know why I'm not involved with his reclusive mother. I was going to bring him to Betsy's baptism, and he would have come to that except he had an emergency call from work."

"Sure that wasn't convenient? Some reason he doesn't want to meet me?"

"Not hardly," I said, laughing.

"What about your mom and dad?" she reminded me.

"They met him. We went to my cousin's wedding. They like him."

"Are they okay with the two of you virtually living together?"

I hesitated. Were they?

"What do you expect?" I said. "You know the moral standards they raised me by. They didn't even like *you* at first, because they discovered us talking about sex as teenagers."

We laughed again. "I remember that," she said. "They had this big confrontation with you, wanted to forbid you to see me since I was a bad influence on their little girl."

"But I stayed loyal to you and here we are. They never considered that I might have been the one to bring up sex and I was the bad influence. We weren't doing anything girls our age didn't do."

"They like me now?" she asked.

"You know they do. They weren't so fond of Dick either, but they never told me that until after the divorce. They've accepted Rusty. They want me to be happy, and they know he makes me happy."

"But the living together?"

I let out a long breath. "We haven't had the discussion. I'm sure they don't want me to be alone. But they would prefer to see us married."

"Because that's how parents think about their baby girl?"

"Something like that."

"Does it bother you?"

"What my parents think?" I stalled, avoiding what I knew her real question was.

"That you're not married. Or don't you want to be married again?"

These were the questions I asked myself when, awake in bed in the middle of the night, I watched Rusty as he slept. I'd never forced myself to answer, especially out loud. But now Dottie Lou seemed to know that I needed to talk the matter out. Although some of my replies had been defensive, I knew she made me face her questions because she cared for me.

Now she gave me some time to get my thoughts together. Finally, I said, "It's okay the way things are. You're worried about my future, right?"

"Right."

"Honestly, I don't know where this is going. Probably nowhere. He's gun-shy about marrying again, due to what he experienced with his parents' marriage, his own marriage, and others he's seen. For me it's better to be with him than not. And for him, too. It would be a mistake to force things, wouldn't it?"

"Some people do force matters. In fact, many do. I don't think it's unusual that one person in a relationship wants marriage more than the other, and that person takes the lead."

"Well, I'm not going to do that. He's got enough on his plate. We just want to make each other happy now, and that's enough."

"Do you believe what you just said? I hope you're not fooling yourself. Do you really know what he thinks?"

"Rusty cares about me and my happiness is important to him. You remember that was what attracted me to him in the first place. But he thinks marriage is what kills relationships."

"But what do you think? What about the future? Joining finances, having a family, all that? Do you want a family?"

What did I want? There I was, back to my uncomfortable feeling there was something missing that I couldn't define. "I thought I did, some time ago," I said. "But if I do want a family someday, I'd need the reassurance of some sort of permanence. If that's ever going to happen…I'm in my mid-thirties already. The clock is ticking."

"He's not thinking about having a family, is he?"

I had to admit that I didn't really know. "He has some decisions to make before that," I said. "What to do with his building? Should he rent his flat? Running back and forth to opposite ends of the city every week to keep things up, plus his mother…it's hard. Maybe he should sell the building? A lot to think about. A lot to happen."

"If he does sell it, you'd live in your apartment for…how long?"

"We'd want to buy a house, probably."

"And live in it without getting married, merging your finances and insurance, starting a family…?"

I knew the answers. I just didn't want to say them. The matter was eventually going to come to a head, and I didn't feel good about the outcome. Everything about our relationship indicated a lack of permanence, even that his company could transfer him at any time. Was that enough for the new life I was seeking?

"I don't know how any of this is going to turn out. I do know I love this man, and I want him in my life. If it's going to end, I'm going to hang on to every minute I can get before that happens."

Chapter 22

AS THE COLD WEATHER SET in and the holiday season approached, I started crocheting stocking caps for Christmas presents. One for John David, one for Betts, one for Angel, and one for Dixon. Rusty insisted that he didn't want one.

"I don't know why you're making one for Dixon either," he said. "He'll never wear it. Knit hats like that don't go with cowboy boots."

"I don't want him to feel left out," I said.

My job at Argonne took a lot of time, but it was always exciting. So much so that I found it hard to relax. Nothing unpleasant was going on, but I just couldn't shut my mind off. I was too jittery to just sit in front of the television evenings, and I'd wake up during the night and not be able to get back to sleep.

My remedy? I didn't want to take pills, so instead of doing less I did more. I began to crochet as I watched television. It kept my hands busy and required just the right amount of concentration to allow me to work and follow what was happening on television at the same time. It relaxed me and I slept better too.

When one crochets for therapeutic reasons, it's always a problem to find projects to make that anyone actually wants. Sweaters have to fit, afghans take months to make, and there are only so many anyone can use. Hats turned out to be the answer. They are fun, easy to do, don't take huge amounts of time, and people tend to like them. Perhaps the crowd at Sami's would start calling me Hatmaker Jane.

Early in November, Rusty came home to change clothes and pick up his pool cue for pool night. Golf was done for the season, but the pool leagues were in full swing. I sat watching the six o'clock news with a skein of navy blue yarn on my lap and a crochet needle in my hand.

"I think I might make a hat for Lindsay too," I said. "To match the one I'm making for John David. What do you think?"

"Terrible idea. I've never seen her wear a hat. She has such luscious hair. I don't think she wants to cover it."

I didn't want to give up. "Winter's coming. I think I'll do it."

Rusty came over to give me a kiss, and then he placed a cup of coffee on the end table and sat down with his arm around me. "Why don't you come with me tonight? You haven't been to Sami's for weeks. Dixon's been asking about you."

I was so busy with my new life, I had been going to Sami's less and less frequently. I still felt attached to my friends there, yet I couldn't dismiss a nagging feeling that the happy life I was living now was temporary. I was reluctant to cut ties I had depended on before Argonne and Rusty became so much a part of my life. I couldn't deny that occasionally something outrageous or wacky happened at Sami's, but that was an added attraction for someone who'd always been intrigued by the unusual and exciting—within the boundaries of safety, of course.

Now that golf season was over, Rusty only saw Dixon at Sami's. Dixon couldn't afford a phone, so there was no way to reach him unless I went to Sami's. I'd meant to stop by, but it just didn't happen. From what Rusty said, nothing had changed with Dixon's ex-wife and girls, and I thought nothing would. Even if the woman found another husband, she'd still find a way to bleed Dixon dry.

Pizza Bob tended bar more often than Sami now. But the place was still called Sami's, and Pizza Bob was still called Pizza Bob. It looked like both names were going to stick, at least among the regular customers. I missed Dixon. And I missed Angel. And I missed Betts. I wondered how his health was.

Rusty was right. It had been a while since I'd been out. The hats could wait.

When we arrived at the bar, the usual clamor was more of a low buzz. There were a lot of long faces, no laughter. Something must have happened. No Betts tonight. John David was there. Pizza Bob was busy behind the bar serving customers. He glanced at us, looking grim. Lindsay was standing near the pool table, chalking her cue. Her opponent was unknown to me. I didn't see Dixon. Maybe he was in the restroom. We walked back to the pool table and sought out Angel.

"What's happened, Angel?" I asked.

"Is Dixon," Angel said, tears in his eyes. "Is hard to say."

My heart thudded and cold dread filled my chest. Angel was an emotional man but I'd never seen him in tears before. This must be bad. I looked at Rusty. He shrugged his shoulders and shook his head.

"I go his apartment. He leave wallet here yesterday. To drop off…I go. He no answer door. I bang and bang, but lights inside. His car is in lot. Neighbor come out…why I bang? I explain. We call police and… he no alive. Ambulance come…take Dixon away."

"Jesus Christ! I can't believe it! That's awful," Rusty said, looking appalled. "When did this happen?"

"Today, in afternoon." It must have been early afternoon, I thought. Dixon worked the midnight shift to get the differential.

We were stricken. I gave Angel a hug, Rusty set down his pool cue, and we went to the bar to talk to Pizza Bob. My eyes burned with unshed tears and a lump in my throat made it difficult to swallow.

"You heard about Dixon, I see," Pizza Bob said.

"I'm…stunned," I said, and gulped. "Does anyone know what happened?"

"One of my friends works at Palos Hospital and was in the ER when they brought him in. She knew Dixon casually from seeing him here, so she kept an eye on what was going on. She said he had a stroke. The ER doc told her Dixon never knew what hit him, gone just like that." Bob snapped his fingers. "Said he probably died soon after he got home from here last night and never made it to work."

Bob walked away to serve some new customers. Rusty put his arm around me. "Are you okay?" he asked.

It was starting to hit me. Tears trickled down my cheeks. I pulled out a hankie, wiped my cheeks and eyes, and said in a broken voice, "I don't know. How about you? He was your golf buddy and pool buddy."

"Yes, but you two were really close. He and I did things together, but we didn't get into each other's heads like you did. He talked to you. I know you liked him a lot."

I gave a weak smile. "Sometimes better than I like you, but it was a different sort of thing. Something between a friend and a brother."

Seeing my tears continue to flow, Rusty fished a handkerchief out of his pocket and offered it to me. I held up the hankie in my lap. "I'm good. Someone I know gave me my own hankies."

He patted my hand and put his hankie back in his pocket. Rusty's eyes were shiny too, but I knew he wouldn't want anyone in the bar to notice.

I waved Pizza Bob over. "Do you know if there will be any services?"

He shook his head. "No services, I heard. Apparently, the only thing he owned was that AMC Spirit rattletrap and his golf clubs. There's no money. The county will bury him, but there won't be a wake or a funeral."

I turned to Rusty. "Can't we do something? Or take up a collection?"

Rusty looked sad. "I wish we could, but we were his only real friends. Who would come? Some of the pool team, that's about it."

"Well, maybe a priest at least."

Rusty put his hand on mine. "I know Dixon meant a lot to you, but you also know he wasn't a religious man, and he wouldn't want a fuss. That wasn't Dixon. Let it be, Jane."

I choked back protests. I knew Rusty was right. But I hated that a man I'd cared for so much was just suddenly gone and there wasn't anything I could do to show my grief or celebrate his life!

My tears slowed as a wave of anger and frustration stuck me. I banged my hand on the bar. "Damn it! I should have found a way to stay in touch with him. He needed me, but I was too wound up in my own life."

Some of the nearby drinkers looked startled at my uncharacteristic outburst. Rusty reached for my hand and held it. I looked into his eyes.

"I knew he wasn't going to take his blood pressure medicine like he was supposed to! I should have been more involved, should have found some way to get his pills for him, dragged him to a doctor, or something. I was the only one who cared about him, the only one he listened to. He deserved better than this. He deserved better from me. I haven't even seen him for weeks! What kind of friend am I? And that damn ex-wife of his, I could just…I don't know, I just…."

After a while, Rusty said, "He was a grown man, Jane. He made his own decisions. He knew he should take the prescription. You told him what he needed to do, and he made a different choice. You don't really know how he died. Maybe the pills wouldn't have made any difference. You can't take care of the whole world. You're not responsible for everyone."

"But Dixon"—I choked over his name—"was my good friend, Rusty—such a gentle, innocent man. I knew better than him, but I just couldn't get him to accept how important taking his medicine was. No one ever thinks it's going to happen to them, and I guess I didn't either."

I pulled my hand away from Rusty's and rested my forehead on my fist. "And I hate that woman for putting him in that position! He had a good job, made a lot of money. He did everything to make his kids happy, sacrificed everything for them, and what did he get for it all? Some greedy bitch taking everything and leaving him the next thing to a street person! I hate her!"

"He had his daughters, Jane. He loved them like nothing else in his life, and he was proud of them. They made him happy," Rusty said.

"Yes, they surely did. I wonder what will happen to them now." I heard the bitterness in my voice as I raised my head and put my chin instead of my forehead on my fist.

"They'll be sad. They'll miss him. But Dixon said his wife was always a good mother. She'll take good care of them like she always did. It was Dixon she punished, not the girls. They're not the first kids to grow up without a father, sad as that may be. They'll be okay."

"She won't have her cash cow anymore."

"No, she won't," Rusty said gently. "But the girls will be fine, I'd bet anything on that."

"I hope they'll always remember how much he loved them. I only wish I had a chance to tell them how much I loved him." I stifled a sob. "And I wish I could tell him too."

Chapter 23

DESPITE MY PREVIOUS RATIONALIZATIONS FOR continuing to visit Sami's, it was hard for me to go there after Dixon's death. I didn't want to be reminded that he wasn't there. Rusty continued to play in the pool league to finish out the season, but without Dixon it wasn't the same for him either. I stayed home most of the time, but Rusty filled me in on any news.

We did plan to go to Poker Dan's wedding. All the longtime regular crowd had been invited. I was eager to meet Karen and see what she and her family were like. Dying of curiosity to see how Sami's crowd interacted with Karen's family and friends. Anxious to find out what sort of new life Dan was making for himself. In other words, I was my usual nosy self.

I knew John David wouldn't want to go, but I went to Sami's one pool night to try to talk Lindsay into coming with us to the wedding. She wasn't comfortable at social events, even when they involved people she knew. "I can't," she said.

"Is it because of John David?" I'd noticed they often came in and left together now, and I often caught her watching him when she was at the pool table. I expected that, as usual, she wouldn't want to talk about anything personal. I must have caught her at a low point, because surprisingly she confided in me once again.

"John David has been really upset since his sister left Lemont to go back to Indianapolis. You remember that rotten business with the

Czacki brothers?"

"I'm not about to forget those assholes," I said, shaking my head.

She looked off in the distance, not comfortable with meeting my eyes, or anyone's for that matter. "John David doesn't have any friends—just me. He was so dependent on her. Now I'm the only one he's got to keep an eye on him, you know? He needs that. I mean, he needs *somebody*, doesn't he?" She looked at me then.

I nodded. "He does, and he cares a lot about you, so I'm sure that's important to him. But you might be making him think he can't do *without* you. Would that be a problem?" I watched her face, but she turned away and looked into the distance again.

After a time she said, "I really don't know, Jane. You know I'm fond of him. He's a smart man, but in some ways he's just like a child. I don't know if…the future…." She closed her eyes and moved her head from side to side.

I touched her hand, understanding all too well. I refused to face questions about my own future, afraid any changes I brought up would cause Rusty to end our relationship.

"Does John David ever think about going back to Indianapolis too?"

She shook her head. "He doesn't want to burden his sister again. She's got enough on her hands already, sadly. No job, alone with her kids, living with her parents—and they aren't in good health either. He'd be just one more thing for her to worry about."

"She probably worries anyway."

"Probably. But at least it's not day to day. Out of sight, out of mind, as they say." She looked at me again. "He says I give him something to live for."

"Wow. I don't know what to say to that. But you care?"

"I do care."

Wow, I thought again. *Two loners finding each other. Is that a good thing, or the kiss of doom?*

We sipped our drinks for a while. Then I asked, "Is he still spending a lot of time at the library?"

"Are you kidding? One of the librarians told me she was with him the first time he came in to use a computer. She said he stared at the keys and at the screen like he was staring at a lover. Then he sat down and just began to type, like a concert piano player making music, like he'd been doing it all his life."

She grinned. "Anyway, he's there when the library opens, meets me for a burger at five, and then heads over here for the evening. The library bought a second computer for other people to use. He says they'll have to buy more computers soon, because they're getting popular."

"What does he do on them?"

"Looks up information. Talks to people from all over."

"You can talk to people on a computer now?"

"Not talk, with actual sound. They have these things called chat rooms. You can see what people are typing back and forth to each other and join the conversation. John David says you can find these rooms on almost any topic and connect with people from all over the world."

"Huh. I didn't know that. We just use our computers at work for word processing, to communicate with other people at Argonne, and sometimes to look things up. Of course, the scientists use them for research, calculations, stuff like that."

We sat with our own thoughts for a while. Then I asked, "Would you think about coming to the wedding without John David? We'll pick you up. You can sit with us, and we'll bring you home."

She shook her head. "I couldn't do that. Sami and Pizza Bob hired a bartender for that night so they can go, but John David would be the only person not going. How's that going to make him feel? At least I can keep him company. Especially since I'm not keen on going anyway."

I grinned at her. "I know you don't want it to get around, but you're a good person, Little Lindsay."

Chapter 24

POKER DAN'S WEDDING WAS HELD on Friday evening the day after Thanksgiving. The weather was unseasonably warm, with a light early-evening breeze.

We picked up Angel. He wore a dark brown leisure suit over a button-down shirt in a tropical print with an open collar. I told him how nice he looked, but I was thinking his clothes went out of style quite some time ago. He probably didn't own anything else except jeans and may have even borrowed the clothes for all I knew. I was glad he made the effort, though.

The Old Stone Church, as it was called, used to be the Methodist church, but now housed the Lemont Historical Society. It was one of the oldest buildings in Lemont, built in 1861 from the famous limestone that had been quarried right here in town. The chapel was small but lovely, as churches from that time were, with dark curved pews, tall stained-glass windows, and a tin ceiling. There were a few flowers for the occasion, and the atmosphere was perfect for the nuptials.

Betts joined us at the church, and we all sat together, Angel on the aisle, then Rusty, me and Betts at the end. Betts bounced his leg and wriggled continuously to the point that I wanted to poke him, but I didn't. He was uncomfortable enough without me turning on him, I thought. He wore a black corduroy sport coat, white shirt and burgundy and gray striped tie and dark gray trousers that would have looked nice except that they hung on him due to all the weight he'd lost. I wondered how long it had been since either Angel or Betts had been in a church. I knew it had been years for Rusty.

Poker Dan, on the other hand, had cleaned up real nice. A little on the stocky side, he had a fresh haircut, a lock over his forehead making him look rather boyish. His dark suit looked neat and fit well, probably newly purchased for the occasion. This was the first time I'd met Karen, the bride. She seemed quiet and looked sweet in a simple sleeveless white lace dress that came to just below her knees. And very young. She carried a bouquet of white roses and had worked one of the flowers into her hair, her light brown curls piled attractively on top of her head. She didn't wear a bridal veil. She was a little thing, barely five feet tall and a little pudgy, with a pleasant face and shy smile. From the way she looked at Dan, she adored him.

I looked around the church. Poker Dan's only sister sat in the front pew on the groom's side with her husband and three little boys. Karen's parents and older brother filled the bride's side, watching proudly with big grins on their faces. A few friends and extended family, I supposed, sat in the pews behind them. From what I could tell overhearing their conversations, they seemed to be nice people. I found myself thinking that Poker Dan had made a good, albeit surprising, choice. I wondered if he would be bored in the little town of Troy Grove, where he now resided.

Pizza Bob, who had found someone to bartend for the night, was the best man. As I would have expected, he looked the part. What I didn't expect was that he brought a girlfriend, Meghan Wend. When I talked to her later, I found out that she and Pizza Bob had been dating exclusively for over three years, a secret he had kept successfully from all of us. She was tall and trim and looked lovely in the pale blue silk dress and jacket she'd worn. Light brown hair fell to her shoulders, nicely setting off her bright blue eyes. She told me she was a physical therapist at Palos Hospital. Who'd have thunk he had a girlfriend? And why had Pizza Bob kept her a secret? I was dying to spend some time with her and find out.

Preacher John met the bride and groom in front of the altar rail, and indeed today he did look like a real preacher in his black pants, shirt, and clerical collar. He held open what I assumed was either a Bible or a prayer book and smiled at the couple standing before him.

"Dearly beloved," he began, his voice deep and reverent. As the traditional words and vows were repeated, I thought of my own wedding to Dick. I had meant my vows when I took them. I never imagined I'd find myself years later sitting next to, and deeply in love with, a different man. It saddened me, for what had been and no longer was. But at the same time, I was so happy to have found Rusty. I felt tears gathering as I looked at him at the same moment he turned to me. I smiled and lifted the hankie I held ready in my hand and pressed it to my eyes. Rusty smiled back, reached for my hand, and pulled it to his knee where it stayed throughout the vows.

The service was short, traditional, and unaccompanied by music. Yet the solemnity and the atmosphere struck just the right note.

Glancing around, I saw that Betts's eyes were shining. When he caught me looking at him, he quickly wiped them with his sleeve. Was Betts more sentimental than I gave him credit for? I didn't think he was so close to Poker Dan that he was emotional because he was saying goodbye to a friend. Maybe there was something sad in Betts's past that the ceremony brought back to him.

I did wonder, however, why the ceremony was held in Lemont instead of the bride's hometown, where the couple now lived. Perhaps it had been important to Poker Dan to have his drinking and card game buddies there to see him off. It was likely that after tonight visits to Lemont would be rare.

I wondered about the whole Sami's crowd here at the wedding today. How many of them saw this event as an ending of sorts? How many of them would be unchanged a year from now, or even still gathering at Sami's? Dixon, and Adam and Eve, were already gone, now Poker Dan, and we didn't yet know how long we'd have Sami with us. Did others see the possibility of our crowd fading from their lives? Where would Angel be a year from now? Or Betts? Were they having the same thoughts as I was? Were we in some respect saying goodbye to each other? Would Rusty be included in that goodbye? The thought terrified me, and I brushed it off.

After the traditional vows, pronouncement of marriage, and kissing of the bride were over, Preacher John turned the couple toward the guests and said, "I don't know how this old bachelor ever got this sweet lady to be his wedded bride, but I can only say his oldest buddy—and that would be me—hopes that God blesses this marriage with every happiness. And don't you be a stranger once you go off to that little town, now!"

The reception was held at the VFW Hall a short distance west of the Old Stone Church. Some of the guests, including Rusty and me, had parked at the hall and walked the few blocks to the church. Betts, who lived nearby and didn't bring a car, walked beside Angel. Rusty and I followed, having our own conversation.

"Our fears were groundless," I said. "Here we'd expected something a bit weird, but it was really a nice ceremony. I don't usually cry at weddings, but...I don't know...the simplicity, maybe? It got to me."

"I was afraid maybe you were remembering your first wedding and that made you sad," Rusty said.

"Oh, no! I'm all over that," I said, although he had been right, but for reasons other than what he thought. We walked in silence for a bit. "I was happy, actually. I was thinking about how glad I was that you're in my life now."

Rusty stopped, linked his arm through mine, and examined my face. "I'm glad we're together, but I hope you weren't imagining us at the altar. You know marriage isn't in the future for me."

Rusty's face showed his concern for me, but his words struck like a blow. I did know. He'd explained how, after watching the disastrous relationship between his mother and father, he thought he'd never get married, and then how hurt he had been when his own marriage, entered into after battling this conviction, came to a bitter end. More than once, he'd mentioned that these experiences had reinforced his opinion that he was a bachelor by nature. He believed in love but was convinced that marriage ruined it.

I knew Rusty had no intention of marrying me, but did I really believe that? I'd refused to let myself dream of marriage to Rusty so I wouldn't be disappointed when I faced the fact it wouldn't happen. I put off deciding how important having a family was. Hoping for marriage would only bring our eventual break-up closer. The best I could hope for was that we'd continue as we were, for as long as we could. During the ceremony I *hadn't* been wishing for him to marry me. But hearing him say the words still hurt. I wished he hadn't picked this moment to remind me.

I squeezed his arm and said, pretending, "I know. I wasn't thinking about any other marriage, and certainly not ours. I was just moved to see the happiness on their faces is all."

I started walking again, looking forward. "I remember a couple of movies where the wedding parties walk from the bride's home to the church. It's a parade that's part of the ceremony. That feels like what we're doing now, doesn't it?"

"I suppose so," Rusty said.

When we got to the VFW hall, Dirty Wally, who hadn't made it to the church, joined us there. He wore nice trousers and a blue button-down shirt, but no tie or jacket. For once, his face and hands were clean and his hair nicely combed. The effort to look presentable was likely the reason he'd been too late to go to the church. Conversely, Sami and Whitney came to the church, but he wasn't well enough to make the reception, and Whitney, who had never warmed up to our crowd, opted to skip it too.

As best man, Pizza Bob toasted the bride and groom. After some funny anecdotes and wishes for happiness, he ended with, "And now, Dan, maybe you can tell me how to solve a little problem you've left me. How am I going to find someone to rent your apartment? And how am I going to explain to a new tenant why men keep knocking on the door at all hours with poker cards and money in their pockets?"

After dinner, the usual removal of the bride's garter and throwing of her bouquet took place. I stood in the crowd to catch the bouquet, but didn't try very hard, and one of Karen's guests caught it. Dan hadn't hired a band for the occasion, but the jukebox played traditional wedding music. After pushing back some tables to make a bit more room for dancing, the newlyweds danced alone to "Unchained Melody." Others joined in until the floor was full. All the regular wedding reception songs followed: "The Hokey Pokey," "The Chicken Dance," "Proud Mary," "Shout," and "The Beer Barrel Polka." Dan and Pizza Bob, the Sicilians in the room, took off their jackets, removed their ties, and rolled up their shirtsleeves to dance "The Tarantella," putting on a show while we circled around them, laughing and cheering them on.

Rusty and I had never danced together before. I wasn't a good dancer, but I knew the basic steps and could move well to the music. Rusty was—well, a little rusty on the dance floor. His moves were energetic, but his timing a bit off, so during the fast dances we wound up colliding more than turning, which kept us giggling.

The evening ended with some slow dances, and there Rusty was a better dancing partner. We glided closely over the floor, feeling no need for conversation. Unlike other men I'd danced with, whose touch seemed to be of the hand on the back variety, I could feel every inch of Rusty's arms and hands in contact with my body. I rested my head in that groove in his shoulder. It fit perfectly, as he was only a few inches taller than me. I felt enclosed by his body, as I had the first night we had sex, and felt again that desperation to keep him in my life. If that meant without marriage, then I was determined to accept that. Somehow, we would work it out.

Everyone, including Dan's poker buddies, behaved themselves, and all the guests left smiling, if not a bit tipsy.

Chapter 25

TWO WEEKS AFTER THE WEDDING, Pizza Bob had another party at Sami's, a small goodbye party for Angel this time. I hadn't been to Sami's since Poker Dan's wedding, but I couldn't miss saying goodbye to Angel.

It seemed the relatives Angel had lived with in Lemont had decided to move back to Mexico, and Angel no longer had a place to stay. The story in the bar was that, after much discussion, Angel's wife had refused to pay for an apartment in Lemont but had sent a ticket for him to return to El Paso instead, where he would move back in with her.

Rusty and I pulled Angel aside to say our private farewells. He was leaving the next morning. I knew it was unlikely we'd ever see him again.

"I try hard this time," Angel said, his expression determined. "Eva say she help me dry out, clean me up, find me work." He grinned. "I mean what I say this time. But she, how you say it…she chicken-peek?"

I laughed. "Henpeck. How will you feel about that?"

He frowned. "Is no fun. But mean she love me, is so?"

I put my hand over his and looked fondly into his eyes. "I'm sure it means just that. I hope you'll be happy, Angel. But promise you'll let us know if you ever get back to Lemont."

"You and Rusty, you be first to know. I have number." He patted his shirt pocket, where he'd put the slip of paper with our phone number that I'd given him earlier. Then he reached for my hand and kissed it. I gave him one of those big, swaying bear hugs, and kissed his cheek fondly.

After Angel left, weeks went by, and I missed him. And I missed Dixon. And I missed Poker Dan. Adam and Eve weren't much of a loss. I rarely saw Sami anymore. I'd never liked Whitney, who hadn't been in the bar for months, ever since they signed the papers that would turn the bar over to Pizza Bob at the end of the year. I didn't miss her. Our little group was dwindling. Me and Rusty, John David and Lindsay, Betts, Pizza Bob, and Dirty Wally. We were all that was left, and I wasn't there much anymore either.

But Pizza Bob was doing a great job with the place. He had plans to expand the bar into the rooms that Adam and Eve had rented. There would be space there for two more pool tables to accommodate more leagues. Which, of course, would increase customers. He was talking about forming summer leagues. He hadn't decided whether to rent the upstairs rooms for living or commercial space yet.

"I don't know if a lawyer, for instance, wants to have clients exposed to jukebox and bar noise. I'm asking around. Something will turn up."

I wondered how many other changes would take place under Bob's ownership. It all seemed to be good, but I missed the old group of lovable characters. I didn't miss the Judge or the Czackis, but fortunately they never came around anymore. Would there be new lovable characters in the new-and-improved Sami's? Would I stick around to find out?

"But say," Pizza Bob said. "I hope you guys don't have plans for New Year's Eve. Keep the night open."

As it happened, we didn't. In past years, I had celebrated New Year's Eve in a small way with my family. Sometimes I just called family at midnight to wish them a Happy New Year and then went to bed. Chicago winters were often brutal and beginning such a late-night celebration in usually inclement weather never seemed worth it. I tried to explain this to Pizza Bob, but the truth was, I was just ambivalent about celebrating the New Year so soon after the hullabaloo that was Christmas, and Rusty agreed with me.

"No, this time you have to come here. I'm having a big party. We'll be celebrating the New Year, but it's also to celebrate my ownership of the bar, which goes into effect on January 1. Lots of food, and free drinks. By invitation only. I'll be upset if you guys don't come."

I guessed we'd be busy this New Year's Eve after all. It might be fun. If not, maybe Rusty and I could get away early. I could always stop going to Sami's after the New Year.

Chapter 26

FRIDAY, DECEMBER 31, 1982: the New Year's Eve party was a great time. I was relieved to find Betts sticking to his plan to cut his consumption of beer in half and that he was eating regularly. Surprisingly, John David and Lindsay stayed to see the New Year in, and we were pleased that Pizza Bob had finally invited his girlfriend, Meghan, for the occasion. Since I was at Sami's so infrequently, I looked forward to a chance to get to know her.

I could hardly wait to see how Betts and John David and Lindsay liked the hats I made for them. It was a little late for Christmas gifts, but I hadn't wanted to make a separate trip. I had a bittersweet moment earlier that day when I wrapped the hats. I kept the wrapping simple, thinking something fancy might be embarrassing since this was the first time I'd given gifts to these friends. When I finished, I stood holding the hats I'd made for Dixon and Angel, fingering them for an emotional moment, imagining how Dixon and Angel might have reacted to their gifts. Then I placed them in my craft box. If I didn't think of someone to give them to, I could reuse the yarn.

Betts was surprised when I handed him a wrapped present. "For me? I don't have anything for you, Janie." For once he seemed at a loss for words, and I saw his eyes grow moist.

"I don't want anything, Betts," I said. "It's just a little thing."

Wordlessly he ripped off the gift wrap and pulled out the stocking cap. He looked up. "You made this, Janie?"

I grinned. "With my own little hands. Do you like the color?" It was navy blue.

"I don't wear hats much," he said.

"Well, when you do, you have one now," I said. I could tell I'd made him happy, despite his words.

"I made one for Angel too, but I guess he won't need it where he's at, even if I knew where to send it. So there's an extra hat going begging," I added. I didn't mention Dixon's hat.

"Don't look at me," Rusty said with a grin.

I punched him playfully in the arm.

Lindsay and John David both blushed and stammered their thanks when they unwrapped the matching hats I'd made for them. Like Betts, they seemed surprised that someone remembered them with a gift. John David would use his, I was sure.

Once the gift-giving was over, Rusty and I moved to the back area, where he watched the pool games while I drifted into my own thoughts, mostly about Dixon and how he should be here with us. My throat burned with sorrow. I closed my eyes to hide the gathering tears and reached for my hankie to wipe them away. My reverie was interrupted when Poker Dan and Karen walked in, grinning and waving, and everyone cheered the newlyweds.

"We can't stay long," Poker Dan said. "It's a long drive home and we want to welcome the New Year with family." As I listened to the couple chatting with old friends, it seemed that Poker Dan, who I knew had never been close to his own family, was enjoying the changes marriage had brought. He told us he was working for his father-in-law, as sales manager for a farm equipment company. The position struck me as ideal. When I met Karen's father, he seemed to be a smart rural type who would be easy to work for. And Dan, who was a natural, friendly, smooth-talking bullshitter, would make a perfect salesman.

Sami and Whitney made a brief appearance around nine. Sami, appearing pale, emaciated, and exhausted, shambled around the room, shaking hands and wishing everyone a Happy New Year.

Whitney wore her usual superior, annoyed expression, but was polite.

Pizza Bob picked up a party horn from behind the bar and blew it for attention. "Let's all sing for Sami," he said, and began "For He's a Jolly Good Fellow." Sami stood in the center of the room, looking baffled and touched, swaying with weakness. I was pleased to see that Whitney took his arm and eased him onto a stool while we sang. Her thoughtfulness indicated to me that whatever was going on in her life, it appeared she was going to stick by Sami through his illness.

At midnight, as everyone was blowing horns, throwing streamers, hugging and kissing, Pizza Bob called for attention. He cleared and wiped a dry place near the center of the bar, lifted Meghan up, and sat her on the edge. She giggled and blushed. Then he dropped to his knees in front of her, pulled a small box from his front pants pocket, and said, "Meghan, will you do me the pleasure of being my wife?"

Meghan's face turned bright red as her eyes filled with tears. "I couldn't be happier," she said, her voice and her smile trembling. Pizza Bob stood, slipped a ring from the jewelry box and placed it on her finger. He wrapped his arms around her and the two kissed passionately while everyone cheered, some patrons making jovial rowdy comments.

Would this ever be me? I pushed the thought from my head and smiled.

After the kiss broke, Pizza Bob looked around and grabbed Preacher John by the arm, dragging him to stand next to the happy couple. "Will you do the honors?" he asked.

Then Pizza Bob opened bottles of champagne. Some of the customers only took a sip to be polite, preferring beer. But the triple celebration of Bob's engagement, his formal ownership of the bar at last, and the turning of the New Year had everyone in high spirits.

Bob and Meghan. *How cool,* I thought. Yet part of me wondered how Meghan would like being the wife of a bar owner, a life of long hours and plenty of stress. Meghan reminded me a bit of myself—an educated professional more interested in quiet pursuits than noisy bars. She, like I, would sooner or later have to make difficult decisions about whether or not Sami's had any place in our lives. I thought I might call her after the holidays and invite her over for coffee. It would be nice to have another woman to talk to nearby.

I'd been uncomfortable at Sami's at first and then gotten to depend on the camaraderie I'd found over time. Yet now, returning to the things I'd loved doing all my life, I had less dependency on Sami's, and with the loss of some of my friends here I was beginning to feel out of place again. I was still reluctant to stop going to Sami's altogether, since Rusty enjoyed being there and shooting pool, and I didn't want to interfere with his interests—he didn't interfere with mine. I wanted to share Rusty's interests with him.

We were supposed to have dinner at my parents' place the next day to celebrate the holiday. My mother had decided she was crazy about Rusty. My dad a little less so, but I figured that was because no one was ever good enough for his baby girl. Besides that, Rusty was strong and handy around the house. Dad *used* to be handy around the house, but advanced age had changed that. Now, although he was grateful when Rusty helped out, it seemed obvious that he was also a bit jealous.

But this night was not one to examine those thoughts. Tonight, we were here to celebrate and have fun, as I'd been doing earlier. And so I ended my drifting thoughts, refusing to allow such conflicting feelings to ruin the evening.

We both enjoyed ourselves, and it was after one in the morning when Rusty and I finally left. It was also only the third time in my life I got tipsy. I wasn't sick yet, but I was floating and weaving and giddy. The alcohol had snuck up on me. We were having such a good time, and despite my good intentions, I had three drinks instead of two, and then sipping champagne did me in. One minute I was happy, then the next I was lightheaded, and I knew it was already too late.

Tipsy! I was way past that. Did I feel high! Oh, me! Oh, my! I couldn't believe how drunk I was. And Rusty, who drank more than me but generally handled it well, had drunk too much also, but he wasn't as bad off as I was. Unlike most drunks, he didn't slur his words. In fact, the tipoff that he'd drunk too much was when his speech became more precise.

I asked Rusty, "Can we make it home? I don't know…."

"Look outside," he said, gesturing toward the door.

I went to the door and stepped out. I was struck by a blast of cold wind and dry snow. The kind of wind and snow that comes with a blizzard. There was only a thin dusting on the streets so far, but the snow was falling fast and would soon pile up. Outside was another world, a silent wonderland glistening under streetlights. I would normally look at such a sight with awe, but now it filled me with dread.

"We can't leave the car and walk home in this. Too far," Rusty said, pulling me back inside and closing the door. He didn't have to tell me that. And then he said, "I'll get us there." I knew he meant he would drive. I didn't think it was a good idea, but I didn't have a better one. Cabs weren't readily available in Lemont at this hour, certainly not on New Year's Eve, and no one at Sami's was available either—no one in better condition to drive, that is. We'd have to chance it, be careful, and hope we didn't get stopped by the police.

But first we had to get to Rusty's car, which was parked over a block away. There had been cars all along the street when we arrived, but now there were no cars at all. When we walked out the door, the bitter cold wind and blowing snow struck our faces. There wasn't a soul out and not a car moving. We were both literally staggering and stumbling and trying to support each other as we struggled down the street. The snow on the sidewalk was getting thicker and we heard the crunch, crunch as we plodded along into the wind, wishing we had boots instead of dress shoes.

Finally, we made it to Rusty's car. Rusty fumbled to get the key in the lock. He opened the passenger door for me, helped me in, and I fell onto the seat. With one hand on the car's hood to help him get around it, he circled carefully to the driver's side, stirring up clouds of snow as he went. He reached his door and fumbled with the key again. I hoped he could unlock the door, because I was afraid if I leaned across the seat to pull up the lock for him, I'd get woozy. I just desperately wanted to get home before I vomited.

Rusty's door opened. Success. He fell onto the driver's seat, pulled the door closed, started the car, and turned on the windshield wipers. Normally Rusty would have been meticulous about clearing snow from the vehicle, but tonight I assumed he was too incapacitated to do so. Fortunately, the wipers easily cleared most of the dry snow from the windshield. Slowly and cautiously, Rusty pulled away from the curb and started down the street.

I was afraid to watch him drive, but I was also afraid that the motion of the car would make me sick if I closed my eyes. Luckily, there were no other cars on the side streets he stayed on, and Rusty carefully made his way down the exact center of the road, his face fiercely determined, that muscle tensed and jumping in his neck. I doubt he drove more than five miles per hour. The car didn't weave at all, thankfully even less than when he drove sober, as normally Rusty was a rather aggressive driver. I breathed a sigh of relief. We would make it home safe.

And we did. Not only did Rusty get us to our parking lot without difficulty, but he managed to fit our car easily and exactly between the two cars on either side of the only parking spot left. All that remained now was to get out and over to our building, unlock the door, climb to the second floor, and go into our apartment. Then we could flop in our bed for the rest of the night. Seemed easy enough.

It wasn't.

In retrospect, that parking place was probably available because, as I soon discovered, the spot was a sheet of ice. Rusty made it around the car to open my door, but when my feet hit the ground, I slid. The next thing I knew, I was lying on my back, with my head under the car door and my feet beneath the car parked next to us.

I heard Rusty say, "Jane, are you okay?"

Surprisingly, I wasn't hurt. I was pretty cushioned by my bulky winter coat—and the alcohol loosened me up some too, I'm sure. I looked up at Rusty and said, speaking calmly and precisely, "I'm not hurt but…I don't think I can get up. Too drunk."

Rusty bent down to help me. He slipped on the same spot as I had and went down on his back, only the other way around, his head at the side of the adjacent car and his feet under his own car.

"Are *you* okay?" I asked now.

"I think so," he said, lying still. Lifting my head, I could just see him gazing at the heavens.

After a moment, I asked. "Can you get up?"

And in a voice that matched my calmness, he said, "I don't think so."

We lay there in the bitter cold, head to toe and toe to head, me looking at the toes of his shoes pointing at the sky and he at mine, the snow swirling around us, starting to cover our coats with a thin layer of white. We weren't really that uncomfortable. I was almost tempted to just fall asleep. But we couldn't stay there all night.

After a while, I asked, "What should we do?"

And Rusty said, "Damned if I know. Let's just stay here for now… see what happens. Maybe…someone will come by."

"The lot's full. I bet everyone's home already. If someone comes in late…I don't think they'll see us." I paused. "Someone night notice the light inside the car…they'll probably think someone came home drunk and left the door open." I giggled, struck by the fact that that was just what happened. "They probably won't even come over to check."

Rusty started to laugh. We both lay there giggling, watching the snow blow and not really caring, because it was all so silly and we were both so drunk.

Later, I couldn't remember how long we lay there and how we finally got into my apartment. I just know we were there for a while, no one ever came by, and somehow, eventually, we were able to get up on our own. I have only a vague memory of pulling off my coat and falling onto the bed in my clothes, and Rusty falling beside me.

I fell asleep feeling grateful for everything I had—for Rusty, for the rewarding work I'd found at Argonne, the direction my new life was going, and for the near-perfect evening with its crazy ending. I'd never felt so close to anyone in my life as I did to Rusty, nor so happy about my future. I felt respected and I felt loved. It could be that so much alcohol had loosened me up and made me soppy, but I didn't think so. I felt happier than I'd been for a long, long time.

For this night at least, I didn't worry about making any changes or about how long this happy life could last. I was sure it would all work out somehow.

The next thing I knew, I was jolted awake by the phone shrilling from the nightstand.

Chapter 27

"IS RUSTY THERE WITH YOU?" Pizza Bob's voice on the phone sounded serious.

I poked Rusty to be sure he was up. We propped ourselves up in bed, our backs against the headboard. I held the phone between us so we could both hear. My head cleared but my heart pounded. Pizza Bob couldn't be calling on New Year's morning with good news.

"It's Little Lindsay," Bob said. "I know you and she were friends. I thought you'd want to know right away. She was killed last night on her way home."

I went rigid. I couldn't wrap my head around what he'd just said. Lindsay was still shooting pool at Sami's when we left the previous evening. She'd been having a really good night on the table. John David had left shortly after midnight. Unlike us, Lindsay was completely sober and when we asked if she needed a ride, she said her car was nearby and she'd get home on her own as soon as she finished the game she was winning. We'd offered as a gesture anyway, since it was obvious we shouldn't be driving ourselves. She likely took that into consideration when refusing our offer.

"Killed? No! Oh my God! My God!" I said now, my mouth suddenly dry, ears ringing. "Was it a car accident?" I managed to ask.

"No…a motorcycle accident," Bob said.

"Just a minute." I took a deep breath and sat taller. Pizza Bob's statement didn't make sense. "That's crazy. She said she had her car and was okay to drive. We asked before we left. I didn't know Lindsay'd ever been on a motorcycle, let alone owned or drove one."

"No, she doesn't drive a motorcycle. But Logan Czacki does," Pizza Bob said.

"The Czacki brothers weren't there when we left," Rusty said.

"No, they weren't." We heard Bob exhaling loudly over the phone. "You know what last night's weather was like. Lindsay left, like she said she would, and I was pushing the last customers out to clean up the place, when she came back in again, snow all over her hair and coat. Her car wouldn't start. The Czackis came in right behind her. Maybe they saw her outside and wanted to poke some fun, I don't know. They were at the top of their form, loud and crude, drunk as skunks. They were wearing helmets and motorcycle jackets. I assumed they'd parked their bikes outside. I heard they'd joined a motorcycle gang recently, but they picked a bad night for that mode of transportation."

"Apparently so," Rusty said. "Who would ride a motorcycle in such weather?" I was sure Rusty was remembering last night's adventure in our parking lot. "But we all know how crazy the Czackis are. Daredevils, playing a dangerous game."

"So there was Lindsay, needing help," Bob went on. "And there were Logan and Warner Czacki trying to get me to serve them after hours—I guess they couldn't find anyone open—me trying to lock up and get out of my place so I could take Meghan home. She was asleep on her feet. I told Lindsay I'd take her home, but I couldn't get out for nearly an hour. And Logan said he'd run her home, no problem, since I refused to sell them any drinks and was throwing them out anyway."

He paused, sniffed loudly a few times, let out a long breath, and then continued.

"I should have handled it differently, of course. But all I thought about at the time was that I couldn't serve alcohol because it was after hours. I didn't want any trouble with my license if the police came by, I wanted everyone, especially the Czackis, out of my bar, and Meghan really needed to get home. I wasn't really thinking so much about Lindsay, I'm sorry to say. I regret that now."

It was like Bob to blame himself. I'd done the same thing with Dixon.

"So Lindsay *did* go with Logan, then?" Rusty asked.

"She didn't *want* to go with him, of course. Wouldn't have wanted to even if he was sober and the weather was good. She made excuses and that made him furious. Who did she think she was, some princess? She couldn't walk home in this weather. Her apartment was over a mile away, but it would be only minutes on the motorcycle. Didn't she trust him? Surely he wasn't so offensive to her she couldn't ride a mile with him. What did she think would happen? He wasn't going to rape her or anything. He had a reputation to keep, after all."

"Yeah, right," Rusty said. "Is there a worse reputation than his?"

"I think it was the whole set-up she didn't like. The weather, the motorcycle, the drinking—and the Czacki brothers. But she couldn't find a way to say no. Logan made a big deal about taking off his scarf and goggles and putting them on her, and she finally walked out the door with him. Warner left too. That was the end of it last night as far as I knew. I was worried, but hoped they'd do as they said and just get her home. Surely they weren't up to trouble *all* the time, and the night was for all intents and purposes over. Other than poking fun, there was no reason they'd actually harm Lindsay. They'd known her for years."

"Obviously it didn't turn out well," I said.

"No, it sure didn't. I got a call a little while ago from a friend of Meghan's, a nurse in the Palos emergency room. She knows me and Meghan well and was there when Lindsay was brought in. Once she overheard that the accident happened after they left my place, she took over the case so she could get all the details, including questioning the cops and the ambulance driver, who had gotten some of the story from the Czackis."

Bob paused again. I wondered if his friend in the ER was the same person who had informed him about Dixon.

"She told me she found out Logan took off with Lindsay clinging behind him, scared half to death I bet. Warner followed behind so he and Logan could meet up again after dropping Lindsay off—probably to continue the night's adventures somewhere or other. Anyway, Warner admited Logan was weaving a bit before the crash. I bet what really happened was that being Logan and all, and knowing Lindsay was scared, he tried to get some of his crazy kind of fun out of it. I mean, every bar was closed, so he was frustrated and wanted some more fun somewhere. Hell, I don't know—maybe the two of them even set her up, disabling her car to get at her. I wouldn't put it past them. And it'd be just like Logan to start hot-shotting to show off, scare her more, speeding, weaving—and sure enough, he wiped out."

I was numb, but drumming in my head was the thought, *Last night I was so happy at Sami's. Now I don't know if I ever want to go there again.*

"Logan was okay, but Lindsay wasn't?" Rusty asked.

"Logan wasn't hurt much, just some street burns from skidding when the bike went down. Lindsay, though, all ninety pounds of her, was so light she was thrown and struck her head on a car that was parked on the street. The impact broke her neck, and she died almost instantly."

Chapter 28

EVEN MORE ALONE THAN DIXON had been when he died, Lindsay was referred to the Medical Examiner's Office in an attempt to locate her next of kin. A distant cousin from out of state handled property and burial matters. Except for the gloom expressed by people who knew Lindsay from Sami's, she, like Dixon, was just gone. To handle my grief, I threw myself into work.

By mid-February I found myself thinking that I'd been at Argonne for over a year, and I owed it all to Rusty. If he hadn't pushed me, I'd probably still be working at Ordman's. Instead, he'd recognized that the things I'd told him about myself—my degrees in biology, how I'd earned my way through college working nights in a hospital typing pool, how I loved to read, and my obsession with grammar—would all come together to make me a perfect fit for a position in the publishing component of a world-class national scientific laboratory.

Although I continued to bring work home and was often physically tired, I never tired of the job. Each month new top scientists from around the world brought their research to Argonne. Not only did I get to meet world-class scientists, but they came to me for help. They respected me and were grateful for the work I did for them and the advice I gave them. It made me feel valued and proud.

What Julia had said about my co-workers when I interviewed for the job was also true. They were smart and dependable, as well as easy to work with. We weren't close friends outside of work, but we were close *at* work and shared the same goals and standards. We were different people who respected and liked each other.

What Rusty didn't know when he recommended me for the job, and what Julia didn't know, and what not even *I* knew until later, was that I also had a natural knack for management. I'd never been in a position to test it before. However, now that I was in my element, comfortable as well as satisfied with my work, my companions, and my superiors, I relaxed and chipped in on decision-making and organizational problems when they occurred.

During staff meetings we were expected to contribute ideas and opinions. My ideas were usually adopted, often enthusiastically. Others started asking my advice. Soon Julia was turning the meetings over to me after describing an issue, leaving me to work out solutions.

Then Julia started calling me in to her office to ask my opinions on the problems she faced.

Meanwhile, scientists came to me to ask for favors or for explanations. They told me they did this because they knew I'd give them a clear, no-nonsense answer, which saved them time.

I suppose this knack was another side of my gift for seeing the good and bad of all sides of an issue clearly, then asking the right questions and spotting the critical points that led to good decisions. It seemed intuitive and obvious to me, but others said I had a talent. I never brought up that it was harder for me to apply the same talent in my personal life—otherwise, why had it taken so long to find my niche, and that mostly a gift from Rusty? Whether it made sense or not, this ability was a real asset on the job.

I told people I loved my work, and that was true. I felt, every day, like I was doing important things for important people. I was happy. What could be more satisfying than what I was doing?

And so, a little over a year after I began work at Argonne, Julia decided it was time to retire, and she told the administration that I was the right person to take over her position.

I was called in to interview, and in the following days while I was waiting to hear if they were going to offer me the job, Rusty and I talked about it.

"Manager, Department of Writing and Editing, Argonne National Laboratory. It sounds pretty good. But are you sure you want to take on the extra hours and added responsibility?" he asked me.

"I'm *already* working extra hours and taking on more responsibility. I like the sound of the title. The extra compensation won't hurt either." My decision was made, but I hoped Rusty would approve of my plans.

As it turned out, no other candidates were even interviewed, and I was offered the position with a twenty percent salary increase. My co-workers weren't upset. They had families, were being paid well, and didn't really want the administrative burdens and extra hours that a department manager had to take on—or so they said. I don't know—perhaps Julia talked the job over with them too and they had turned the opportunity down. What they told me was that they were happy to know I was the one who would be taking over.

Shirley had returned part-time after her maternity leave. She was willing to take on a few more hours and help train a new transcriptionist when I moved to management. It amazed me that having only one leg seemed to have no effect at all on her ability to juggle home and work.

"How can you manage all this?" I asked her. "A new baby, little kids and a house plus your job?"

She laughed. "You didn't mention that I do it all on one leg." Shirley was not at all hesitant to talk about her missing leg, which she told me had to be removed at the hip when she was a teenager due to cancer. She went on. "Two-legged women handle home, baby and career all the time. Did it ever occur to you that getting out of the house to work would be relaxing for me?"

So, I had no problems at work. Outside of it…well, not problems exactly. Let's say room for improvement.

I was happy living with Rusty, but that feeling of impermanence resurfaced, which was a little disturbing. I suspected Rusty sensed my feelings, but we avoided talking about it.

I was busy with work, reading, music, and hobbies, as well as my occasional phone conversations with Dottie Lou. If I needed a social outlet I could always go to Sami's with Rusty, but I rarely went there now. I missed Little Lindsay and Dixon. Remembering how they died made me too sad. Pizza Bob was usually too busy to talk much, and even conversations with Betts gravitated toward depressing topics. Everyone else I knew was gone and the new crowd that the bar was attracting didn't seem to have much interest in me, or vice versa. Rusty was even talking about quitting the pool league.

But with Rusty spending weekends away, the separation of our families and finances, I began to feel like something was missing. The feeling wasn't strong enough that I wanted to end the relationship. Quite the opposite. I felt I had to savor every moment we spent together. In many ways, that desperation to keep him in my life as long as I could made our love more intense. But there was a lack of sustainability that overshadowed pure happiness. Call it bittersweet.

Knowing that Rusty was gun-shy about marriage, I was determined to take things as they came and leave the decision entirely in his hands. I knew how he felt, but now I asked myself if he had any idea of how *I* really felt. I was afraid to turn things sour by discussing my fear that without a marriage commitment I would never feel secure that he'd stay with me. Or my fears about not having a family, or having a family without the permanence of marriage. I'd never been a strongly religious person, but my Catholic upbringing had instilled the concept that we were living in sin. Although clearly I had decided Rusty was more important to me than my religion was, I harbored the idea that someday I wanted to feel right in both.

If I told Rusty this, I was afraid he'd say, "Yeah, you're right," and leave me. That was the worst possible outcome, so I said nothing. I supposed I was sending signals that our current arrangement was just fine with me. For the most part, it was. Rusty was the man I loved, and I desperately didn't want to be alone again. So I hid my fears from Rusty. If we were ever to be married, he not only needed to be all in, marriage had to be his idea.

After I accepted the management position at Argonne, Rusty took me out for dinner that Friday night to celebrate. It wasn't to McDonald's this time, but instead to Jack Gibbons Gardens, a steakhouse in Oak Forest. We'd been told it was the best steak in the southwest suburbs. And as an added bonus, Jack Gibbons was one of our choices in the Entertainment coupon book that bought us two meals for the price of one.

It was a storybook evening. The steak was as good as promised, the service excellent. We'd had wine with the meal, chatted and laughed about some recent gossip and happenings in the news. We'd watched the last episode of *M*A*S*H* together earlier in the week. I asked Rusty now if it brought back memories of his days in Vietnam.

"I didn't have it as tough as most draftees," he said. "I was on base almost all the time, working the communications desk, operating the teletype, and routing messages." He grinned. "I had top-secret crypto clearance, remember."

I didn't remember. This was the first time he'd bragged about his role in the Army.

"They called me the Trick Chief. That meant I was the guy in charge of the communications center whenever the sergeant wasn't available—and that was most of the time!" He chuckled.

After the meal our conversation turned more serious while sipping after-dinner cocktails. We started talking about how our lives might change with my new administrative responsibilities.

"I don't really think things will be much different at home," I said. "More meetings, I suppose. And late nights now and then. I may bring home issues to talk with you about." I smiled and pointed a finger at him. "You're good to bounce things off of, you know. In fact, I've never known anyone with more common sense than you."

He laughed. "Not even close. You take my advice once in a blue moon, when you decide my common sense is better than your rational sense."

I laughed with him. "You know me too well."

"Apparently so." His face grew serious, and he looked down at the table. Then he looked up again, rather bashfully I thought. What was this? Rusty never looked bashful.

"I think maybe…I wouldn't mind being married after all," he said.

I sat stunned and speechless, blinking at him.

"I mean…I think I want to marry you," he said. He looked into my eyes and grinned.

I stared at him. He stared back.

"Will you?" he asked, leaning forward. "Do you want to marry me?"

I couldn't believe it. Talk about out of the blue! What's the word— gob-smacked? Elated? Stunned? Thrilled? Overjoyed? I couldn't find the right one.

Then doubt crept in. I smiled at him but leaned back in my chair and waved a forefinger at him. "You're just saying that because you've seen how happy Poker Dan and Pizza Bob are. Or maybe you're feeling guilty because you didn't get me a gift for Valentine's Day this year."

I remembered that day during lunch at Argonne when he'd confessed his attraction to me. That was shortly after Valentine's Day too. A whole year ago. It didn't seem that long.

But was this just a whim? Had he been thinking about marrying me for a while, or did the idea just come to him tonight? Would he regret his impulse? I searched his eyes and said, "Will you still want to marry me tomorrow?"

He smiled back. "Do you want me to wait until tomorrow and ask you again?"

A thrill passed down my back and hit the pit of my stomach. *This is really happening.* I took a slow breath to control my racing pulse and calm my elated thoughts, allowing peace and contentment to fill me. Then I grinned and leaned forward. "You can if you want. But meanwhile, of course I'd love to marry you. If you still want to tomorrow, that is."

He reached out and squeezed my hand. Then he motioned to the waiter and asked for coffee. The evening wasn't going to end yet.

We started making plans right away. He would keep the three-flat in Rogers Park but rent his apartment. Who knew how long he'd be consulting at Argonne, but it didn't make any difference. He could be sent anywhere, so we could live near my work—full-time. If he got transferred farther, to the East or West Coast, for instance…well, we'd figure it out when the time came. Together.

I knew there were a lot of changes in store for Rusty. He'd be giving up some of his attachments to independence and his life on the North Side. I hoped he realized marriage would bring him benefits he'd previously thought he could do without.

"Let's buy a house," he said. "Not to make money, just for you and me to live in. On a large lot so we can have a garden. I've never had one, but I always wanted to. You can't grow much of a garden on commercial property."

Chapter 29

THE NEXT MORNING, I RUSHED Rusty out of the house to tackle his routine Saturday chores in the city. As soon as he left, I poured a cup of coffee and sat down to dial Dottie Lou's number.

"Can you talk?" I asked, hoping her husband and kids were out of the room.

"For a little. The monsters are all playing relatively peacefully in the basement playroom, Betsy's content in her playpen for the moment, and Tom's working overtime again. What's up?"

"Oh, not much," I said. "Only I was wondering if you'd do me a favor?"

"Of course," she said. "Any time. I hope it's nothing serious." She sounded worried.

"Oh, it's serious," I said, pausing dramatically. "I wanted to know if you'd be willing to be my matron of honor again."

She screamed and I could hear what sounded like a hand slapping some hard surface. "Oh my God! He proposed! Or did you?"

I laughed. "It was him. Sort of. He said he'd been thinking that he wouldn't mind being married to me. But it was his idea—he brought it up and I didn't put any words in his mouth."

She laughed along with me. "I can't believe this. What did you say, besides yes?"

"I said if he still wanted to marry me in the morning, I'd accept."

"And he did?"

"Yes, he did."

More screaming and delighted laughter. "Well, if you didn't realize it already, I'm very happy for you. I won't have to keep thinking about you living all alone anymore. I mean, I know you aren't now, but this will be permanent. Do you have a ring?"

"Not yet. Too spur of the moment. We're going to go shopping for one, but there's no hurry. I don't think I want an engagement ring with a big stone. I'm thinking just a wide wedding band with some smaller diamonds in it. But you haven't answered my question. Will you be my matron of honor—again?"

"Of course I will. Don't we always stand up for each other?"

I giggled. "In many ways."

Chapter 30

AFTER I TOOK OVER AS manager of the Department of Writing and Editing at Argonne, I rarely went to Sami's. I was either too tired, rehearsing or singing, or just relaxing with a book. I had started keeping a journal, toying with the idea of writing a novel someday. I don't think Rusty took me seriously about my dreams of being an author. And, of course, there was a wedding to plan.

By March, we'd talked to a priest. I was raised Catholic and believed that being married meant having the blessing of the church, and to be married in the church we had to have our previous marriages annulled. Rusty really didn't care either way but wanted me to be happy. Therefore, we both began the annulment process. We couldn't make wedding plans until our annulments were granted.

Rusty's paperwork was easier than mine, because his first marriage hadn't taken place in the Catholic church. Mine, however, required meticulous answers to questions I had previously avoided answering, and gathering witnesses. It was a painful process, but one that turned out to be beneficial. Once I had to put into words the reasons to dissolve the marriage, I was more convinced than ever that I had done the right thing.

After the papers were mailed off, we had to wait for an unknown amount of time. There was no reason to stall housing, however, so we registered with a real estate agent and started looking at homes for sale in Lemont.

Although I tagged along with Rusty to Sami's so infrequently now, that didn't mean I didn't care for my old friends. I frequently asked Rusty for updates.

We had suspected that Pizza Bob would change the name of the place, maybe from Sami's Saloon to Bob's Bar.

"I'm not going to change it," Bob said, during one of my infrequent visits. "Sami had a good business until just before he sold it, and that's how the place is known. I don't want to confuse people or go through that "under new ownership" bullshit. The alliteration works better as Sami's Saloon than Bob's Bar anyway. More syllables to trip over the tongue."

I suspected the real reason was as a tribute to Sami. Bob and Sami had been friends. Sami had finished his cancer therapy, but there was a question of whether the disease had spread, and we suspected that Whitney, although she was still in Sami's life, wasn't very supportive. I didn't think Bob wanted to take the name of the bar away from Sami too.

Rusty told me that recently the Czacki brothers had started coming back to Sami's. Word on the street was that Logan had hired a shyster lawyer who had gotten him out on bail pending trial for vehicular manslaughter.

"After the accident, you'd think the last place they'd come would be Sami's," Rusty said. "But lately they've been coming in now and then. Could be they wore out their welcome other places...I don't know."

"Pizza Bob doesn't throw them out?"

"He can't, so long as they don't cause any trouble. Bartenders can't refuse service unless someone is underage, obviously intoxicated, rowdy, or harassing customers or staff. They've been behaving themselves."

"So instead, he has to watch for trouble whenever they come in. I bet Bob loves that," I said, shaking my head.

I was proud of Betts. He was sticking to a promise he'd made to himself to drink less and eat better. He hadn't gained any weight, but he hadn't been hospitalized again. He was always glad to see me when I came in, and glad to hear about how things in my life were going.

"Don't think I can sit through one of those longhair concerts of yours, no matter how good a' friends we are," he said, with his typical bark of laughter.

I laughed. "Rusty doesn't care for my music either. He prefers to volunteer as an usher, so he doesn't have to sit down and listen—or fall asleep."

"Ain't gonna do that either," Betts said. "Can you see me as an usher, in my only dress pants half fallin' off me?"

I couldn't unsee that once he said it.

John David was absent from Sami's for a few weeks after Lindsay's death, which I assumed he needed to deal with her loss. When he returned, he seemed even more odd than he had been before she died, when all he did was sit staring at the top of the bar and mumbling under his breath. People used to joke with him back then, but he'd never react, and they'd quit poking fun when they couldn't get a rise out of him. Now guys would come in and say, "Sorry 'bout Little Lindsay." His responses tended to be either inappropriate or off topic, and sometimes he acted as if he didn't even hear the person talking to him.

"John David must have been seriously torn up," I told Rusty. "I feel so sorry for him. I can't begin to imagine what he thinks about the Czacki brothers. Not only because of what happened to Lindsay, but they were responsible for that mess with his sister and her husband over that bar business."

"True. They screwed them over, literally. I'd forgotten that," Rusty said. "The thing is, of course, no one wants to make jokes about John David anymore after the tragedy."

A couple of months went by, busy and happy months full of hard work and joyful plans. I was looking forward to that "forever" move that people dream about, finally secure and content with the direction our lives were taking.

One night in early April Rusty came home and I asked as usual how our friends were doing. He told me John David was getting stranger and stranger.

"One night he walked in clutching this wooden box against his chest, as if protecting it. He set it on the bar and climbed on his regular stool and just sat there with one hand on top of the box. Pizza Bob came over and asked him if he'd put the box on the floor by his stool instead, but John David gave him a determined look and shook his head, so Bob let him be."

"What did it look like?" I asked.

"The box? Like nothing special, just the size and shape of a shoe box, but made out of unvarnished wood, with a couple of tiny rough holes drilled through it and a little key lock hanging from a latch. He brings it with him every time he comes in now—just sets it on the bar while he has his drinks. Of course, when anyone asks what's in it, he just shakes his head, turns away, and mumbles, 'Nuttin', like when people used to ask him about his ears. So we stopped asking after a while, realizing he was just John David being John David and he wasn't ever going to tell us about the box like he didn't about his ears."

"That's weird, though," I said.

"It is," said Rusty. "Even more weird, sometimes sounds come from the box."

I stared at him. "What kind of sounds?"

"Like thumps, or rustling noises. I can't tell if they're actually coming from inside the box or if he's making them himself—you know, with that hand he keeps on top of the box all the time? I've tried to catch him at it, but I'll be damned if I can see him move a twitch."

"Surely he needs to go to the bathroom or get up now and then. Doesn't anyone try to peek?"

Rusty shook his head. "Takes it with him. If anyone tries to touch it, he gives them a real nasty look and they back off. I'm sorry to say this, because I know you feel sorry for the guy, but he's getting nuttier and nuttier, and people are a little scared of him now, or at least a little spooked, maybe I should say."

"I am sorry. But to tell the truth, I got that feeling from the very beginning. I talked myself into trying to think well of John David because of Lindsay."

"Well, the poor guy has never hurt a soul. I still feel sorry for him," Rusty said.

Chapter 31

ONE NIGHT IN LATE APRIL, the weather finally warmed up and it was too beautiful to sit inside. Rusty's pool team, the Slot Shots, was scheduled to play the best team in the league, the Bank Bosses. It had been a while since I'd been out, so I decided to go along to watch Rusty play. We brought both of our cars so I could leave early if I didn't want to stay until the games were over. I doubted that would happen, though, as I really hoped Rusty would do well and I wanted to be there to congratulate him.

I sat with Betts, but I asked him to move from his usual place near the front door closer to the pool table so we could see the games. We passed John David near the middle of the bar as we moved to the back of the room. As Rusty had forewarned me, John David didn't look up to acknowledge us but sat staring down at the wooden box on the bar in front of him.

Rusty seemed nervous. I could see his jaw jumping like it did when he was intense. He tended to be highly competitive, which sometimes gave him a winning edge, but other times interfered with his skill at the table. I was worried about which way it would go tonight. His game was second to last, so of course he was hoping his teammates would take enough points before it was his turn to shoot.

I heard the front door open and Betts said, "Oh crap, excuse my language. I thought we were done with those guys."

I looked up to see the Czacki brothers. They were loud and jostling each other, the way they did when they were looking for what they called fun but everyone else knew as trouble. Looked like their tame spell was over.

Feeling nervous, I glanced at Pizza Bob. How was he going to handle them? His expression looked angry, but he said calmly, "Can I get you guys a Coke? On the house?"

"Fuck no," said Warner. "Give me a double scotch on the rocks, and the same for my brother here. None of that top shelf stuff, we're gonna be here a while."

"Damn straight," said Logan, poking Warner and giggling.

"I think you've had enough already," Pizza Bob said. "Why don't you guys take yourselves down the street?"

"Fuck you! We like it here, and we're staying. And don't get any fancy ideas about sending for the cops if you like that arm you got there," said Warner.

Pizza Bob hesitated. I was scared. This wasn't going well already. It wasn't likely that other patrons would want to get physically involved with the large, muscular Czacki brothers. Would Bob be able to control the situation? Would he back down and serve them?

Between where Betts and I sat and the front of the bar, I saw John David stand up next to his stool.

What the hell is he doing? I thought. Later, when what followed replayed over and over in my mind, I found it ironic that as John David got up the jukebox was playing the Eurythmics' "Sweet Dreams Are Made of This." The song and the scene were forever linked in my memory.

John David reached into a front pants pocket, pulled out a key, and unlocked his box. "Look here," he said to the man sitting next to him. John David's hands shook, his eyes shining with something that looked like excitement or joy. He pulled up the lid of the box about an inch so the man could peek inside. "Look what I got in here! It's my frog!"

The man, clearly surprised, didn't seem to know what to do. Instead of looking into the box he pulled back, but John David didn't stop.

John David had drawn the attention of other drinkers. He went to the next man, closer to the door, and said, "This is a very *special* frog! Look at him but be *very* careful not to *touch* him. I don't want you to *hurt* him."

That man peeked in the box. "It's a frog in there, all right," he said to the room, nodding and raising his eyebrows. People nearby had stopped their conversations to watch.

The Czacki brothers were staring at John David by then too. They knew him, of course, and John David was always fair game for their kind of jokes. They grinned and winked at each other.

John David kept moving down the bar, holding out the partly open box. "This is *my* frog. See him, but don't *touch* him—that's very important. In fact, don't even touch the *box*."

The bar patrons didn't have to be told not to touch—they had no wish whatsoever to do so. Most didn't seem like they even wanted to look at the thing. Some laughed weakly, at a loss for how to react. Some seemed surprised or curious. I certainly was. After weeks of the box being a secret, and John David who never talked to anyone, tonight he wasn't acting at all like John David…what the hell was he doing?

I felt Betts's elbow jab into my side. "Look at the Czacki brothers," he said in my ear. "Are they pissed! John David just stole the center of attention from them."

Logan walked up to John David. "Let *me* see that frog, if it's so special." He reached into the box and pulled something out before John David could stop him. Logan held up a little frog by one leg, pinched between thumb and forefinger, waving it in the air for everyone in the bar to see. It wasn't very impressive. Just a skinny little thing, about two inches long, struggling and jerking frantically. The only thing unusual about it was its bright yellow color.

John David was going crazy. "Don't! Don't! You mustn't! Put my frog back in the box!"

Instead, Logan wrapped his fist around the frog and squeezed.

Juicy reddish stuff came out between his fingers. Logan said, "That's what I think about your fuckin' frog!" He threw it on the floor and rubbed his dirty hand on his shirtsleeve.

Giggling, almost out of control, Warner slapped Logan on the back. Then he reached down and picked up what was left of the frog. "Aw, Logan, you shouldn't drop things on the floor like that. You got to pick it back up and put it in the box so this fuckin' idiot can see how nice you fixed his fuckin' frog." He wiped the remains of the frog off his hands on the edge of the box and then held it in front of John David's face and said, "Look at that. Isn't it a fuckin' improvement?"

At which point he threw the box on the floor and stomped on it, caving in the top. He and Logan continued laughing and carrying on.

I was shocked and disgusted. And speechless. I turned to see if Rusty had seen any of this. From the grim look on his face, he had. He walked over to stand next to me.

John David screamed, "No! Don't do that! You can't touch my frog!"

He picked up the largest piece that remained of the box and shouted, "Give me a rag, somebody give me a rag, quick. Don't step there! Give me a rag!" He grabbed Pizza Bob's bar towel, knelt beside his box, and frantically started wiping the floor.

Everyone in the bar was staring at John David, but I caught sight of Logan. He was weaving unsteadily, a look of panic on his face. He grabbed his chest, let out a startled cry, and slid toward the floor. Then Warner—the same thing—and they were both writhing on the floor, shaking and struggling for breath. John David was on the floor too, scrubbing furiously with the bar towel, at the same time holding it carefully, and yelling, "Call the paramedics! Get help, stay away! Poison, poison! Nobody touch anything! Oh, God! Nobody's supposed to touch it! Get help! Please! Get help!" And then he bent forward sobbing.

Chapter 32

PIZZA BOB PICKED UP A phone behind the bar. Holding the receiver between his head and shoulder, he yelled, "Everyone! Move outside and wait there. Watch where you step. I'm calling police and emergency. Don't go anywhere. I think the police will want to talk to everyone."

I thanked God it was Pizza Bob taking control. Sami would never have acted so quickly and smartly.

Those of us who had circled around the scene peeled away one by one, filing out as ordered, leaving Pizza Bob behind the bar as we passed John David blubbering, mumbling, and still scrubbing. The Czacki brothers gasped and writhed nearby. A man bent over and loosened both men's collars and then stepped back. No one seemed to have any idea how to help them. I joined Rusty and Betts outside the front door, and we stood shivering against the brisk cool evening breeze that had picked up. There were thirty or more of us milling around on the sidewalk under the glow of a nearby streetlight, waiting for the police to respond.

"What the hell happened in there?" complained one of the pool players I didn't know. "We didn't play our games yet!"

A man who had been sitting near the Czacki brothers said, "Two guys collapsed. Someone yelled something about poison. Could be there's a contamination issue. The bartender said to hang around in case the police want to talk to witnesses."

The same pool player said, "Well, I didn't witness anything! Are we going back in to finish our games?" I guessed he was the captain of the Bank Bosses.

"We'll just have to be patient and wait to find out," Rusty said.

Betts, standing at my elbow, said, "I looked at those two lugs as we were leaving. Warner was breathing real heavy and drooling on the floor. He didn't look good. And I don't think Logan was breathing."

"I didn't see anything either," another pool player said, rubbing his hand up and down his cue stick. "Why do I have to stay?"

"Aren't you curious?" another man asked.

If he wasn't curious, I sure the heck was! Why the hell did John David have a frog in a box? Why did he pick tonight, of all nights, to show it to people? He knew the Czacki brothers were in the place, looking for trouble. What happened to Logan and Warner? What was wrong with them and how bad off were they? And what was this talk about poison?

A police car, sirens blaring, screeched to a halt in the street. An officer jumped out as a second car arrived. We stepped back as the two police officers pushed hurriedly through us and entered the bar. Less than a minute later, an ambulance drew up. Two attendants, a man and a woman, got out and disappeared through the bar entrance, carrying large black cases.

A freight train roared by across the street, a mere forty feet from where we stood, the engineer laying on the horn, making conversation impossible for the ten minutes it took the railcars to pass. Shortly afterward, the paramedics came out, went to the ambulance, and rolled out a stretcher. Some five minutes later a third police car and a second ambulance arrived simultaneously. Apparently the first officers on the scene had radioed for backup. Two uniformed cops, one man and one woman, exited the police cruiser. Two male attendants got out of the ambulance. All responders disappeared into Sami's.

It seemed like an hour but was probably only a few minutes later when the paramedics wheeled out two stretchers. I recognized Logan on one of them. He wasn't moving. I saw Warner, strapped to the second, rolling from side to side, moaning and pulling violently against his restraints. The stretchers were loaded into the ambulances and they immediately pulled away, sirens screaming.

A policeman and a policewoman walked out, supporting John David between them. John David's head drooped forward. He mumbled, stumbling on unsteady legs. He pulled himself into the back seat of the cruiser. The policeman got behind the wheel, but the female police officer signaled him to wait and went back into Sami's. She returned wearing rubber gloves and carrying a plastic garbage bag with something small and heavy in it. I guessed this was John David's wooden box, maybe with the remains of his frog. She got into the passenger seat and the car pulled away, following the ambulance.

Pizza Bob came out with the other two policemen. "Sorry, folks," he said. "We're going to have to close for the night. But these policemen want to talk to you first if you witnessed what happened. The rest of you can go home after you give them your contact information."

"Shit," said one of the pool players, brandishing his pool cue, his face flushed and angry. "What about our games?"

"Call me about rescheduling," Pizza Bob said. "I'm sorry, but there's nothing that can be done tonight. The police have to conduct an investigation, and the place has to stay closed while it's evaluated for possible contamination. Shit happens."

"Yeah, right," Betts whispered in my ear. "Especially when the Czackis are around."

"Contamination! Are we exposed? What can you tell us?" called the captain of the Bank Bosses.

One of the officers stepped in front of Bob. "I'm Sergeant Stephen Talcott," he said. "We can't tell you much at this point. The gentleman who brought that box in here told us he had a frog in it that was from some place in South America. He said it secretes a very strong poison. He's being taken to the hospital to be checked out too, but he seems to be okay, just a little shaky. Of course, that frog, what's left of it, will be evidence and will be tested." He paused and rubbed his left ear.

"Meanwhile, we have to treat this as a hazardous materials

situation and call in people who know how to clean up the bar. Until then it will have to stay closed."

"Hazardous materials?" called one regular patron. "What kind of hazard are you talking about? Are we in danger? Should we go to the hospital too?"

Should we? I turned to Rusty, who frowned and shrugged.

Sergeant Talcott held up both hands. "Now, don't panic. If you didn't touch that frog or go near where it was, there's no reason to think you're at risk. That should be almost all of you. If you want to be checked, drive yourself over to the Palos Hospital emergency room and tell them what happened. They'll be handling the situation because that's where the victims were taken."

"Who's going to pay for that?" another patron called.

"Give them your insurance, and we'll straighten that out later. I'm sure Bob here has liability insurance if it comes to that." He looked toward Bob.

"Of course," Bob said, nodding.

"Now, if you didn't see anything, give Officer Porter Grant here your name, address, and phone number, and go on home or to the hospital, or wherever you want to go. The rest of you wait right here until I talk to you."

After Rusty, Betts, and I told Sergeant Talcott what we'd seen, I asked him if he believed John David's story. "I'm sure you've never had this happen before. John David has a reputation for being weird, and Pizza Bob probably told you he was acting even stranger than usual. Wouldn't you think his story about the poison frog was either made up or a delusion?"

"I would have..." Talcott said, rubbing his forehead with the fingers of one hand. "...except for the fact that we had two big, burly men on the floor for no apparent reason. Bob talked us into taking the gentleman seriously in case what he was saying was true. Bob is well known around here—has a reputation for good common sense. We thought it would be risky not to give the story some consideration until we could prove otherwise."

He had a point. Far-fetched as the whole situation seemed, the Czacki brothers had clearly suffered some sort of trauma, yet no one had touched them. They had, however, both touched John David's frog. Or...maybe the frog had nothing to do with their collapse, and something had happened before they came to Sami's. I wanted to believe that.

"What a night!" I said to Rusty as he drove home. "I wonder if they're going to be all right."

"At least John David walked out on his own."

"Thankfully. But the officers and paramedics did a good job, didn't they? Quick, professional, competent. You hear so many complaints about our responders these days. Based on tonight, I'd say they've been getting a bad rap. I have nothing but praise for how they handled the situation."

"True" Rusty said, "but I still can't fathom what happened. We may never know."

But I *had* to know...to make sense of it and satisfy my insatiable curiosity. I'd find out somehow.

Chapter 33

SAMI'S WAS CLOSED FOR A full week while a hazardous materials clean-up was performed. When the bar was declared safe once again and reopened, Rusty and I both went to see Pizza Bob for an update. The bar was full, but when Bob saw us, he signaled to his relief bartender that he was going to step away and motioned us to a side table. As we waited for him to join us, I hummed along to the jukebox: "Billie Jean" by Michael Jackson.

"Everything's good here now," Pizza Bob said, sitting across from Rusty and me. "We had to wait a couple of days for the clean-up company to fit us in, then after the job was done, there was a scheduled wait period, and a retest."

"So the frog *was* poisonous, as John David claimed," Rusty said.

Pizza Bob rubbed his forehead with both hands. "Apparently. The police brought the remains of the frog to the hospital so the medical people could see what they were dealing with. Presumably they acted on the assumption it was poisonous, because they called poison control. I understand the police got the frog back and sent it to the state lab, but as far as I know there's no result yet."

"Who told you the story this time?" Rusty asked.

"I talked to both Sergeant Talcott and Meghan's ER nurse friend, Roberta Bossert. She's the one who told us about Little Lindsay. Roberta wasn't on call that night, but of course the staff talks among themselves, and the night supervisor told her. A lot of odd things happen in ERs, but this one took the cake, so they talked about it for days. Roberta passed the details along to Meghan, who told me."

"How did everyone make out?" I asked. So much for privacy in an ER, I thought. Someday they'd have to do something about that.

Bob shook his head. "Not well. None of them. Logan and Warner won't be bothering us anymore. They made it to the hospital, but it wasn't long before they both went into cardiac arrest. The doctors couldn't revive either one."

I was stunned. I had expected them to be treated and released after a short stay. Watching too many medical shows on TV, I supposed.

"None of them, you said? What about John David? Did he make it? Did the police blame him? Did he get arrested?"

"When they left here with him in the police car, Talcott said the intent was to get him checked in the ER, to be sure both he and the frog were available for whatever information they could provide, and then bring him in later for questioning. I don't think they knew whether or not they were going to charge him with anything. It was all preliminary at that stage."

"But…?" Rusty said.

"But when John David was examined, he was found to have some neurological problems. Despite all they could do, even following suggestions from poison control, nothing helped. He developed temporary paralysis, and by the time he eventually came out of that, they found he had suffered some nerve and organ damage that wasn't reversible. He's lost some of his memory, and he has mild dementia and seizures, which the doctors say may or may not improve. He's still at Palos, but Meghan says he's going to be transferred to Hines soon for the VA to take care of him—probably permanently."

Rusty shook his head slowly, his lips compressed. "That's terrible," he said. "He should have been checking into the VA all along, for his depression or whatever mental diagnosis he had since he was discharged from the Army after Vietnam. I guess he didn't want to do that. But now…well, the VA can take care of him. Even housing if he needs it. Sounds unlikely he'll ever be able to live independently again."

Bob pressed his lips together and nodded.

I saw Rusty's point. I was glad the VA was there for John David, knowing how hard it would be for his sister to help. But my gut told me he'd rather be living by himself.

"Oh, and guess what?" Bob went on. "That rumor about John David's ears? They had to remove his hat in the ER, and it turns out the rumor is true. His ears were cut off. Of course, we still don't know the hows and whys of that."

I took a sip of my drink and thought through all I'd heard.

"So what do you think really happened here?" I asked then. "Do the police think this was a freak accident? I'm sure someone told them about John David's past history with the Czackis, his sister and brother-in-law, and Little Lindsay. Didn't they think he might have made this happen somehow?"

"Sergeant Talcott has been in a few times during the week to follow up. The detectives have the investigation, but from what he told me, I don't think John David's free and clear on the criminal end—after all, two guys died. But Talcott says it's going to be a hard case to prove. For one thing, John David never touched them. He even warned them not to touch the frog. It was their own meanness that did them in."

"True," I said. "I mean, if I came into the bar with a gun, and they grabbed it away from me and shot themselves with it, would that be my fault?"

"I guess it would depend on whether or not you had the gun legally," Pizza Bob said, chuckling. "I doubt there are any laws on the books about poison frogs. Anyway, Talcott said they could charge him with reckless conduct for bringing a poisonous frog into the bar, but that carries a relatively minor penalty like one to three years' incarceration. Under the circumstances, he's not even fit for trial, so why bother? I could be wrong, but I doubt they'll charge him. He's still in the hospital anyways."

"What's the talk in the bar about it?" Rusty asked.

"Pretty much everyone thinks it was a weird accident. No one seems to think John David was smart enough to plan something like this. Even though he had motive, even if he brought the frog in on purpose, how could he know both brothers would grab it? Or even be there?" Bob said.

"Maybe if they didn't grab it on their own, he had a plan to get them to touch it, rub it on them or something like that," I said.

"Well, from what I heard, by the time they got John David to the hospital he was in pretty sad shape himself and didn't seem able to tell a coherent story. I doubt we'll ever know."

Rusty leaned his elbows on the bar. "So the police only had what John David told them at first, and what witnesses saw. They couldn't talk to the Czackis nor to John David after they got to the ER. And he was such a loner, there was no one to say what was going on in his head, and of course, he couldn't—or wouldn't."

"That's about it," Bob said. "A lot of people saw what happened. They heard John David tell everyone not to touch the frog. They saw him try to keep the Czackis from grabbing it. He tried to clean up and warn everyone. And no one thinks he's smart enough to put together a complex plan like this. But everyone's asking the same questions. I suppose the police are too."

"Could John David be faking it now?" I asked.

Rusty and Pizza Bob exchanged glances and shrugged.

"Was anyone else hurt?" Rusty asked.

Bob shook his head. "No one else touched anything. No one reported any symptoms. Of course, this place took a hit while we were closed, and my insurance is probably going to go through the roof." He shrugged again. "You have to expect ups and downs if you're in business. But already the word is out that Sami's is safe again, and people are flocking in. In fact, I have even more customers than usual. Everyone wants to tell their story and point out where it happened." He laughed. "The ghouls are coming out."

"Do you have any idea where John David got the frog?" I asked.

"He told the police about that while he was still here that night. Said he was using a computer at the library and found someone in

South America that was willing to ship the frog to him for a price. I doubt he was telling the truth. I never realized he knew how to use a computer, or if something like that is even possible."

But I *did* know he spent lots of time on the library computer. Whether or not he could find such information, and a willing seller, I couldn't know. Technology was developing more and more each day, but this was beyond what most people, including me, were using their computers for. I worked at the right place though. I'd bet someone at Argonne could tell me.

I rubbed my chin. It seemed to me that John David must have been up to something. Why would he even bring the frog to the bar? Why would he wait until the Czackis came in to disclose what was in the box? His actions indicated some element of intent.

"Do you think the deaths were accidental?" I asked. "Do *you* think John David killed the Czackis intentionally?"

Bob shook his head. "Don't see how. Seems pretty far-fetched to me. But then again, the whole damn business is so weird, I don't know what to think."

I wasn't done yet. "I don't know either," I said, "but somehow I'm going to find out."

Chapter 34

I COULDN'T LET MATTERS REST. After what I'd seen with my own eyes and what Pizza Bob told us, I had to know more. John David said he found the frog using a computer. I was in the right place to investigate. Throughout its history, Argonne competed with other scientific research centers in developing one of the most powerful, if not *the* most powerful, computers in the world. With that in mind, I turned to a friend at Argonne to help get answers to my questions. If anyone knew what could be done using computers, Hermes Peiffer was the guy. A week later, working together, I finally satisfied my curiosity and made some conclusions.

The day I spent with Hermes was quite revealing. I could hardly wait to tell Rusty what we'd found out. But Rusty had called to let me know he wouldn't be home until seven in the evening.

Of all nights to be late!

I wandered through the apartment, straightening things that didn't need straightening, picking up papers on my desk and putting them down again unread. I put a frozen pizza in the oven at six forty-five so it would be ready when Rusty got home.

"Sorry I'm so late," he said when he finally arrived twenty minutes after seven, hanging his keys and topcoat on hooks inside our apartment door. "The management team couldn't agree on anything and the meeting went on forever. I'm beat." He dropped a kiss on my forehead, then looked at the plates I'd set on the kitchen table. "Aren't we going to eat in front of the TV?" he asked.

I shook my head. "No TV. I want to talk."

He knit his brows.

I laughed. "There's no problem. Just want to tell you what I found out today about John David and his frog."

He looked away and sighed. "Okay—just let me change out of my suit first."

I waited impatiently, listening to the bumps and rustling from the bedroom, then the sound of the bathroom door closing, and soon afterward the toilet flushing. *Why is he taking so long?*

He strode into the room at last, looking fresher than when he'd arrived. He picked up his plate, grabbed two pieces of overcooked pizza, scooped some salad into a bowl, and finally joined me at the table, where I was sitting with my own plate of food. He looked up and raised his eyebrows. He was trying to humor me. I appreciated that. I knew he'd change his attitude once I started telling him all I'd learned.

"So, what did you find out? Did you talk to Pizza Bob today? Did he have more information?" he said, through a mouthful of salad.

"Not Pizza Bob. I did some detective work from my office. You know I use the internet from time to time from my desk, double-checking data while editing some of our papers. But I don't know much about what other activities people may be doing on computers from home—or at the library." I gave him a significant look.

"You're referring to John David at the Lemont Library?"

"That's right. So, you know Hermes Peiffer, Director of the Department of Computer Sciences at Argonne?"

"Sure. He's got his finger in everything. I run across him every now and then."

"Our departments have a lot of contact, so I know him pretty well. I went to him to find out what's happening in the world of private computers—figured he'd be playing around at home, not just at work. And I was right."

Rusty swallowed, wiped his mouth with a napkin. "What did he tell you?"

"Hermes said before long people will be doing their shopping using computers. We won't have to go to stores at all—everything will come to us."

"I thought maybe he'd be sick of computers after working on them all day, but go ahead. What did he tell you about John David?"

"Well, he brought me to his computer and showed me. It's pretty amazing. You'd be surprised how easy it is to find information on the internet. Hermes said someday everyone will have home computers. We should think about getting a computer and modem, Rusty. I'm not sure what exactly we'd do with them, but we'll see. Should be fun."

Rusty picked up a wedge of sausage and mushroom pizza and took a bite from the pointed end. "Something to think about," he said after he swallowed. "As if we don't have enough right now…work, the wedding, shopping for a house…."

"Well, later. Anyway, the beauty of it is that when you want to locate something, the computer does the work. You just type in what you want to know and before long up pops a screen listing a bunch of things to read. You click on them and there's the information you asked for. And fast! Some pages come up in only a couple of minutes. Better than sitting for hours at the library, searching card catalogs and shelves for books, taking notes, and lugging a bunch of books home with you. It's as easy as watching television. Some of the links we tried did take a while to download the information, and Argonne uses the fastest modem available. But I bet this will get faster with time."

Rusty set down the remaining half of his pizza slice and followed it with a few swallows of wine. "So, your idea about John David?"

"Yeah, well…using the computer at the library—we know John David spent a lot of time there. It would have been just as easy for him to find out about frogs as it was for me today."

"You found out about frogs, then? With Hermes? He had time for your questions?"

"Are you kidding? Once I told him what happened at Sami's and what I was looking for, he was like a dog with a bone. He loved showing off what his computer could do—I couldn't have stopped him if I tried. But of course, I didn't try." I chuckled.

"Glad you found him with time on his hands. That's rare."

"I think he was just having fun putting the pieces together. You know how intense these computer guys can get." I grinned. "Hermes is like me. Suffers from FOMO."

"FOMO?"

"Fear of missing out."

"You got that right." Rusty glanced at my plate and pointed. "You haven't touched your food. It's getting cold."

I stared at my plate. I wasn't thinking about food. Even so, I liked cold pizza anyway. I took a bite to humor Rusty.

"So you two found John David's frog? Go on," he said.

I swallowed and washed it down with a sip of wine. "Well, we found quite a bit. Enough to make what happened believable, anyway."

Rusty raised his eyebrows. "Really? Like what?"

"There's this frog from Colombia. The golden poison dart frog. There are other poison dart frogs in other parts of the world. The name comes from the fact that natives used the venom from these frogs to make darts to use as weapons. Pretty much everyone has heard about poison darts, but most people probably don't know where some of the poisons come from. The Colombian one, the golden poison dart frog, is the one that seems to fit John David's frog. Its scientific name is Phyllobates terribilis." I laughed. "I doubt I'm pronouncing that right. Anyway, *this* frog makes a poison called batrachotoxin, a deadly neurotoxin."

"So you think John David's frog, the one you saw Logan squeeze, was a golden poison dart frog?"

I held up and shook a forefinger to make my point. "It fits the description perfectly—about two to three inches long, slender, and a bright yellow color."

"And deadly, you say."

"And deadly. I'm not sure how reliable information on the internet is, but if what we read is true, this particular frog's poison is twenty times more toxic than other poison dart frogs. An amount equivalent to only two or three grains of salt is enough to kill a human."

"How did these natives get the poison on their darts then, without killing themselves in the process?"

"They found the frogs on the jungle floor and pierced them with a stick. They never touched the frog itself. They held it on the stick over an open fire and the heat would make the poison collect in little blisters. Then they rubbed their blow darts against the frog's blistered skin to coat the tips. Voila! Ultimate Human Weapon Number One! Supposedly, the poison stayed effective for a year."

"Pretty smart, those guys. Glad they don't live around here. Them or their frogs." He sat for a moment thoughtfully. "Makes you think twice about touching public door handles, or gym equipment, doesn't it?"

I chuckled. "I for one will never be casual about that again."

Rusty laughed, then sobered. "But why would the poison kill Logan and Warner right away, when John David had a delayed reaction, paralysis, and he lived? Shouldn't it have killed all three of them right off?"

"Hermes and I talked about that. We thought it might be due to the way the poison acts. It collects in the skin of the frog and is released when the frog is threatened in some way. The immediate effect is neuromuscular—tingling, followed by difficulty swallowing and breathing, drooling, and then very quickly muscle paralysis, particularly the cardiac muscles, leading to cardiac arrest. The onset can be pretty rapid, almost immediate, or it can take a couple of hours. There really isn't any treatment, except to try to treat the symptoms." I shook a finger again to emphasize. "This is a really wicked poison, but it can't permeate skin. If there's a cut or abrasion, however, you're a goner before you have time to say, 'Oops that frog is poisonous'—at least in the case of p. terribilis!"

"So you think the poison killed Logan and Warner right away because they had cuts on their hands, but John David didn't, and got a lighter dose?"

"Something like that. Hermes thought the Czackis could also have had an allergy that made them react so strongly to the toxin, being brothers and all. Whereas John David didn't have an allergy, or cuts on his hands, and knew how to handle the frog carefully."

"Okay, so how could John David be sure the Czacki brothers had cuts on their hands?"

"Logan and Warner worked in construction. I remember hearing them talk about doing demolition work. I'm sure they handled a lot of things that cut and scraped their hands, and they probably banged them a lot too. Guys who do the same jobs for a long time wear gloves, learn to minimize the beating their hands take. But Logan and Warner moved from job to job a lot, probably weren't good about protecting their hands. They were macho guys anyway, probably thought gloves were sissy stuff—real men don't wear gloves. And it's spring, right? A lot of cleanup going on. Moving bricks or stone, or breaking up concrete slabs, stacking the pieces. That would be something they would generally do, and that's pretty abrasive. What do you think their hands were like?"

"Point," he conceded.

"And, contrary to some people's opinion, John David was *not* dumb. He sat at that bar all day, looking down, not talking, but I bet you anything he was listening. And watching. People didn't notice him much once they were used to him, but really, he noticed a lot from that position. I bet he didn't miss much. He probably knew everything about everybody and remembered every word that was said. And if the Czackis came anywhere near him, I bet he saw their hands. He didn't start bringing the box in until he figured they were working and had cuts and rough raw skin on their hands. And he was ready when the right time came up eventually."

Rusty looked doubtful. "Well, okay, so that could be how the frog killed them. Admittedly we know he had it, but how did John David *get* the frog? He wouldn't have found one at Ordman's, Sears, or Goldblatt's. And he doesn't have a car. Did you figure that out on the internet too?"

I grinned. "Actually, we did. Ever hear of CompuServe?"

"No."

"If you access CompuServe on your computer, you'll find news articles, data, and something called 'chat rooms.' Hermes said the CompuServe Company realized that people who are really into computers want to interact with other people on them—it's a fad that's really growing. There are these forums you can check into where people talk to each other by typing into their computers. You can find just about any topic you're interested in to chat about, all over the internet. And all over the world."

"So he found someone through a chat room to send him a frog? Wouldn't that have been hard to do?"

"I imagine it *was* hard. But John David didn't do much else, did he? When he wasn't at Sami's, he had all the time in the world. He could have started out checking into chats about terrariums, saltwater fish, people who like lizards, snakes, amphibians, exotic animals. Eventually he could have found someone in Colombia, got that person's email address, and communicated with him from there."

Rusty pushed his plate away and leaned back in his chair. "So, once he found someone who was willing to send him a frog—for a price, I presume it wouldn't have been cheap—how did the seller or the buyer handle the thing without coming into contact with the poison?"

"That occurred to us too. But apparently the frogs only make the poison if they're in their natural habitat. If born in captivity, they aren't poisonous."

"And I'm sure you found out why that is?"

I grinned again. "We did!" I pushed my cold pizza away too but took a long swig of wine. "Scientists think the frogs eat a species of ant that only lives in their natural environment, and having that ant as part of their diet is required for them to make the poison. In captivity they don't have access to that specific ant. So dealers can offer captivity-born frogs, since they are perfectly safe."

"So how does that explain how John David got the poison version of the frog?"

"It doesn't. We can only guess."

"Right. And your guess is?"

"We think he spent a lot of time on research. We think he researched not only the frogs, but also the ants, and somehow, he found a way to get the right ants to feed to a captivity-born frog. Maybe he just got lucky, tried something that made sense to him and it worked. Or maybe the seller found a way to get a wild-born frog, which could retain its poison for years, of course. But we thought it more likely the same person got him the ants and he fed them to the frog."

Rusty frowned and shook his head. "Isn't this pretty convoluted? You really think John David was smart enough to do this?"

"People only *thought* John David was simple. Lindsay, who knew him best, said he was only very shy and didn't know how to act around people. Do you remember how obsessed he was with Lindsay? People who can be that obsessed certainly have increased levels of determination and abilities we can only guess at. When obsessive love turns to obsessive hate, God only knows." I paused and searched his eyes. "It could happen."

Rusty appeared skeptical. "Well, he certainly had motive. He could have done it, I suppose. But where'd he get an idea like that? He was always strange, and that lends itself to crazy ideas, but a poison frog? Aren't there easier ways to get revenge?" He paused. "I wonder…John David spent time in the jungles in Vietnam, didn't he? I wonder if he heard about poison frogs there."

"Bingo!" I said, slapping my palm on the table. "Hermes and I thought it would have something to do with Vietnam too."

"But John David never talked about Vietnam. So you're only guessing."

I held up two thumbs. "Guessing, but with some credible information to guide our opinions. Hermes deals with a lot of government contacts, and he called a friend to look up John David's service record. Guess what?" I leaned back, wrapped my arms across my chest, and grinned. "John David was a tunnel rat."

I didn't see light dawn in Rusty's eyes like I'd expected. "You were in Vietnam too—you must know about tunnel rats."

Rusty had finished eating. "Look," he said. "If you're not going to eat anymore, let's move to the living room to finish this conversation. I promise I won't turn the television on until we're done."

I agreed and we moved, Rusty to his recliner and me to a corner of the sofa nearby, where I stretched out my legs, facing him. We both held glasses of wine to sip while talking.

"So," Rusty said. "Tunnel rats. I don't know as much as you might expect because they just discovered tunnels near Saigon while I was stationed there. We knew the Viet Cong had secret operations in the tunnels. The army was asking for volunteers to train as specialists to retrieve intelligence or supplies, take prisoners, and destroy the tunnels—that sort of thing. I was asked because I'm on the short side—five feet seven inches. They wanted small men because the tunnels were short and narrow, only two feet by three feet for the most part. But I was a little too big—five-foot five inches or less is what they wanted. Even if I'd been the right size, going into tunnels wasn't my thing. I wasn't that brave, and I'd have had to re-up because my tour would have ended by the time I finished training."

Rusty was looking away as he said this. Since he so rarely talked about Vietnam, I had very little idea of his experiences there, but my excitement over the day's research adventures faded amid a surge of gratitude that he'd returned. If he had any emotional battle scars, he hid them well.

"I didn't know any of this," I said softly. I wished I was close enough to hug him, but we were both comfortable and still had a lot to talk about. We sipped our wine, both thinking for a few moments.

I sighed. "Well, we found out a lot about Vietnam tunnel warfare this afternoon. I'm glad you didn't train for it, because it was really dangerous. With the tunnels so narrow, only one man could pass at a time, and they kept twisting and changing levels so you couldn't see if there was an ambush ahead. Not only could you run into armed Viet Cong, but the tunnels were filled with booby traps. Things like poison gas traps, punji stakes tipped with poison, even venomous snakes tethered in the tunnels. Everything a man touched could mean his death—every inch through that dark labyrinth could mark a soldier's last breath."

Unbidden, my mind formed an image of myself in such a tunnel. I shuddered and winced, closing my eyes as if in pain.

"What's wrong?" Rusty said, alarmed.

I opened my eyes and the image went away. "Just *thinking* about what it would be like, I almost had a panic attack."

"And this is what John David did? No wonder he's scarred."

"Yes. Who knows what horrors he saw."

"But how does this relate to poison frogs? Did they have those in the tunnels too?"

"Not that we could document. There was some anecdotal stuff hinting that the punji sticks could have been tipped with neurotoxins, but as far as we could tell, poison frogs are only in South American rainforests. We did think John David's training would have included learning about poisons and toxins, in order to avoid traps in the tunnel. Or maybe he came across somebody in Nam that used other poisons found in the jungle, and that's where he got the idea."

"Some spooky little old guy in a dirty little shop down a dark mysterious alley in downtown Saigon, something like that? Okay, I'll give you it's possible John David could have come up with the idea, and maybe even found a way to get the frog and feed it, although that's a stretch. You think he wanted revenge against the Czacki brothers, for killing Lindsay and ruining the lives of his sister and brother-in-law?"

"Yeah…something like that…maybe he just started looking into poisons out of interest, because of his experiences in Nam, and the idea popped into his head. Eventually he found what he was looking for in Colombia. He may not have meant to kill them to begin with, just started toying with the idea, eventually wanted to see how far he could go, whether he could make it happen. You can't deny he probably wanted them punished in some way. And it came together over time just like he envisioned."

"You really think John David thought this all through, planned it, and pulled it off?"

I nodded. "That's what I think, yes. I thought at first that he just wanted to make them pay and his plan turned out to work much better than he ever intended. But from the first time I met him, I sensed a sharp but disturbed mind. The more I thought about it, the more convinced I became that he planned their murder. And paid a price himself in the process."

"It would have been brilliant of him to do them in using their own meanness to pull the trigger, so to speak," Rusty said.

"Quite brilliant, yes," I said. "Part of the beauty of the whole plan is its sneakiness. The Czackis never saw it coming. They had no reason to believe they had an enemy in John David. Unlikely they ever knew the innocent, strange little guy was in love with Lindsay, and the brother of one of their victims. If they had known, they'd have laughed about it because they never took him seriously. They barely knew he existed, except as an object of their warped sense of humor."

"If he knew this frog was so dangerous, why didn't he protect himself better, use rubber gloves or something?"

"I haven't got a clue. Maybe he thought wearing gloves would tip them off. Maybe he just screwed up. Maybe, as I said, he didn't think it would go that far. Maybe he just didn't care—didn't think he had much to live for. I just don't know."

Rusty said thoughtfully, "I still question the idea of this being planned. If John David really wanted to get back at the Czackis, it seems like there would have been a simpler, less bizarre way to go about it. Why would he go through all this complex set-up?"

"You have to admire his craftiness. He was a meek little guy up against two mean-minded brutes. How and where would he approach them, if not at Sami's? His plan made sure everyone else in the bar stayed safe at the same time that he gave himself an alibi by warning everybody not to touch the frog. He would know the Czackis would do the opposite. As for how he got the idea, that's back to guesswork, like I said. Maybe he got interested in frogs in the jungle, had been thinking about getting one for other reasons, and the plan just fit. Maybe it's a product of the way his mind works. Only thing I'm saying is, he *could* have. And I have a feeling he did."

"Murder by frog. Who'd have thunk it? Well, far-fetched as it may seem, I don't have a better explanation," Rusty said. "It happened, after all, didn't it?"

"It did. What's the talk around the bar? Does anyone there think John David planned this?"

"I think Pizza Bob and Betts suspect it. They won't share that opinion with the police, though, or even other people at the bar. First of all, there's no proof, and secondly, they'd both defend John David over the Czackis any day of the week. As for others, well, all the people who knew John David seem to think it was just an unfortunate accident."

Rusty raised his recliner and picked up the remote control but then sat staring at a wall with it in his hand. After a moment, he asked, "Was there anything in those records that mentioned John David's ears?"

I slapped a hand on the arm of the couch. "I forgot to tell you that part. Not directly. He had been getting frequent commendations for bravery and accomplishments as a result of his work in the tunnels. Then suddenly, after a short stay in a field infirmary, he was transferred to a desk job. Part of that record was classified. But, partly based on stories we heard at Sami's and partly because of our research, Hermes and I had the same idea."

"And that is?"

"There were only about a hundred tunnel rats, and due to the extreme danger they encountered as a way of life, they developed a special code that ensured that no rat, wounded or dead, was ever left behind in a tunnel. Hermes and I thought that if John David had to leave another rat behind, regardless of whether or not any other action was possible, the other rats may have turned on him."

"And cut off his ears?"

"Maybe."

"And that's why he finished his service at a desk? And that part of the record was sealed?"

"Right. This is all speculation, remember."

"That's no harder to believe than the rest of your theories."

Rusty picked up our empty wine glasses and brought them to the kitchen. "Maybe I need to try out this internet stuff. Could be the greatest thing since remote control."

I sucked in my cheeks and turned my head so Rusty wouldn't see my grin. I couldn't pry the remote from his hand unless he fell asleep. This from the guy who thought when remotes first came out they were the height of laziness.

"But there's something wrong about this internet too," he went on. "Inviting all this technology into our homes? Isn't that going to threaten our privacy? What about Big Brother? It's almost 1984, isn't it? And if we're buying stuff using our computer, is our money going to be safe? I don't know. Some people might see this as an opportunity to take advantage of innocents like us."

I got up too, and after piling dishes in the sink, we grabbed a few cookies each and settled back in the living room. This time Rusty sat on the sofa near me instead of on his recliner. We sat thinking for a while. Finally, he said, "Not many of our friends from Sami's are left, are they?"

"That hurts," I said. Paused. "Hurts a lot."

After another minute, I said, "Sami made it all possible for us, I guess, because without his place we wouldn't have known each other. But he was always so about himself, you never felt like he was your friend, more like he was out to get as much as he could from you. Pleasant enough, but it was all banter, not like he really cared about us. A one-way friendship, you could call it. I'm sorry he's not around anymore, but you could kind of see he would end up the way he did, sort of a self-destruct thing. I hope he survives his cancer, though."

"You don't seem as upset about Sami or even Lindsay as you were about Dixon," Rusty said.

"Probably not. Lindsay…I don't know…there was always a sort of hopelessness about her, a feeling of here today, gone tomorrow. Maybe that had a lot to do with why it was so hard to get close to her. And of course I *wasn't* close to her. She was a friend, but not an intimate. Anyway, there wasn't any feeling of permanence, of her being in my life for a long time. I don't think too much about her, sad to say, but when I do I miss her."

I felt my eyes burn with unshed tears and swallowed painfully. "Dixon, on the other hand, I thought he would always be there, just my buddy Dixon, and we'd always be friends. Even after I stopped seeing him as often, after I started working at Argonne and dating you, I thought he'd be there any time I wanted. I'd just drive over and there he'd be with his gentle smile and his worn-down cowboy boots. We'd just pick up, like I'd never left, like I do with Dottie Lou. I miss him tremendously."

Rusty gave me a quiet smile. "Should I be jealous?"

"Oh, God, no! There's nothing for you to be jealous about. There was never the slightest attraction between Dixon and me. We were just the best friends that could ever be. That's pretty rare." I checked my pocket for my hankie, but it was empty so I wiped my face with the back of my hand and closed my eyes for a moment. "Poor self-sacrificing Dixon. What a sweet guy he was."

"You're not still blaming yourself for him, are you?" Rusty asked.

"No," I said. Then, "Not much. Maybe a little. His death just hit me right between the eyes, you know? I never expected it, and I felt so bad for not staying in touch. I could have found a way, made time. We depended on each other that year. He helped me so much and I helped him, and then I found you, and my job, and made my own life and never gave a thought to whether maybe he still needed me. I should have made an effort to see him more, acted like the friend I claimed to be. Too late now. I regret that."

"And now there's John David."

"Yes, and now there's John David. One can't help but think of him as an innocent somehow, even if he *did* do everything I said. It's sad to have him end up locked in body and mind the way he is now. Poor guy—never seemed to fit in anywhere his whole life."

Rusty allowed me a moment of silence. I was surprised he hadn't turned on the television yet. Then he asked quietly, "Want to share any more thoughts?"

"It's all so sad," I said. "Not only Dixon and John David but all these people who were my friends. So many endings...so many *sad* endings! I didn't think my friends were sad when I was with them, of course, but now I can't help but wonder. Most everyone seemed to live pretty lonely lives when they weren't at Sami's, which is why they went there, to avoid their loneliness. I was lonely then too. But there was more to it than that. They had something missing, and they found that thing at Sami's, or at least reason to deny for a time that anything *was* missing.

"So the question is, did they come to a sad end because they never found what they were looking for, and gave up on life? Did they go to Sami's to begin with because they thought the place was a solution to their problems? Or did going there ultimately *cause* their problems, and their sad end? And then I have to ask myself, why did I go there, really? How deep is that!"

"It's not all sad," Rusty said, smiling. "You and I met there."

I smiled too. "How fortunate we are, you and me. We've moved on. Thinking about them hurts, but I'm thankful that time is over. I'm well out of it, I think."

I paused again. Sami's had given me the strength to find my new life. I didn't have to go there anymore. I had everything now that I wanted or needed.

"You can continue your pool leagues if you like," I said. "But I won't go back there again—to Sami's. There's nothing there for me now, and it would be too painful. Keep an eye on Betts and say hello to Pizza Bob for me. This last thing with John David, I wish I hadn't been there to see that. I would rather have remembered the place the way it was."

"Do you mind if I turn the TV on?" Rusty asked, holding up the remote.

I slid over, leaned against him, and pulled my feet up on the sofa. "Not at all, hon."

Author Note - Smokey Row

Lemont was not always the semi-isolated, quiet suburb it is now. Before 1900 the town was notorious throughout Chicagoland for its sin strip, Smokey Row. Just a short ride down the I & M Canal from Chicago was an abundance of places for gambling, liquor, and loose women, not to mention the entertainment of bar fights and even organized illegal prizefights.

As early as the 1860s, a small area on the northeast side of the canal that ran through Lemont to Chicago served men who worked on barges, quarries, and railroads. Most of these men were single and poorly paid. Their work was hard and their hours long. In the little free time they had, they sought out dives near the canal where gambling, liquor, women, and other entertainments were available. The name Smokey Row probably originated from the presence of African American entertainers as early as the 1870s.

Lemont was an inland port for commerce between Chicago and the Mississippi River. It was a tough, violent place, where assault and even murder were commonplace. The village had no police until 1873.

Smokey Row and the honest citizens of Lemont co-existed side by side for years until the early 1890s, when the beginning of construction on the Sanitary and Ship Canal brought a huge temporary work force of primarily single men to the area. Following "Shovel Day" in 1892, Lemont's population went from 5,800 to almost ten thousand over a period of two to three years. These canal workers were a mixture of hardworking, honest Americans and immigrant labor, plus the rowdy, nameless drifters such projects attract. Economic times were hard and laborers in town—canal, quarry, rail, and barge workers— sought ways to spend their money.

At the close of Chicago's 1893 Columbian Exhibition, an economic depression faced the nation. Lemont, due to the canal construction, was one of the few places in the area that offered jobs and a favorable economy. Therefore, after the fair, seedy businesses and those who patronized them brought Chicago's sin strip to Lemont, where Smokey Row was already going strong. The result was an enormous expansion of Smokey Row. By 1895, it was estimated that over a hundred "dives" were in operation.

From the *Joliet News*, June, 1895:

"...The saloons and dives are doing an immense business and probably 60 percent of the $600,000 [canal payroll] paid each month goes into their hands...Most of the good folk of the town lock their doors at night and pull the covers over their heads. Some few rake in the money."

The town was wide open. Canal Street was said to be one of the toughest streets in all of America, wilder and more sinful than Dodge City, Deadwood, and Tombstone combined. It had the flavor of a port town, with a red-light district and men speaking various languages, refugees from all over America and the world.

Most of the saloons were "buckets of blood," where men could not, and bartenders did not, control their drinking. Many men came to such taverns with the intent of engaging in or watching fights, an additional entertainment. For gamblers, action could be found twenty-four hours a day: cards, dice games, billiards, and an occasional boxing match. Every night the strip was wild and rough, but weekends were a nightmare. Murders and assaults averaged two a week and the local police, along with the Sanitary Canal police force, found it hard to maintain order.

The hundred or so "establishments" that composed Lemont's Smokey Row between 1893 and 1897 called themselves saloons, clubs, gambling halls, brothels, or dance halls. They had names like *The Standard Club, The Big Casino, The Palace Saloon, The King of Hearts, Ted Boyle's Place, Jawoski's Place, Mazzie's Place,* and *The Silver Dollar.* Typically, in addition to liquor and gambling, women were part of the "trade", and entertainment such as nude dancing was readily available.

The women and the saloons changed their names as frequently as they changed their clothes. The "female companions" of the day were extremely greedy. On payday, after the workday ended, the tops of the workers' heads could be seen bobbing along as they approached Smokey Row, and the competition began. Women didn't wait for the men to arrive but rushed out clothed in exotic dress—and a range of undress—to entice and latch onto a "gentleman" for the night. Often, the "ladies of the evening" fell to battling each other over patrons, sometimes wrestling in the front yard of a resident.

The cost of a prostitute in a house of ill repute could be as little as twenty-five cents. Prostitution wasn't legal, but the "ladies" kept business going by paying protection to town officials. Saloon and gambling-house owners similarly passed a few dollars for "blind eyes."

One such lady, Hattie Briggs, was over six feet tall and weighed 250 pounds. Her trademark was a long red coat. Hattie made her fortune by stealing from her customers, grabbing a victim, taking his money, and throwing him out the door. She was so successful that her friends flocked from out of town to join her, setting up their own businesses. The result was an increase in rentals of vacant buildings, so that honest businessmen profited from Hattie's trade too.

Another middle-aged woman, Sarah Brown, gave her name as "Sarah Bernhardt." She was so popular among the patrons of Smokey Row that when she was arrested in one of the town's infrequent raids, a mob estimated at over a hundred men fought each other to post her bail.

As bad as crime was in Smokey Row, it did not adversely affect the life of most Lemonters, as the revelry stayed mostly on three downtown streets. Also, its profits contributed to the welfare of the town through license fees and taxes from the establishments to the tune of $500,000 a year by 1894. Each license cost five hundred dollars, a large sum in those days. The village found itself torn between the money these enterprises brought and the disorder and lawlessness they caused. Without the revenue from Smokey Row, the village of Lemont would not have been able to construct the Village Hall and the school on McCarthy Road, the electric streetlights and street signs at a time when most of the country was in an economic recession.

Mayor John McCarthy wasn't too worried. He enjoyed the crowd and the big spenders the strip brought to town. He wanted to take advantage of the income and excitement that would likely die on its own once the canal was finished. With only three policemen in Lemont, little could be done anyway.

Rev. J. Franklin Clancy was thirty-three years old when he arrived at the Lemont Methodist Church in 1894 with his wife. They found a devoted congregation and a beautiful stone church with new Italian stained-glass windows. However, from the quiet church one could look down on Canal Street and part of Smokey Row. Crime was rampant on the street, and the town did little to control it. Clancy soon realized that some of the youth did not attend Sunday school or services. There were far too many more exciting pleasures in town. In his opinion, gambling and drinking were creating unhappy families and broken homes.

A Sunday closing law was on the books, but it wasn't being enforced. This was because quarry and canal workers, as well as unskilled laborers, worked long hours six days a week, leaving Sunday the only day for socializing. Immigrant groups, such as German and Irish workers, made up a large part of the residents, and their social life traditionally occurred in family saloons. They protested that the closings were directed against them.

Clancy began his campaign by conducting meetings at the very gates of Smokey Row, in canal worker camps, and in the town, handing out small Bibles to working men. His preaching tours began at the Palace Saloon, and all along the route at eighty or more establishments he spoke of the evils of gambling, drink and other sins. Some patrons listened attentively, but he was more often subject to heckling, especially from the "ladies" of the strip. The liberal newspapers at the time painted Clancy as a fanatical temperance crusader and Mayor McCarthy as a practical politician. The conservative papers described Clancy as an idealistic young man and McCarthy as an evil, corrupt official.

On September 6, 1895, Clancy was able to persuade a Chicago

judge to issue warrants for the arrest of Mayor McCarthy on charges of bribery and for twenty-eight saloon keepers and inmates of disorderly houses. A ten-car train had been side-tracked on nearby River Road to await transport of those swept up in the raid.

Once begun, word quickly spread through town that a raid was in progress. Customers fled from the dives by a variety of escape routes. Women in stages of nudity hurried down the towpath, awkwardly trying to dress as they ran barefooted, carrying their shoes and stockings. Lemonters came from throughout town to watch the excitement.

By six p.m. the prisoner train was filled and ready to head for Chicago. Friends, tavern keepers who had not been arrested, and members of the watching crowd boarded another train on a second line, intending to support the offenders. This second train of onlookers arrived at the courthouse before the prisoners, where they gathered to welcome them, waving and cheering them on.

All the offenders were taken to court. The seats were soon filled with joking and laughing Lemonters. The judge set bonds at five hundred dollars each, which were posted by Lemont's alderman, who could well afford to do so. All prisoners were released within an hour and back in Lemont by 1:00 a.m.

That night the streets in Smokey Row were so crowded that it was hard to pass. It seemed that each person who returned from the city brought a friend back with him, and extra parties were held at every place and into the next day.

McCarthy was released the next morning on $5,000 bond. A year later, his charges were dismissed.

As courageous as Rev. Clancy had been, he had angered some townspeople, and a number of unsuccessful plots against him were uncovered later that year. As a result, it was necessary for his congregation to provide a bodyguard. For a time, Clancy welcomed parishioners on the steps of the church each Sunday, standing next to a man holding a double-barreled shotgun.

The majority of Smokey Row businesses had rented property

from land in the downtown area of Lemont that was owned by early pioneer settlers. Many of these people were important and well respected. Unhappy due to pressures put on them after the raid, the demise of Smokey Row establishments followed. Within six months only twenty-five saloons remained.

Smokey Row gradually closed down, not because of Clancy's battle against the sin strip, but because the portion of the canal through Lemont was finished. By early 1897 over 3,500 people had left the area.

Lemont's last brothel closed in 1906. Pete Kane, a popular local policeman, grew tired of raiding the place up to three times a week. He arranged for resettlement of the "girls" in Chicago, personally renting a place for them, arranging for their protection, then renting a wagon to pick them up along with their possessions and driving them to their new home.

Lemont today retains its friendly, small-town flavor. It continues to have a large number of popular drinking establishments, some of which are located in the same buildings as in the days of Smokey Row. For many residents, social life still takes place in the neighborhood taverns, as well as at many restaurant bars in and around town, but especially in the downtown area where Smokey Row once thrived.

Two businesses in town retain the name of Smokey Row: The Inn at Smokey Row, and Smokey Row Antiques, at 112 Stephen Street in downtown Lemont. The Old Stone Church, the Methodist church once led by Rev. Clancy, is now the home of the Lemont Area Historical Society.

Resources

Kallick, Sonia Aamot, *Lemont and Its People*, Chicago Spectrum Press.

Lemont Area Historical Society, *History & Anecdotes of Lemont, Illinois, 6ᵗʰ Edition*, revised by Pat Camalliere.

Acknowledgements

Last Call at Smokey Row is a work of fiction. Sami's Saloon and all the characters in the book are products of my imagination. That does not mean that places like Sami's don't exist. In creating the setting for this story, I used bits and pieces of taverns I knew when growing up on the South Side of Chicago, or as an adult working in Chicago's Loop, living on the North Side of Chicago, and from more recent years in Lemont. I wanted to keep my book in Lemont, the setting for my Cora Tozzi Historical Mystery Series, although none of the characters from that series appear in *Last Call at Smokey Row*.

Although Sami's is not a real saloon, Lemont has a number of taverns where this story could have taken place. Perhaps the closest resemblance of Sami's would be Peterson's Main Inn. Like Sami's in my novel, Main Inn is located on Main Street, one of the Lemont streets that comprised Smokey Row in the 1890s, across from the railroad tracks less than a block from the center of town. The building has been a tavern most, if not all, of the time since the Smokey Row days. And it has in-house pool leagues that pack the place most nights. Main Inn has the flavor of the fictional Sami's, and it fit the requirements of the story I wanted to tell. The story itself is completely my imagination and does not represent any real people or events that took place at Main Inn.

I am grateful to Linda Peterson and Tanya Gongol, the owners and operators of Main Inn, for allowing me to imagine what the tavern may have been like in the 1980s, and to take a photograph of the building to be used on the book's cover.

Since the story takes place in the 1980s, one of the challenges was to accurately describe how emergency units would have responded to calls to the bar. I am extremely grateful to Matt Peksa, Deputy Chief of Operations of the Lemont Fire Protection District, who was kind enough to spend a number of hours reading scenes from the book and answering my questions in person as well as subsequent calls and emails. Matt saved me from errors, such as pointing out that 911 was not active in most suburbs until after 1985.

I am also grateful to Daniel Dykshorn, Commander of the Village of Lemont Police Department, who spent an equal amount of time helping me understand how Lemont police would have responded to situations that happened at bars in the early 1980s, laws at the time, and the likelihood of arrests and convictions.

I did not move to Lemont until 1998. Since then, I have been fascinated by Lemont's quirky, yet important history. I am grateful to my friends in town, at the Lemont Public Library District, and at the Lemont Area Historical Society for helping me learn the history of Lemont. In particular, I would like to mention the late Sonia Kallick, one of the founders of the Lemont Historical Society and the author of Lemont's definitive history, *Lemont and Its People*. I would also like to thank Barb Bannon, my co-worker and genealogist at the historical society, who has lived in Lemont all her life and straightened me out on little details throughout the writing of the novel. Thanks also to my good friend Sue Roy, the owner of the last two businesses that bear the name of Smokey Row, The Inn at Smokey Row and Smokey Row Antiques.

Thanks to my writers' critique groups: Rod Brandon, Luisa Buehler, Mim Eichmann, Jon Payne, Jesse Severson, and Lee Williams, and to Write-On Joliet. The writing is never done until their astute comments are heard. You guys are the best!

To my editors, Donald G. Evans and Diane Piron-Gelman, for their insight and detailed edits, as well as their encouragement and belief in this book. And to my designer, Jeff Waggoner, whose understanding and creativity are unparalleled. This trio have my back and elevate my work.

To my family, who put up with my incessant chatter about all things writing, who excuse my forgetfulness and are patient with my distractions. Your love and support mean more to me than I could ever say.

And last, but in my mind always first, love to my husband, Chris, who lived along with me some of the experiences that provided ideas for this book, and who patiently took care of day-to-day details at home to allow me to keep writing.

About the Author

Pat Camalliere is the author of The Cora Tozzi Historical Mystery Series. Camalliere has lived in the Chicago area all her life. After moving to Lemont, she became intrigued by the unusual, sometimes mysterious region along the Des Plaines River Valley and Sag Valley in the Southwest suburbs of Cook, DuPage, and Will counties in Greater Chicagoland. Wanting to share that fascination with others, she began writing historical mysteries set in this locale, finding that a hint of the paranormal fit perfectly into the setting for the stories she wanted to tell. Her books relate a mystery from the past to a mystery in the present while enlightening readers with details in both time periods through storytelling that surprises even lifelong residents. *Last Call at Smokey Row* is her first historical novel outside of the Cora Tozzi series.

A cancer survivor, Camalliere has also written a best-selling memoir, *Staying Alive Is a Lot of Work: Me and My Cancer.*

Camalliere holds a Bachelor of Arts from Saint Xavier College. She lives with her husband in Lemont, Illinois, serves on the board of the Lemont Public Library District, and oversees the archives of the Lemont Area Historical Society. She writes a blog on local history and speaks to organizations and book clubs on a variety of topics related to writing, local history, and her cancer experience. She is a lifelong avid reader and enjoys classical choral singing. Visit her website, www.patcamallierebooks.com, or contact her for speaking engagements, interviews, or at any time at Pat@Patcamallierebooks.com.

www.ingramcontent.com/pod-product-compliance
Lightning Source LLC
Chambersburg PA
CBHW031343020726
47499CB00005B/1371